Arthur, *Dux Bellorum*

A Light in the Dark Ages, book four

By Tim Walker

Text copyright © 2019 Timothy N. Walker

All rights reserved

Arthur, Dux Bellorum

"*Then Arthur fought... with the Kings of the Britons, but he himself was Dux Bellorum.*"

Nennius, *Historia Brittonum* (History of the Britons) c. 820 AD

Acknowledgements:

Proof and Beta reader and critique partner - Linda Oliver
Copyeditor - Sinead Fitzgibbon (@sfitzgib)
Cover picture - *Arthur Dux Bellorum* by Gordon Napier aka dashinvaine (deviantart.com)
Cover design - Cathy Walker (cathyscovers.wixsite.com)

Published by:

http://timwalkerwrites.co.uk

Arthur, Dux Bellorum

Table of Contents

Place Names and Map   04
Character List   06

PART ONE   07
Chapter One   07
Chapter Two   22
Chapter Three   43
Chapter Four   57
Chapter Five   67
Chapter Six   81
Chapter Seven   93
Chapter Eight   104
Chapter Nine   120
Chapter Ten   132

PART TWO   143
Chapter One   143
Chapter Two   158
Chapter Three   169
Chapter Four   180
Chapter Five   195
Chapter Six   204
Chapter Seven   217
Chapter Eight   227
Chapter Nine   241
Author's Note   251

Place Names and Map

PLACE NAMES	(Roman)	(Briton)
Britain	Britannia	Albion (ancient name)
Ireland	Hibernia	
Wales	Cymru	
Scotland	Caledonia	
Winchester	Venta Bulgarum	Dunbulgar
Exeter	Isca Dumnoniorum	Exisca
Silchester	Calleva Atrebatum	Calleva
London	Londinium	Lundein
Gloucester	Glouvia	Glevum
Lincoln	Lindum	

Arthur, Dux Bellorum

York	Eboracum	Ebrauc
Bath	Aquae Sulis	Caer Badon
Carlisle	Luguvallium	
Hadrian's Wall	Vallum Hadriani	The Wall/Great Wall
Fort on Hadrian's Wall		Vindolanda
Fort on Hadrian's Wall		Birdoswald
Fort near Durham	Vinonium	Guinnion

Character List

Artorius/Arthur	Son of Uther and Ygerne
Merlyn	Healer and adviser to Ambrosius and Uther
Ygerne	Uther's widowed queen, mother of Arthur
Anne	Ygerne's daughter, sister of Arthur
Morgaise	Ygerne's daughter, fathered by Gorlois
Geraint	King of Dumnonia, husband of Morgaise
Morgana	Uther's first-born daughter
Velocatus	Morgana's husband, Chief of the Brigantes
Mordred	Son of Velocatus and Morgana, King of the Britons
Caradoc	Chief of the Catwellauni, commander of the king's army
Pascent	Son of Vortigern, slayer of Uther
Gerwyn	Bard and spy for Merlyn
Varden	Bodyguard and military trainer/adviser to Arthur
Gawain	Knight, commander and ally to Arthur
Percival	Knight and escapee with Arthur
Tristan	Knight
Iseult	Wife of Tristan
Bors	Knight – commander of Vindolanda
Bedwyr	Cavalry commander and future knight
Herrig	A Jute and Arthur's bodyguard
Dermot	A cook and member of Arthur's group
Pryderi	Merlyn's wife
Ulla	Merlyn's adopted son
Hector	Knight and adoptive father of the boy Artorius
Gayle	Adoptive mother of the boy Artorius
Maddox	Chief of the Coritani based at Lindum
Ambrose	Son of Maddox and friend to Arthur
Meirchion	Chief of the Rheged
Gunamara	Arthur's wife, daughter of Meirchion
Colgrin	King/chief of Deira
Venutius	Chief of Brigantes, succeeds his brother, Velocatus
Lot	King of the Goddodin
Icel	King of the Angles
Ceredig	King of Alt Clut in Caledonia

Arthur, Dux Bellorum

PART ONE

Chapter One

A COCKEREL CROWING its defiance to rivals always marked the start of his day. Shifting uncomfortably on a straw-stuffed sack, he turned away from the damp wall to see how far the first fingers of daylight had stretched across worn paving slabs. But the cockerel's call was distant, muted and distorted – filtered through a narrow opening high up in his cell, making his first waking thought a cruel reminder that he was no longer in the sanctuary of his parents' farm. Absent were the homely sounds of dogs barking, birds fighting, workers busying themselves, and the fountain splashing an invigorating melody.

Artorius sat, scratching at his woollen garment, then pushed aside the filthy blanket and ruffled his long, tangled hair, freeing some strands of straw. The rattle of keys interrupted his woeful reflection, signalling the entry of his jailor, Ahern, with a bowl of weak gruel and a pewter mug of water. He was a sullen, wordless giant who expressed himself with grunts and kicks.

"You are a happy man, Ahern, for you have found your true calling in life," Artorius muttered, receiving a snarl in reply. Three months in his narrow cell had afforded him plenty of time to reflect on the words of Merlyn that had led to his arrest. Merlyn had exposed him to a cheering crowd as the true heir to his father, Uther Pendragon, and had showed him how to pull the sword of Ambrosius smoothly from the cleft in a rock, made possible by the removal of pressure due to Merlyn and Varden's subtle easing back. A trick to fool an expectant crowd. No sooner had he entered the royal hall than the doors were barred behind him, and Caradoc, the army commander, had him arrested. Merlyn too, and Gawain the knight who had supported his claim. But not Varden, the ex-soldier and Merlyn's bodyguard. He was at large and represented his only hope of rescue.

"But my destiny as the son and heir to Uther, if indeed I am, has proven to be a false calling," he moaned to the closing cell door. He had received no visitors or news from the outside, but the fear of execution had receded as the weeks had passed. They had locked him away and would no doubt parade him or dispose of him once the reign of the new king was bedded in – the boy-king Mordred, whose mother had tried and failed to free the sword on his behalf. He gloated over the memory of Morgana's desperate and unsuccessful struggle.

Left alone with his thoughts, he shouted his anger and frustration at the impassive stone walls. "It was a conjuror's trick that landed me here! It was YOUR ambition, Merlyn, not mine!" He had practised it over and over. This is what he would say to the mysterious healer should they ever meet again.

THE BEST PART of Ygerne's day was the hour she was allowed to spend in her enclosed garden in the company of her daughters, Morgaise and Anne. They would tend to the roses and dwarf apple trees, and collect vegetables and herbs for their evening meal. They had been confined to their rooms since that strange day when Merlyn had unveiled Ambrosius's sword. Ygerne had been shocked by his revelation that the youthful Artorius was the baby she had believed dead, although Morgana had once revealed her suspicion that he had been stolen. But that was typical of Uther's mischief-making daughter. Morgana's long investigation had revealed nothing, so the baby remained officially dead, despite a faint maternal flutter that tugged at Ygerne's heart, the vague feeling that maybe the child still lived. She had experienced it during Uther's victory parade in Corinium, as if her son's eyes were on her.

The widowed queen invited the squabbling girls to sit beside her on a stone bench and be still whilst she shared her thoughts with them. "Could it be true?" Ygerne asked her daughters, not for the first time.

Anne, a girl on the cusp of womanhood, answered first. "I think so, Mama. I have always felt that I have a brother, and have often imagined playing with him. When I saw Artorius, my heart jumped."

"You are Uther's daughter, without a doubt," Ygerne laughed, "impulsive and firm in your belief."

The older Morgaise, daughter of Ygerne's first husband, Chief Gorlois of Cornubia, scoffed at the suggestion: "It was all a trick by Merlyn to place a farm boy on the throne so he could rule this land."

"And yet, I would look into that boy's eyes and decide for myself," Ygerne replied. Her worn face, lined by thin strands of greying hair, was troubled.

"I would like to try and visit the cells to talk to him," Anne said, making a curved line with the pointed toe of her slipper in the gravel at their feet.

"They will not let you," Morgaise replied sharply. "And besides, it would be interpreted as plotting by Caradoc and Morgana, who rule over the boy-king. They would have your pretty head on a spike."

The sisters glared at each other. Ygerne reached out and held their hands, silencing them. "I am less inclined to do nothing, as time goes by. Let us apply our minds to thinking of a way to contact Artorius. Perhaps, sweet Anne, you could find a way to go to the dispensary where they are holding Merlyn and try to talk to him when his guards are not looking?"

Morgaise's face lit up at the prospect of something to do to break their dull routine. "Yes! And I can go with her to distract the guards. But what should we ask of him, dear mother?"

THE FOLLOWING MORNING, Morgaise reported to their guards that Anne was sick with stomach ache and urgently needed to be taken to the dispensary to see a healer. The guards were visibly alarmed by the sight of Anne rolling on the floor, groaning, with white foam dribbling from the corner of her mouth. Caradoc himself appeared, some minutes later, wearing Uther's purple cloak edged with gold, Morgaise noticed, and a silver medallion bearing an eagle's head swinging on his chest.

"Carry her on a litter to the dispensary. Hurry," he tersely commanded the guards.

"May I accompany her as I know her diet and history of ailments?" Morgaise asked innocently.

Caradoc nodded, then promptly turned his back and marched out.

They had not been outside of the enclosure of royal apartments in three months, and now Morgaise enjoyed looking about her at the passing traders and market stall women who turned away from her stare and stilled their chatter. Where the cobbled street ended, a dirt track took them to a row of wooden thatched huts that clustered around the dispensary, a large stone building standing apart from the more typical rows of townhouses and livestock pens.

They entered through a wide archway and were greeted by the women who tended to the sick and injured. The two guards and two litter-bearers were directed through a door and out into an airy and light courtyard where a fountain dribbled spring water into troughs from which servants collected fresh drinking water in jars for the patients. Morgaise followed the litter-bearers into a room smelling of herbs and was soon face-to-face with Merlyn. The ageing healer was still an imposing presence and easily the tallest man there. Her keen eyes noted his long grey hair tied neatly behind a black gown; his narrow features and tattoo swirls were partly hidden by a closely cropped beard.

Merlyn's brown eyes flitted from Morgaise to Anne lying still on the litter, and he pointed to a table laid out with a white cloth.

"What ails the young woman?" he asked.

"She has eaten something that does not agree with her delicate stomach," Morgaise replied.

"Stand outside," he commanded the guards and litter-bearers. They hesitated, exchanging looks, before silently withdrawing to guard the door. Morgaise sniggered at his authority over his jailors.

"I may be a hostage, but I remain a valuable resource to them. This is my dispensary, developed over many years under Uther's reign. I preserve here the skills and knowledge of Roman physicians now long departed." He looked at Anne's tongue and touched the back of his fingers to her forehead, whilst Morgaise looked around her. Glass jars contained plants and body parts, and assorted clay pots with symbols scratched on them occupied the shelf space around the room.

Merlyn, once satisfied that Anne was in no danger, indicated a woman, who stood by the stool where a boy sat grinding a pestle into the mortar hugged to his ribs. "You can trust Pryderi, who assists me. The guards do not know she is my wife, so please keep this a secret." Turning to the quiet woman he said, "My dear, may I introduce Queen Ygerne's daughters – Morgaise and Anne." If Pryderi was shocked or surprised, she didn't show it. She bowed slightly to the royal princesses and busied herself on a nearby workbench.

By now Anne was sitting up. Merlyn asked Pryderi to bring a potion to ease stomach pains. "What did you take to make you unwell?" he asked her.

"I crushed up some fennel and dog wort from the garden and made a potion with sheep curd. It gave me stomach cramps and produced foaming of the mouth," she cheerily quipped.

"Indeed, it would," Merlyn replied. "Now drink this to settle your stomach," he said, as Pryderi handed over the remedy.

Turning to Morgaise he asked, "Pray tell me, what it is that you have come for?"

The confident young woman faced him and held his gaze. "Our mother is concerned about the fate of the youth, Artorius. We are not convinced that he is the son of Uther, as you claim, but we would like to help rescue the boy from what may yet be an unfortunate end."

"Have you heard that Caradoc has plans to kill him?"

"No, but our mother has a feeling that once the people are more accepting of Mordred as king, then he will be disposed of."

Merlyn took the pewter vessel from Anne and passed it to Pryderi. "You should start to feel better now, my lady," he said, smiling. She managed a half-smile in return. "I also am of a view that the young man needs rescuing, and soon. I had not expected allies from within the royal enclosure, although I'm pleased that you have come." He bowed slightly to Morgaise.

"We are so bored imprisoned in our rooms that we are ready to do anything for some excitement."

Anne coughed and added, "But I have long harboured a feeling that I might have a brother, and would welcome the chance to meet with Artorius and question him."

Merlyn kept his thoughts to himself. A jailbreak would almost certainly be followed by a swift escape for all involved. There would not be much time for a family reunion. "I have six men or more camped in the woods who are in readiness to act. But first we need to plan his release. Can you draw me a diagram indicating where he is held on this wax tablet?" Merlyn turned to a table and handed a curved stick to Morgaise. Anne joined her and together they made a crude sketch of the interior of the underground chambers beneath the king's hall.

"Is this the only entrance?" Merlyn asked, pointing to the sketch.

"Yes," Anne replied. "It is guarded day and night by two guards. It can be reached from the kitchens at the back of the hall. If I know when you are coming, I can let you in through this door." She indicated a gap in the outer wall of the enclosure.

"I know the place," Merlyn said. "The moon will be at its brightest two nights from now and will help with our escape. We shall come to this door when the moon reaches its highest point in the night sky. I shall knock like this." He rapped his knuckles on the table in a broken beat.

"Then one of us shall let you in," Morgaise replied.

"We can do no more than that," Anne added, "and must return to our rooms before the alarm is raised."

Merlyn hesitated before speaking, "You may only have the briefest of moments with your brother, you must realise." He did not want any words left unsaid on their plan. "But I shall send word to you where he can meet with you and your mother once we have made good our escape. That is all we can do. Remember this boy, Ulla, for it might be him who brings you news." He ruffled the dark brown hair of the quiet boy in the corner.

Anne nodded, knowing this was the best that could be expected from a midnight jailbreak, whilst harbouring the faint hope of a snatched moment with her brother.

MERLYN LED HIS gang through the streets of sleeping Venta, beneath the glow of a pale moon. He glanced about for any signs of movement before rounding a corner, where he came face-to-face with a large, growling dog, its bared teeth and arched back indicating a readiness to strike. He held an arm up to indicate his followers should stop and dropped to eye level with the dog. He whispered in a soothing tone and slowly pulled a piece of roasted boar skin from inside his tunic and offered it. The dog approached, sniffing. Merlyn carefully patted its head and was relieved to see its tail wagging. "Come on," he urged his followers, allowing the dog to tag along beside him.

They avoided a watchman's tower at the corner of the wooden stockage that housed the royal buildings, and lined up in the shadow of a warehouse opposite the doorway to the kitchen. Merlyn checked both ways and studied the parapet above the wooden barrier across the street before running across to the door. He rapped the code and waited for a response. Sure enough, he heard bolts being withdrawn and he stood back, gripping his staff in both hands, ready to strike.

Morgaise's face peered out from under a hood and he smiled with relief. "Come quickly," she whispered. "The guards are drunk and sleeping."

Merlyn waved for his men to follow and then entered the compound. Once all eight were inside, Varden, their leader, detailed one man to watch the doorway and two others to scout the yard and be in readiness to cover their escape.

Merlyn turned to Morgaise and asked, "Do you know where the sword of Ambrosius is?"

"The one Artorius pulled from the stone? Yes, it hangs on the wall in the Great Hall, behind the throne and under Mordred's banner."

When Varden returned to his side, Merlyn conveyed this information in a whisper. With a nod from Merlyn, Morgaise led them into the kitchen and out into a passageway that connected the hall to the sleeping quarters. She met Anne halfway along the narrow hallway, who indicated they should take a left turn. At the top of a circular stairwell Anne whispered to Merlyn, "At the bottom you will find the jailor sleeping on a wooden bed, but the night watchman is awake. He has the keys to the cells."

Merlyn nodded. "Anne shall lead us down and Morgaise shall remain here to keep a look out and wait for our return. Varden will go to the hall and get the sword."

"No," Morgaise whispered, "the hunting hounds sleep in there by the hearth. They will attack him."

Varden and Merlyn were confounded by this information. "Barking and snarling hounds would wake the guards," Merlyn said, deep in thought.

"I sometimes feed the hounds," Morgaise said softly. "They know me. Let me go there with a plate of meat from the larder and pick the sword on my way out."

"Will they attack you in the dark?" Varden asked.

"Not if they smell the meats on offer," she replied.

"Then let us try it," Merlyn said, not wishing to delay further. "Varden will stand by the door with two men, ready to come to your aid if the hounds are restless," he added.

Morgaise led Varden back to the kitchen to raid the larder for joints, whilst Merlyn and the rest of the men descended the stairs behind Anne. At the foot of the stairwell was a chamber lit by a solitary torch glowing from a bracket on the stone wall. To their right was a wooden bed on which slept the large form of Ahern, the jailor, snoring on his back. Anne crept forward towards the row of cells and bumped into a startled watchman, holding a lantern in which the candle had died.

"Oy, what are you doing here?" he growled. Merlyn and his companions shrunk back into the shadows, leaving Anne to answer him.

"I... followed my cat down the steps. Have you seen him?"

"No, I have not..." was all he managed in reply as Merlyn stepped forward and banged his head with the ball at the end of his wooden staff. The young gaoler fell to the floor, unconscious, and they checked whether the sleeping man had been disturbed by the clatter of the lamp on the floor. Ahern grunted and rolled over, facing the wall. Anne picked up the keys from the stricken man and passed them to Merlyn. They moved cautiously down a flight of a dozen steps to a tunnel lined with locked doors. A burning torch fixed to the wall lighted their way. Anne plucked it from its sconce.

Merlyn led the way to the first cell door with Anne following behind. The second key clanked in the lock and Merlyn pushed the door open, peering into the gloom. He moved towards a hunched figure lying on a bunk with his back to him. Merlyn put his hand on the sleeping man's arm, and rolled him onto his back. The light from Anne's torch fell on Artorius. He woke with a gasp and Merlyn put his hand over the young man's mouth. He ceased to struggle when he heard a familiar voice by his ear.

"Merlyn!" he croaked through dry lips.

"Be quiet, my boy," Merlyn whispered. "The jailor still sleeps."

Merlyn led Artorius, whose heart galloped now, to where he saw a young woman staring at him. "This is your sister, Anne," Merlyn said, stepping back. Artorius stood, mystified, but Anne stepped forward and looked closely at his face.

"I believe there is a resemblance," she said, and then hugged the bemused youth.

"We'd better get going," Merlyn whispered, looking around.

"Wait," Anne replied, "there are two knights held here. Perhaps they are friends of Artorius?"

Merlyn looked to the hunched youth who shrugged his thin shoulders. "Then let us quickly look to see who they are and if they are worthy of our help."

They combed the dungeons, finding some stray wretches, and soon identified Gawain and Percival, held in separate cells. Gawain could stand, bruised but otherwise unhurt, but Percival cried out in fear as they approached, in the voice of one who has endured a terrible torment. It soon became apparent that he was in much pain and couldn't walk, his leg badly broken.

"What of these other wretches who are unknown to us?" Gawain asked, indicating three reed-thin men.

"Let them follow us out of here, then they can decide if they wish to come with us or escape to the forest," Merlyn replied.

Whilst Artorius and Gawain briefly hugged, Merlyn called up two men to help the lame knight. "Let us hope you don't have to make a run for it," Anne whispered to Merlyn as they made their way to the stairwell.

At the top of the stairs Merlyn paused to peer in the direction of the hall. "Anne, lead them out through the kitchen door. I'll follow soon." With that Merlyn strode into the gloom towards the hall, leaving Anne and Varden's men to escort the shuffling escapees towards the exit.

Merlyn found Varden and his two companions hiding in a recess in the wall, daggers at the ready.

"She is still inside with the hounds," Varden whispered.

"We have rescued the prisoners and now must get away from this place," Merlyn muttered, the tension apparent in his tone.

"You go and lead them to safety. I'll wait for Morgaise and the sword," Varden replied, his eyes shining with resolve in the dim glow of an oil lamp. Merlyn paused for thought. Ideally, they should all leave together. Just then, the hall door creaked open and Morgaise slid out, shutting it behind her. They gathered around her as hounds whined and scratched at the closed door. With a triumphant smile, Morgaise produced the unsheathed sword from a fold in her skirt. Varden took it from her and Merlyn gave her a gentle hug around her slender shoulders.

"Let us make haste, for our luck will soon run out," Merlyn whispered, turning to lead them back towards the kitchen. They passed out into the cool night air, finding their fellows hiding in a shadowy porch. Clouds shrouded the moon making it much darker than before, causing Merlyn to sigh his relief. The biggest man was able to carry Percival on his back, and they filed out through the open door and into the night. Artorius and Merlyn were the last to leave, exchanging hugs with the two young women. Morgaise was hurriedly introduced to Artorius, to add to his wonder of the events still unfolding.

Anne sniffed back her tears as she kissed Artorius on the cheek. "I hope we meet again soon, dear brother, together with our dear mother who longs to hold you once more."

Merlyn pulled Artorius away and they melted into the night. "Let us not tempt the fates by delaying, Artorius," he whispered. "Our horses are outside the town's walls. It is but an hour to sunrise."

Artorius started at the sight of a large guard dog emerging from the shadows. His alarm soon turned to bemusement as it wagged its tail and lolled its tongue at Merlyn who bent to pat its head. The beast trotted beside them to the unguarded gates and watched as they slipped out into the night, leaving the sleeping town behind.

Chapter Two

THE INQUEST HAD begun in the Great Hall at Venta Bulgarum. The boy-king, Mordred, sat on Uther's throne, his dangling feet the only movement apart from commander Caradoc's pacing. His mother, Morgana, stood silently beside the nine-year-old, her eyes searching the faces of the assembled household for signs of complicity.

"They must have had assistance from inside to escape unnoticed!" Caradoc bellowed, his cloak swishing with his every turn. The thirty or so who lived within the royal enclosure were lined up in two rows – servants and guards on one side, nobility and their attendants on the other. Caradoc strode between the two rows, swinging his head from side to side, trying to catch a guilty eye.

"And they stole my sword!" Mordred squeaked.

Caradoc stopped abruptly before Ygerne. "The youth, Artorius, claims to be your son, my lady. What do you know of his rescue?"

Ygerne held his stare and calmly replied, "I know nothing of this matter, my lord."

Caradoc grunted and moved to stand before Morgaise. "You are fond of the hounds, Lady Morgaise, perhaps you came and fed them in the night?"

"I slept soundly, my lord," Morgaise replied, her superior air causing Caradoc to stiffen.

"Then perhaps the hounds can sniff out their friend," he said, signalling to his Master of the Hunt to bring the beasts into the gap between the two rows. The six wolfhounds sniffed the boots, skirts and leggings of the assembled group. One of the hounds approached Morgaise, its tail wagging, but when it sniffed her hand it recoiled and moved away. On the opposite side, three hounds stood before one of the kitchen attendants, wagging their tails as if expecting a snack.

"Take her away," Caradoc thundered. The weeping woman's protests were mocked by the king and his mother as she was dragged from the hall. "And the gaoler's boy, together with those two guards found drunk by the kitchen door. There is plenty of room in the cells to fill."

Caradoc continued to pace up and down, glaring at Ygerne and her daughters. "Be warned, my ladies. The king shall not be mocked. We shall soon recapture the prisoners and then they shall tell us who aided their escape. King Mordred's leniency towards you may soon wither like the vines in your garden. Return to your rooms."

The unhappy gathering funnelled out into the corridor, walking two abreast. Anne whispered to Morgaise, "How did you rebuff your favourite hound?"

"I rubbed some crushed pepper seeds onto the back of my hand."

"You're not as clever as you think, my sister – some clay from the kitchen yard fell from your boot as you left the hall." They exchanged glances but kept their faces fixed in the look of a solemn funeral procession.

DAWN DID NOT so much break but creep with cold reluctance into a dull and overcast morning. A dozen riders, followed by a horse-drawn cart, picked their way northwards towards the ruins of Calleva.

"Why do we head northwards, Merlyn?" Artorius asked, bouncing on the back of a lively pony beside the taller chestnut mare of his mentor.

"They will search for us to the west and south. We shall head northwards where we can find friends and allies. Firstly, there is someone I hope to find in the ruins of that once important town, Calleva." They lapsed into weary silence, aside from the ever-vigilant Varden, who sent his men out to scout in four directions, receiving their reports from time to time. It had the effect of both soothing the travellers, but also putting them on edge whenever a rider returned.

By midday they reached the forest edge, next to a clearing where stood the crumbling stone walls of the former legionary transit town. The Roman garrison had kept a cleared space around the town, free from cultivation and occupation for as far as an arrow could fly, to give defenders clear sight of an advancing enemy. Now, the space between them and the walls was busy with thatched huts, cultivated plots and enclosures for animals.

Merlyn called Varden to him. "We shall make camp in the forest. You must search deeper in for a suitable place. I shall enter the town with Pryderi and the boy on the cart, with Percival in the back. I hope to find a friend who is skilled at fixing bones."

Artorius had appeared behind them. "May I come too?" he asked.

"It is not safe. Soon Caradoc's spies will be looking for us. You stay close to Varden – perhaps he will remind you how to wield that sword."

Varden grabbed Artorius by his slender arm, as if evaluating a slave at an auction. "Aye, we may have need of everyone who can fight soon enough. I'll assess those two wretches who have chosen to follow us."

"Ah yes," Merlyn mused, "I have not yet had time to question them. One has the look of a Saxon. If he is, he is not to be abused, Varden. We may have need of him, if he speaks their tongue. You may question them and find out the circumstances of their capture."

Varden led the group to a suitable site to make camp. Merlyn had the cart emptied of supplies and the barely conscious, emaciated form of Percival, attended by Pryderi, placed in the back on a bed of straw and moss. The boy, Ulla, sat beside Merlyn, holding the reins of the big bay horse, its feathered fetlocks swishing over its hooves as it picked the best course towards the cobbled road. In a short while they entered the town through the south gatehouse, now unattended. Merlyn scanned the battlements for Caradoc's guards, but none were evident. They made their way in slow progress towards the forum at the town's centre, looking like a family of farmers come to trade.

Merlyn was saddened by the destruction of what once were neat rows of houses, taverns, warehouses, shops, and public buildings – now stunted and roofless stone ruins sheltering crude new dwellings constructed of wood and thatch. Wandering pigs, dogs and fowl joined the cacophony of noise in the filthy streets where traders touted their wares. The lack of order seemed incongruous when contrasted with the learning that had planned and built a functional town dissected by two straight, paved thoroughfares that divided the town into four neat quarters. The Romans had gone and, to Merlyn's eyes, left a legacy that was unwanted, neglected and being crudely dismantled by Britons moved only to eke out a simple living, without interference from a ruling elite. Galvanising the people into collective endeavour would be extremely difficult.

"The collective will of the Saxons will surely sweep our people away," Merlyn muttered, drawing a curious sideways look from Ulla. He smiled at the boy and indicated he should direct the horse through an archway into the town's forum. They emerged from a tunnel into a bright and busy space, bound on four sides by crumbling imperial buildings, once the administrative centre of a region. Under canvas awnings, stalls displaying vegetables, dried meat, pots, utensils, tools and ornaments lined the generous courtyard, as townsfolk bartered with traders in the exchange of goods. Merlyn searched for something familiar.

"Stop," he commanded, and jumped from the wagon, marching with purpose towards a large tent, with a blue circular design painted on a banner outside, that might once have housed a Roman officer. Inside, he found the man he was looking for leaning over a patient. There were twenty or so patients on beds or seated on stools lining the edges of the musty space.

"Ah, Drummond, we meet again," Merlyn said, waiting patiently to be acknowledged. After a moment, the healer turned and faced him.

"Merlyn, it has been long." The old friends embraced. "I shall be with you shortly." The white-robed Drummond turned back and finished tying a splint to a young woman's arm.

"Still setting bones, I see," Merlyn said.

"There is always injury and illness. It is a fact of life. Are you well, my old friend? I heard you had been detained at Lord Caradoc's pleasure."

"It is true. I have not properly taken my leave, so do not speak of my passing through this place. My friend, I need your help to set the bones of a companion's leg. He is outside."

"But you can set bones, Merlyn. Why bring him to me?"

"You shall see. It is broken in two places." Merlyn guided Drummond out to the cart, where he lifted the blanket covering Percival and inspected the twisted leg. Percival was groaning and barely conscious.

"Bring him inside," Drummond commanded of his followers, who manoeuvred the thin knight onto a wooden board and conveyed him into the tent. Drummond carefully cut away his soiled leggings and ordered an attendant to wash the patient.

"I will assist you, my friend," Merlyn said, washing his hands in a basin.

"You were right to bring him here," Drummond replied. "It is a double break, probably inflicted with clubs. It will take the two of us to set these bones. I'll give him some essence of poppy seeds."

Once Percival was fully unconscious, Drummond discussed the procedure with Merlyn, and they set about the task of setting the thigh and shin bones, then tightly binding wooden splints to both calf and thigh.

"There is a chance he will recover, but he must stay off his feet for some time. After one month, he can try to walk with a crutch under his arm. Now let us share a drink and you can tell me of the politics of Venta." The old friends sat for a while and Merlyn recounted the events that followed the death of Uther and of his captivity in his dispensary. He omitted mention of Artorius – it was too dangerous to risk being overheard.

"Soldiers may come looking for me. I hope I shall not bring you trouble, dear friend."

"I will deny all. Besides, I am the only healer in this area and many of my customers are soldiers." He instructed his attendants to return Percival to the cart, and gave Merlyn a small vial of poppy seed essence. "He will be in much pain for many days, but slowly the bones will meld together, if he remains still, and he will heal. Good luck, Merlyn, in all your endeavours." Drummond gave a knowing smile, indicating he suspected his old friend was involved in more intrigue than he admitted to.

Merlyn returned the smile and embraced his friend, pushing an ounce of silver into his hand. "Take this to replenish your supplies. My thanks, and good fortune to you, Drummond." A boy came running and whispered to Drummond.

"It seems a dozen mounted soldiers have arrived at the south gatehouse, asking questions. Come this way and leave through the east gate. The boy will guide you. Go!"

With that, Merlyn mounted the cart and they followed the boy who trotted before them. Outside the town they quickly navigated along tracks between farms and into the dark embrace of the forest.

BROWN LEAVES WERE falling from oak, beech and ash in the ancient forest. Varden had directed his group of outlaws to set up a camp that might shelter them for several days. Lean-tos were constructed from cut branches and covered with moss and grassy sods, and campfires lit. A hunting party went out into the forest, and camp followers drew water from a stream and collected mushrooms, edible roots and berries for the evening meal. Varden gathered the escaped prisoners together and each spoke of the circumstances of their internment and their treatment. Of the three fellows rescued with Artorius, Gawain and Percival, one had opted to make off on his own and two had chosen to follow Merlyn.

Varden was keen to hear from the wiry fair-haired man.

"I am Herrig, a Jute captured by soldiers on your south coast," he began, speaking slowly in the Brythonic tongue of his audience. "My fellows fought their way to our boat, but I was knocked down and taken prisoner. They held me at the fortress called Portus Adurni for a year, during which time I learned your language. Then the king's men came and took me to their town and I was questioned about Jute settlements on the Isle of Vectis. I told what I knew, not much. Just a village around a rough port on the east of that island. From there, settlers trade with our homeland."

"How many of your fellows have come to Vectis?" Varden asked.

"About two hundred in all, including wives and children. Plants for eating will no longer grow for our fathers as the rising sea has turned our fields to salt marshes. Also, the Saxons push into our lands from the south, saying that they, in turn, are being pushed by tribes coming from the east." He sat back and held Varden's gaze, wondering what his fate would be.

Varden wondered briefly what the true number of Jutes was on Vectis, but switched his attention to the other man, a thin fellow with dark brown hair and narrow features. "And what of you?"

"I am Derward of the Cantii people, from the south and east. The Regnii raided our village and I was taken as a slave. My captor beat me for little reason, until one day I struck him. He fell hard and was injured. After that, I was whipped in the square and thrown into the cells, where I remained until you let me out. My lands are now overrun by his sort." He glared at Herrig. "But in truth, our tribe is enslaved by both Jutes and Regnii, or scattered, so I have no home to return to."

"This is a sad tale, Derward," Artorius said. Gawain, chewing on a grass stem, nodded his agreement.

Varden grunted at the pair. "You have both been treated harshly. I know Merlyn is a fair man, for I have served him for many years. He will offer you both his protection in return for your loyalty. What say you?"

They both nodded their assent. "And no settling of old scores," Varden added. "You will both have fresh starts here, and we are all friends, even with a renegade Jute." He insisted that they all lock forearms in the Roman greeting.

As the light began to fade, Merlyn entered the camp. A boar had been slaughtered and the aroma of its meat roasting over a fire filled the glade. "That is a welcome smell," he groaned, climbing wearily from the wagon. "I trust all is well?"

"Aye, all is well, and soon will be even better when we eat," Varden replied.

"I found my physician friend and he has fixed Percival's shattered leg. With good fortune he will recover and walk again. Our exit was hastened by the arrival of soldiers. They are looking for us, as expected."

Percival was carried from the cart and laid with his back to a tree and his splinted leg stretched out towards a fire. He was still delirious from the poppy infusion. Soon the company of thirty were assembled for their meal and Varden introduced Herrig and Derward to the group, finishing with, "Although Herrig is a Jute, he has been freed from captivity and shares a common enemy with us. He speaks our tongue, has chosen to join us and will be treated as an equal."

"Bravo," Merlyn said, putting his seal on the matter. "I have always liked an odd band of fellows. The most important thing is honesty and respect. We must be true to each other, for in that our strength lies, and our best hope of evading capture. We shall remain for two days whilst our weaker members regain their strength, then head west to Gawain's home settlement where we can expect a favourable welcome. Now let us eat and enjoy the bounty of the forest."

THE FOLLOWING MORNING, Artorius rose early and found Gawain by the stream, shaving his chin with a short, sharp blade. He would stop periodically to look at his reflection in a polished piece of obsidian.

"I also wish to shave the whiskers from my face and keep it free of hair, in the Roman manner," Artorius said, sitting beside him.

Gawain laughed. "Then you will need a sharp knife and a looking glass, my friend. Then we shall both keep our looks in the Roman manner, unlike our tribal cousins. Wait till I have finished and I will shave you."

Once his face was free of hair, Artorius bathed and then busied himself in helping the wives of Varden's soldiers prepare breakfast. This consisted of fetching water and filling an iron cauldron that hung over a fire. Oats and barley were poured in to make porridge. He chewed on hard bread and honey as he stirred the cauldron. He was feeling much refreshed after his shave, wash and a sound sleep, and felt his energy returning as he waited for Merlyn, yet to emerge from his hide, longing for the opportunity to have some time with him alone.

"Ah, Artorius," Merlyn croaked through a dry throat, "I know why you are loitering outside my shelter. Your mind is full of questions, and all shall be answered in time." He put his arm around the young man's stiff shoulders and led him away from the camp. Although still bitter and needing an explanation, Artorius's anger had been assuaged somewhat by his relief and gratitude at being rescued in such a daring manner.

"First, let me pay a call to nature, then we shall talk. Please fetch me a drink of warmed water and honey." Merlyn disappeared in the bushes and Artorius returned to camp, searching for a pewter beaker. Pryderi, silent as ever, appeared in front of him, holding a drinking vessel. Artorius smiled and nodded his head in the direction of Merlyn. He knew her sad story – the abuse she had suffered at the hands of cruel Hibernian slavers that had caused her unwillingness to speak. Merlyn had bought her at a slave market and set her free, but she had willingly joined the enigmatic healer's band of followers. She dipped the mug into the cauldron of warming water and added a drizzle of honey from a jar, stirring it with a twig. She then handed the mug to Artorius and, after the briefest of eye contact, turned to attend to Ulla.

Once Merlyn had slaked his thirst, he led Artorius along a track away from camp. "I know you must think ill of me for seemingly leading you into a trap..." he began.

"A trap! Yes, indeed!" Artorius shouted, causing startled birds to leave their roosts and take to the air. "Without any explanation you made me perform a trick with Excalibur, and then you made a public speech declaring me to be the one true son of Uther..."

"But you are the one true son of Uther. It was I who… made a pact with King Uther to take you away from a place of danger and settle you for safekeeping with the noble knight Hector and his doting wife, Gayle. They had lost their son that very summer in battle with the Saxons, and were happy to take you."

"But why?" Artorius blurted. "Why was I in danger, and from whom?"

"Do you remember when two assassins came to your farm? They were sent by Uther's daughter, Morgana, to find and kill you."

"Yes, I remember. It was I who followed one of them to Glevum…"

"…And I appeared just in time to save you from the sharp tip of his sword," Merlyn interrupted. "It was a dangerous time for you, young Artorius, and Morgana had ideas of her own about Uther's succession. I took you for your own safety and protection, against the day when you could return to Venta and claim your birthright."

"But that didn't go well," Artorius moaned, hanging his head and kicking at clumps of brown leaves.

"For that, I owe you my deepest and most sincere apology. When some of the knights came forward to support your claim, I felt our cause would prevail. But I had underestimated the strong will of Morgana and the ambition of Caradoc. Politics is a dirty business, Artorius, and the prospect of power casts a strong spell over the hearts of those driven by lust and ambition."

"But now we are outlaws, to be hunted down like wild animals."

"I will take us north where we will find allies. The people are desperate for protection and will look for a strong leader. That leader is you, although you may not see it yet. But I have seen it in my visions, when my head throbs with their potency, and know it will come to pass…"

"Not if we are slain!"

Merlyn tousled the sullen youth's nut-brown hair. "I have looked after you since you were born, dear Artorius. You are like a son to me, as you are to Hector. You have many friends who will fight for you. We shall gather allies as we move northwards, starting with the settlement from where Ambrosius plucked a young Gawain to be his squire, many years ago. Come, let us join the others and share some of that sweet-smelling porridge."

FOR TWO DAYS Varden patrolled the edge of the forest and sent scouts into Calleva, searching for intelligence of Caradoc's men. They had not stayed long, riding west, by all accounts, and were unaware that Merlyn had been there. The freed captives ate well on game from the forest, slowly recovering their strength. Even Percival was able to talk and a smile returned to his long, narrow face. The brutality of his capture and rough treatment had turned his hair white, despite being barely fifty years of age. Gawain had endured his ill treatment with stoicism and by chance had escaped serious injury.

Both Percival and Gawain now regaled the group with their accounts of how they had earned their right to be knights as youngsters, no older than Artorius, under Ambrosius's leadership at the battle of Maisbeli, where the Saxon army was routed and Hengist slain. They had become skilled commanders of King Uther's army, and had fought many engagements against his enemies. Merlyn was pleased to see their spirits rekindled. After consultation with Varden over the movement of Caradoc's guards, he decided they should leave the next day to travel the thirty miles westwards to the ex-legionaries' commune where Gawain's family lived.

With raised spirits, they broke camp the following morning. They travelled along rough trails, barely wide enough for the wagon, to the edge of the forest and the Roman Portway road that linked Londinium, now Lundein, in the east with Aquae Sulis, now Caer Badon, to the west. Gawain rode ahead, whilst Varden and his scouts fanned out on either side and covered the wagon. It was decided that the half dozen or so camp followers would walk with the wagon, whilst the remaining eight riders would hang back and follow at a distance, just keeping them in sight. They passed by the occasional hut, where women and children would offer vegetables and dried meats in exchange for small Roman coins or bartered goods. Merlyn kept his hood up for fear of being recognised, and Percival was advised to stay under a blanket if anyone approached the wagon.

Dark clouds inched towards them as the day advanced, the gloom causing Gawain uncertainty when he identified the turn-off to the farming commune where he had grown up.

"I believe this is it, but there is no longer a signpost standing to mark the place," he reported to a sodden Merlyn crouched on the platform of the wagon.

"You ride ahead with Varden and introduce yourselves to the occupants, but do not speak of recent events as they may not have heard. We shall remain here at the junction, but hidden from the road until you return," Merlyn replied, indicating that they should move off the road into the trees and seek shelter. Artorius was eager to accompany them, but Merlyn, ever cautious, asked him to remain and attend to Percival.

Unwilling to light fires, they huddled under canvas sheets until Varden and Gawain returned. "We are to be welcomed," Varden announced. "Come, let us make haste whilst there is still some light in the day."

The straggling party followed the track for half a mile, past fields of stubble where crops had been harvested to their left and the wall of the forest to their right. The settlement was guarded by a stockade fence and ditch, and two soldiers with long spears stood on a parapet above the wooden gatehouse, wearing Roman helmets and wrapped in red cloaks.

"Welcome, weary travellers," boomed the deep voice of a tall, silver-haired man standing with five others before a long hall, all wearing cloaks of red. "I am Flavius Albus, the caesar of this settlement we call Nova Roma. We are the descendants of Roman legionaries, officers and scribes, settled here by a former Governor of Britannia Prima."

Merlyn climbed down from the wagon and stood with Gawain and Varden. "Our thanks for your welcome, Flavius

Albus. We were all servants of King Uther, now sadly deceased, and have in our company two distinguished commanders in Gawain and Percival. It is a homecoming for Gawain, who was born here and hopes to find his kin. We are travelling northwards and ask for your hospitality for a few days."

"It is given. Our people shall house you in the barrack block, and you shall be our guests in the mess hall for our evening meal. We get few visitors and look forward to your news of events in this worried land. Welcome home, Gawain, although I cannot remember you."

"My father was Gaius Drusus, an optio with the second legion, sir. He and my dear mother are dead. But I have cousins still."

"Ah yes, Drusus – a good man," Flavius said.

"Thank you, sir. Yes, the best of fathers."

Percival was taken to the dispensary where Merlyn fell into discussion with the commune's healer. Gawain took Artorius with him to search for the house of his cousins, under strict instructions from Merlyn to say as little as possible about events in Venta Bulgarum. It was Merlyn's intention to judge the strength of support for their cause with the commune's leaders before divulging too much about their predicament.

They were summoned to the meal by a horn blast, and found long banqueting tables laid out with benches on their side. The visitors were invited to sit along one side, facing senior members of the commune.

Gawain's return to the locale of his childhood had subdued the sunny knight. He appeared to be lost in the memories it had stirred, for he said little as they prepared to eat. Twice his head cocked and his eyes lit and then dimmed in disappointment, as if he heard a longed-for voice in the hubbub and then realised himself to be mistaken. He roused himself when Merlyn nodded faintly to him and raised his drink. "To our elders," he said and pressed his own goblet to his lips, before looking properly at the bustle around him.

Serving boys and girls dressed in white togas waited on their guests, moving efficiently in the light of lamps placed to illuminate hanging tapestries depicting classical scenes.

"Our harvest is in and we are set for the winter," Flavius explained. "We keep cows, sheep, horses and fowls and have a good grain store to see us through the dark days."

"You live well by Roman rules and manners," Merlyn observed, bowing to his host.

"We have continued the traditions of our fathers, including weapons training for our young men. We can put one hundred to the parapets if attacked," Flavius replied, pouring wine for his guests. "And we make our own wine and ale."

During the meal Flavius and Merlyn sparred, each trying to uncover what information the other had. "A herald came two months ago, announcing that Uther was dead and the new king was his grandson, Mordred," Flavius said, watching Merlyn keenly. He stripped meat from a bone with his teeth and continued. "After we loosened the herald's tongue with our ale, he admitted that the transition had been contested and there was an imposter in jail claiming to be a lost son of Uther."

"I have also heard that," Merlyn replied, thinking they must keep the silver goblet he sipped from for honoured guests.

"And what was your position in Uther's court?" Flavius asked.

"I was his healer and adviser."

"But your services are not required by the boy-king Mordred?"

"He is catered for by Lord Caradoc and his followers. There has been some tension around the appointment of a child as king. Some feel that a man with a strong arm is needed to lead the army with resolve and rally men to his banner. We live in dangerous times."

"On that we can agree, my lord Merlyn. Without the protection of Rome's legions, this land is ripe for plunder by uncouth tribes who were kept at bay by an organised military. Despite the best efforts of Ambrosius Aurelianus, I feel this fragile peace will slowly be whittled away."

"And Uther spent much of his time in the saddle. It seems to be an endless task. This land's riches are also its curse." Merlyn had decided this was enough information to impart for now, and switched the conversation to other matters.

"I notice you have a temple to Mithras, but have you no Christian church?" he asked.

Flavius grinned and considered his answer. "There is a small Christian church behind this hall, a mere wooden shelter, visited once a week by a priest from a nearby village. The women and some of the men go there. Most of our men still look to Mithras, the bull-headed god of the legionaries, for protection. As you may know, the worship of Mithras demands more than prayer – a man must also live up to an oath of loyalty and engage in acts of bravery to prove himself worthy. This instils a code of noble conduct and loyalty in our young men."

Merlyn nodded sagely. "I am tolerant of most beliefs, but fear the intolerance of the Christian faith."

Flavius laughed. "The priest wants to collect all our souls for Jesus. He has told me!"

OVER THE FOLLOWING days, Merlyn took Flavius into his confidence and disclosed the identity of Artorius. The grizzled veteran was suitably impressed and, knowing that Gawain was held in high regard and would be a commander of any future army, agreed to let them have horses and six of his best men. Merlyn also asked if Percival could remain with them, along with the women and children, as they must move northwards as a battle-ready unit.

Merlyn gave the unwelcome news to his followers on the day before their departure. Percival protested, but could not insist on joining them as he was unable to ride. Pryderi and Ulla were also told that they must remain, with Merlyn trying his best to sweeten his instruction by adding that he could think of no better and safer place for them to see out the winter months.

By morning, they were ready – a well-equipped troop of sixteen riders, dressed as Roman cavalry with body armour, rounded helmets and oval shields. Of their fellow escapees, Herrig the Jute now looked the part of battle-ready soldier, in contrast to Derward, who had shown little interest in wielding a sword and willingly took on the role of cook. Merlyn had also forsaken his flowing black robe for more practical dress: leather riding leggings, boots and a padded leather tunic. His one concession to military dress was a plain, rounded helmet.

The leader of the six guards from the commune came forward and introduced himself to Merlyn. "I am Bedwyr, a captain of the guard. My sword is at your service."

Merlyn smiled and motioned Artorius to come to his side. "Artorius, this strapping captain of the guard is Bedwyr. He shall watch over you, together with Varden and Gawain. These three fine warriors are destined to be your commanders."

Bedwyr bowed, but Artorius just looked bemused, not quite believing in Merlyn's vision. "You and your men are a most welcome addition to our group, Bedwyr," was all he could think of to say. A smile cracked Bedwyr's broad face and he scratched his short black hair before donning his helmet.

Merlyn addressed Flavius and his followers from the saddle. "We shall endeavour to return or send word when the flowers of spring cover the meadow. Until then, farewell, dear friends!"

Chapter Three

MORGANA, HER BLACK hair bundled into a net at the nape of her neck, paced before the throne and the fidgeting king, swishing the skirt of her gold silk gown with every turn. "You must learn your letters before swordplay, my son. But first, we shall discuss matters of state." She stopped pacing and stood beside her burly husband, Velocatus, as Caradoc entered with his guard.

"Have you found them?" she demanded.

Caradoc's jaw was set like granite and his black eyes just as hard. "We have not, my lady. They have melted into the forests and we have no clues as to the direction they have taken. One of the wretches was captured, but he insists, under torture, that he has no knowledge of their plans. He was allowed to go his own way once they left the town's gate. We search south and west as that is the most likely..."

"Merlyn is clever," Morgana interrupted. "He will most likely have headed north or east to make good their escape. I advise you to look there."

Caradoc sat heavily and ordered some ale be brought. "We have another problem. A Saxon force has laid siege to Lundein, and we must send men to relieve the garrison. Perhaps Velocatus and his Brigante warriors could assist in this matter?"

Velocatus exchanged looks with Morgana before answering, "I too have received unwelcome reports of Picts invading my lands to the north. I am of a mind to return there."

Morgana touched his arm and purred, "Then perhaps do both. Ride east, keeping a look out for the fugitives, then chase off the Saxons at Lundein before riding north, my love."

"Can I come, Father?" Mordred shouted, jumping down from his throne.

Morgana hugged her son and said, "You shall stay here with me until your safety is assured, my little king. Until Merlyn and Artorius are killed or captured, we shall have no peace of mind."

"The harvest is in and I shall raise a levy of men from the south and west," Caradoc said, between sups of ale, "for we shall need to bolster our army and coastal forts to counter these interminable raids. Are we agreed that Velocatus will ride to relieve the siege of Lundein and then move northwards to his tribal lands?"

"Aye," Velocatus confirmed. "My scouts shall scour the countryside as we go, looking for any signs of the fugitives. We ride at daybreak."

BEDWYR GUIDED THEM northwards, through forests and around low-lying marshes, avoiding small settlements whose smoke trails twisted into the grey sky. By the end of the first day, they had reached the base of a steep hill.

"We shall camp here," Merlyn announced, "and in the morning our way takes us on the pathway of the ancients, over the high ground."

The camp was established and a thick game broth was soon simmering over a fire, stirred by Derward. Artorius sat close to Merlyn by the campfire and asked the question on which he brooded. "Where are we heading, Merlyn?"

"We will lead our horses upwards at first light, but on the top of the ridge path we can ride high above the plains, seeing all about us for a great distance. In time we will reach the White Horse carving and see the place where Uther fought his last battle and was slain. Gawain was there, and can recount the tale of that battle with devilish Saxons." He looked over at Gawain, who nodded.

"We shall camp there, amongst friends, and continue the next day, over the River Tamesis and northwards until we meet the Roman road, then make our way to the town of Lindum where we can expect a warm welcome from the kinfolk of Ambrosius's mother, Queen Justina. It is my hope that we gather allies to your banner and grow our numbers."

"Do you expect conflict, and if so, with whom?" Bedwyr asked.

"We are being pursued by Caradoc's men, and if they find us, we must fight for our lives. His tribal lands are close, and we shall continue to avoid settlements to the south of the ridgeway. On the north side, in the Vale of the White Horse, we will be welcomed. At Lindum, we shall find a settlement with Roman manners, like your commune, Bedwyr, and will seek their wise council. For I do not have all the answers, and the future may unravel in a number of ways." He poked the fire with a stick, sending sparks dancing upwards, and they lapsed into silent reflection over their meal.

They set out early in a steady drizzle, leading their horses along the sheep herders' path that wound upwards. "It is dry underfoot," Merlyn explained to Artorius, "because of the white rock that devours the rain. We can expect to see travellers and drovers of sheep who use this path for safety as you can see a long distance in all directions. Bandits, bears, wolves and even storms can be seen approaching. There are few trees or bushes on top of the ridge. It is cold and windy because it is exposed, but it offers safety and a direct route towards the north and east. Ancient peoples live here, unaffected by the Roman occupation, and may offer us hospitality." He stopped briefly to catch his breath, then continued, "…and the way is marked by ancient forts where our forebears protected themselves from attack by men, wild animals, giants and dragons."

With aching legs, they reached the top of the hill and saw they were at the start of a long upland ridge that snaked into the distance before them. They were now below blue skies and above low, scudding white clouds.

"We have ascended to the heavens," Gawain gasped in awe, as they mounted their horses.

"Follow me in single rank and keep your eyes open for movement of horsemen below," Merlyn said, leading the line. The wind had died and their way was pleasant along a worn dirt track, lined by tufts of hardy moor grass and sage scrub, undulating across the ridgeback. After an hour they saw burial mounds on a high plateau, with sheep grazing about them and an indifferent boy sunning himself on a hillock. He briefly looked up as they slipped by, although his dog gave chase to the skittish horses. Shortly after they came upon their first hill fort.

Merlyn called a halt by the gates of the wooden stockade, the tell-tale curls of smoke signalling that it was occupied. "I'll go ahead with Varden to speak to the occupants," he said, dismounting. They approached and pushed the unguarded gate open, slipping inside.

Artorius sought out Gawain and asked, "Do you believe Merlyn's story that I'm Uther's one true son?"

Gawain smiled and replied, "Yes Artorius, I believe it. I cannot say I have evidence, for although Hector was my fellow knight, I did not see him again after Uther sent him into retirement to his farm in the west, and Merlyn also disappeared from court at that time. But you have the look of Uther – his dark and searching eyes, the same unruly hair and shape of his face. He was bigger in the body, mind, but there is still time." Gawain squeezed Artorius's bicep and they shared a laugh. Artorius was mildly content with his answer, but reserved his judgement.

Varden beckoned them to come to the gate and they filed into the fort. Inside, there were two wooden huts built on to the stockade side, a pen with an assortment of animals, and some crude thatched huts in a semi-circle facing a fireplace with a cauldron bubbling over it. About twenty people – family groups – turned and stared at them. Merlyn was deep in conversation with a bearded druid and they stood waiting patiently.

"You are welcome, friends of Merlyn," the older druid said, indicating that they should tether their horses on the fence of the pen. Dirty children came running with arms full of hay for the horses. Drying animal skins and clay pots, and sods of peat cut for burning were the only signs of industry in the place. They were invited to sit by the women, who served elderberry-infused water in wooden beakers to quench their thirst.

"We shall eat and rest for an hour and then continue," Merlyn said, unpacking some object from his saddlebags and entering the hut of the druid.

Varden saw the quizzical look on Artorius's face and whispered, "Best not to ask."

"Is Merlyn a druid?" the curious youth asked.

The burly soldier jabbed a stick at a tuft of moor grass and considered his reply. "He often seeks out the company of lonely druids hidden in remote places. They are rarely seen in towns, where Christian priests would round on them and publicly denounce them. And so Merlyn goes creeping around in swamps and wooded places. But he is not a druid, although he shares some of their beliefs. I think he is searching for something or someone."

Artorius regarded his companion with a quizzical expression. "Why do you think he is searching for someone or something, and who or what?"

Varden laughed, drawing the attention of others. "That I do not know, nor dare to ask. All I know is that he says he is guided by visions and the wisdom he finds in books and scripts – and he has an understanding of our world and what lies in the hearts of men beyond that of ordinary folk. Remember, he was an advisor to two kings."

They shared some biscuits with the silent locals, in exchange for a bowl of meat and vegetable broth. It was clear they cared not for conversation, offering one-word responses when spoken to, or sometimes merely nodding in the direction of the druid's hut.

"There is not much joy here," Gawain muttered, drawing a snigger from Artorius.

BY EVENING, THEY had reached the White Horse, bringing their horses to a standstill above the head and eye of the great carved beast. Below them stood a flattened hill, and beyond was a large village enclosed by a wooded stockade.

Merlyn turned to a curious Artorius and said, "We cannot see the spectacle of the White Horse from above, only from below. When we get down to the village, look up to see it racing across the hillside, and marvel at the Britons who designed and carved it long before the coming of the Romans."

Gawain joined them and remarked, "That flat hill below is called 'Dragon Hill' and is the place where King Uther met his end. He was sick from poisoning and planted his banner beside his wagon, rallying his remaining soldiers about him to fight the oncoming Saxons."

"And where were you?" Artorius asked.

"I was in command of one hundred mounted soldiers. Our task was to harry the Saxon rear ranks and discourage them from attacking the hill. There were too many of them, they outnumbered us three to one, and half of our men had also been poisoned from the well in Verulamium. We could flee no further and were forced to fight them on that unhappy day."

Artorius wondered why Gawain had not fought to the end to defend his king, but kept this thought to himself. "Where were you, Merlyn?" he asked, after a moment's reflection.

"I had not been by Uther's side for some years, my dear boy. I was out of favour and in my marshy hideaway to the west, where I kept an eye on you. It was Caradoc who was his adviser, but they had split their force at Lundein, and Caradoc had returned to Venta."

"It was there that I found Caradoc," Gawain continued, "after I had recovered Uther's body and taken it to Queen Ygerne."

Merlyn led the group off the high ridge, down a winding path that passed the Dragon Hill. He took the trail that wound around the hill, and they spilled out onto the curiously flattened and grass-free top, as the last rays of the sun turned orange at the end of the Vale to the west. "It is said that a noble warrior named Gaarge did slay a dragon on this site, spilling its blood into the earth upon which nothing grows," Merlyn said, dismounting. They all followed him and kicked at the dusty grey earth. No evidence of a battle remained, apart from deep ruts where a heavy wagon had stood. "This must be the place of Uther's last stand."

Gawain came beside him and added, "Yes, I recovered Uther's body here, and noble Vortimer who died by his side. Their bodies were stripped and their swords snatched."

Artorius crouched and ran his fingers through the dry earth, keeping his thoughts to himself.

Merlyn patted his shoulder and said, "Perhaps Uther Pendragon, son of Marcus, son of the dragon, was destined to die here, his blood mingling with that of the ancient beast. Come, Artorius. We'll make haste to the village before darkness sets in."

WITH CARE AND vigilance, the troop of riders moved without incident for two days, following the Fosse Way northwards into the well-cultivated region of Linnius and to the town of Lindum. Merlyn dismounted and gathered the party behind a blackthorn thicket when pale stone walls came into view. Looking at the drooping shoulders of his tired companions, he reassured them.

"This town was built by the Romans as a colonia – a commune for retired legionaries, much like Bedwyr's home. Many of the occupants will be the descendants of ex-legionaries and we can expect a favourable welcome."

"How do you know that?" Artorius asked. "They may be friends to Morgana and Mordred."

"I know because last year I spoke to their council. Lindum is governed by a council of elders from the Coritani tribe, and they elect a leader, in the Roman way. They revere Ambrosius and his mother, Justina, as if they were gods."

"Are they not Christians?" asked Artorius, who had read scripture to his tutor on Hector's farm.

"The Christian faith is also strong."

Merlyn scanned their attentive faces and continued, "However, Artorius has a point. Since the time of my visit much has changed. They may have pledged allegiance to King Mordred and regard Artorius as a fugitive and so, to be cautious, I shall go ahead with Varden and Bedwyr to announce our arrival. The rest of you stay out of sight in the trees. If armed soldiers come pouring out of that gate instead of us, then flee to the forest."

"Would they not also regard you as a fugitive, Merlyn?" Artorius asked.

Merlyn laughed, "Perhaps, but I have faith in their friendship and hope they would allow me my liberty. I feel this is a more likely outcome – let us go."

A pensive hour passed before Varden returned and bade them follow him into the town.

To Artorius's keen eyes, the bridge approach over a dry ditch and stone gatehouse were almost identical to Venta's, but in well-maintained condition. Inside, the town was a bustle of activity with a multitude of people going about their business. Varden led them along the straight central thoroughfare, past two-storey townhouses interspersed with livestock pens, to an open square lined with market stalls. This was dominated by an imposing imperial building, ringed by a columned portico reached from a dozen steps.

Merlyn and Bedwyr stood at the top of the stairs, flanked by ten or so men dressed in white tunics belted at the waist in the Roman fashion. Once dismounted, attendants took the reins of their horses and led them away.

"Come and join us!" Merlyn shouted down to them, as a curious crowd started to gather. Looking about, and noticing the guards, Artorius could see why Merlyn was content for Flavius to dress them like Roman cavalry.

"Welcome, my brothers!" a white-haired elder called, beckoning them to climb the steps. "I am Maddox, elected chief of the council governing Linnius, the region that surrounds our town. Please enter our senate building that we may hear of your journey."

The elders led the way into a huge hall with a high ceiling held up by white stone columns carved in the Greek manner. The walls were draped with tapestries depicting an odd combination of hunting scenes and Christian saints. Their hobnail boots echoed as they were ushered across a marble floor to sit at benches flanking long banqueting tables. The elders took their seats on a raised platform. Spring water treated with herbs was served, whilst Merlyn gave an account of their escape from Venta and journey to the farming colonia near Calleva. He introduced Gawain and Bedwyr to the elders, each standing to bow in a knightly fashion, and then walked to Artorius and clasped his shoulders in both hands.

"This is Artorius, the true son and heir of King Uther Pendragon, of the bloodline of Ambrosius."

The elders leaned forward to peer at the young man and fell into whispered conversations. Maddox took to his feet and said, "We thank you for these introductions, Merlyn. You are known to us, thus your testimony carries weight. Indeed, King Uther's army did pass through our lands some three years before, and he did eat in this hall. I can see some resemblance to the boy… but is there any hard evidence for your claim?"

Merlyn smiled and replied, "There is no written evidence, but it is widely known that Queen Ygerne gave birth to a boy child seventeen summers past. I beseeched King Uther to give the boy into my care for his safety. He was raised on a farm near Glouvia by Sir Hector, a knight to Ambrosius, and his wife, whom Artorius came to know as his parents. When the king fell into poor health, I took the boy to my farm in the west to await the right moment to bring him to court at Venta. Sadly, King Uther was slain in battle before this could come to pass, and now Uther's daughter, Morgana, has taken the crown for her son, Mordred." He bowed to indicate he was finished. Artorius's expression conveyed his admiration at the smooth telling of the tale, causing Merlyn to smile as he took his seat.

The elders huddled in private discussion and soon Maddox announced, "You shall stay here in our barracks as our guests. We have much to talk on, Merlyn, as much has changed since your last visit. You are all invited to dine with us this evening. But first, go refresh yourselves after your travels. Please avail yourselves of our bathhouse."

They were shown to the legionary fort and one of the barrack blocks that had been hurriedly cleared out for them. Wooden beds with straw-filled mattresses made for a welcome change to sleeping rough in the woods and the men sank their saddle-sore bones onto the dry, clean sweetness, content in the knowledge their steeds were also in good hands. Gawain and Bedwyr took Artorius to the bathhouse where they soaked in the warm, mineral-rich waters.

In due course, Maddox's servant appeared before the newly spruced visitors. He led them through a gate into a walled garden at the rear of the hall.

"My friends," Maddox gushed, "I want you to see our Garden of Heroes, that you might gain an insight into our history and the beliefs that support and guide our community."

He led them along a gravel pathway that ran through a well-kept garden of cut grass and flowering bushes, lined with statues carved in marble or stone. "Here is the great general of Rome, Julius Caesar, the first to try and conquer Britannia; then, the great emperors who followed him: Augustus; Claudius, who completed the task of conquering Britannia started by Caesar; Hadrian, who had the foresight to build a wall to keep the northern barbarians out; Septimus Severus who waged war on the painted people north of the wall and died in Britannia at Eboracum; Magnus Maximus, who some say was from this isle; and Constantine the Great, also born here in Britannia and declared Caesar by his legion in Eboracum on the death of his father, Constantius. We also have the great usurper, Carausius, who held this island against Roman authority for ten years."

"Why is he a hero if he rebelled against Rome?" Artorius asked.

"Ah, a good question, Artorius," Maddox replied with a beneficent smile. "It is because he was a great and fair leader who supported a Roman way of organising us, even minting his own coins, and he built the great sea forts that we now hope will keep out the Saxons."

The slow procession brought them to three less-weathered statues, standing white and polished by the rear entrance to the hall. Maddox stood on the steps and turned to address his captive audience. "These last three statues were recently carved by our stone masons to honour our own connection with the great, imperial history of this island. These two on my right are King Constantine and Queen Justina," he announced with pride. "Justina is the daughter to my predecessor as leader of this civitas, Severus Senovara."

He coughed as he noted Merlyn's quizzical raised eyebrow. "Not my immediate predecessor, you understand. There were two between us. Justina became Queen to our first post-Roman king, Constantine. They continued the Roman manners and methods that have helped to halt our slide into barbarian ways."

He clasped his hands in front of his white robe, edged with purple, whilst grinning at his guests. "And finally, to my left, is Ambrosius Aurelianus, their noble son and the last leader of Roman manners to unite our people and keep the barbarian hordes at bay. But I shall leave the telling of their stories to a wandering bard who has composed an epic tale that he shall regale for our pleasure after our meal. Please, come this way."

Maddox led them through the rear of the hall, past a kitchen busy with cooks and attendants, from which sweet smells of herbs and roasting meats assailed their nostrils and tickled their rumbling bellies.

Chapter Four

FOLLOWING THE PORTWAY road eastwards, Velocatus marched his rabble of northern warriors to the gates of the stockade at Stanes, a settlement that guarded the approach to the Romans' first bridge upstream of Lundein, the Ap Pontes, spanning the mighty River Tamesis. The watchman on the parapet above the gatehouse studied the unfamiliar banner of the new king, Mordred, recognising only Uther's red dragon emblem. Velocatus approached on his black stallion and was challenged by the wary guards.

"Who goes there?"

"Velocatus, chief of the Brigantes and father of King Mordred. We come in peace on our way to Lundein." He dismounted and removed his helmet as the gate opened and the headman came forward to greet him.

"You are most welcome, my lord," the elderly man panted, "and your coming is timely as there are Saxon ships on the river. My men are on the bridge as we speak, firing arrows and throwing spears and rocks to hold them back. Come quickly and see."

Velocatus called on his men to follow him at a trot through the wooden gatehouse and along the main thoroughfare to the stone bridgehead. The scene before him was of one dragon-headed ship in the stream, oars out, with warriors holding up shields to deflect arrows and spears, and two ships beached on the shingle downriver, from which Saxon warriors were spilling out and racing towards them.

"Form a line!" Velocatus shouted. "Spear men to the front!" He quickly arranged his warriors in three ranks on the riverside path, each thirty men wide, to meet the onrushing Saxons. His fifty riders were sent across the bridge to reinforce the far bank. Velocatus then deployed his archers and javelin throwers on the bridge and sat behind them, watching from his horse. War cries and the clang and thud of arms clashing echoed beside the bubbling waters.

The Saxons numbered barely one hundred and fifty between three boats, and were not expecting the town's garrison to be bolstered by reinforcements. The ship in the stream gave up its assault on the bridge and floated backwards, under a continuous hail of arrows from the bridge and far bank. On the path, the one hundred Saxon warriors were being overpowered by the superior numbers of Brigantes, some falling to spear thrusts. They soon broke and ran, chased back to their boats by the whooping Brigantes whose tails were up. Many were cut down and only a handful managed to push their cumbersome vessels back into the stream and climb on. The three boats made ungainly turns mid-stream and headed around the bend in the river, chased by riders firing arrows at them.

"Sound the recall," Velocatus commanded, as his riders disappeared from view, enthusiastically pursuing the ships. Two horn blowers moved to the bridge railing and sounded loud blasts. "Kill their wounded and form a burial party. Headman, we shall camp here and continue our journey at sunrise."

A SMILING AND portly bard named Gerwyn, clad in a green woollen smock, cloth breeches and boots of calf leather, plucked random notes on a harp to quieten the boisterous hall. A troop of six children stood behind him, holding hand drums and ready to dance and mime. Items of costume were not quite hidden behind an improvised screen.

Maddox turned to his guests, arrayed in a horseshoe of banqueting tables, and nodded slightly to the roll call of leading families in the region of Linnius. "And now a treat indeed, my honoured guests. This wandering bard, Gerwyn, will regale us with his tale of the coming of Constantine and of the mighty Ambrosius Aurelianus!"

Maddox clapped to signal Gerwyn should commence, and conversations around the tables fell away. The storyteller bowed low and stepped forward, plucking the strings of his harp and accompanied by a steady drum beat.

"Our Roman masters with scorn did leave, tired of repelling troublesome Picts from the northern lands and raiders from the seas that lap on the shores of our beguiling island. They did sail on an ill tide that took their galleys out of our rivers into the Saxon Sea; but no sooner had they departed than the greedy Saxons, with lustful eyes, did sail their dragonhead boats to land on our unguarded shores."

Boos rang out, accompanied by foot stamps and mugs crashed on tables.

"...For the groans of misfortune carry far on a whispering wind. Our holy bishop, Guithelin, did take to ship and summon the noble and Christian prince, Constantine, from our cousins' land of Armorica, to come to our aid." Cheers and mug bashing broke out again.

"He did quell dissenting chiefs and called a council at Londinium, where he was crowned King of Britannia! Our noble

chief, Severus, of the Coritani, did attend that council and offered his beautiful daughter, Justina, in marriage to Constantine. And so, our people's blood did mingle with the Armorican king and three princes were born to them over the years of peace and prosperity that followed."*

A brief interlude took place in which Gerwyn plucked a tune on his harp and danced a few steps, mimicked by the boy drummers. Mugs of ale were replenished and platters of meat and bread served, improving the mood of the hall.

Gerwyn returned to his spot and resumed. *"Ten years did Constantine reign, with the mighty warriors, Allectus of the Alani and Marcus Pendragon, as his generals, patrolling the land and keeping the peace. Invaders were repelled and soon learned not to return."*

The telling of the well-loved tale was oiled with brays, hisses and generous applause for the antics of the children, who leaped about waving wooden swords, gurning at each other and the merry guests.

"Then a rebellious noble named Vortigern did make a surprise attack on Lundein, as that town is now called, with an army of Gwessians from the west and cruel Picts from the north, overpowering the guards and laying waste to that imperial place."

Artorius and Gawain were amused and leaned forwards in their seats, laughing and pointing at the fox-brush wigs the boys now donned. Merlyn sat back and watched them, chuckling occasionally and stroking his beard.

Gerwyn continued, *"In the ensuing battle, many brave soldiers did fall, including our noble king, Constantine. But his champion, Allectus, did lead the royal family to the port and put them to ship, before he was himself cruelly slain.*

"But one of Justina's three sons was missing. Little Prince Aurelius was lost in the chaos of battle, but was saved by the fierce queen of the Regnii, Nathair, who did bear him away to Calleva where she placed him in the care of the mighty and noble commander, Marcus Pendragon."

Gerwyn paused for a mouthful of ale, whilst the boy representing Nathair, the Regnii queen named for the feisty hare, boxed the air, flicked the floppy ears he wore, and groomed his imaginary whiskers, much to the amusement of the guests.

"In time the boy, Aurelius, was sent to Armorica across the Gaulish Sea to be reunited with his mother, our gracious queen, Justina. He did grow to be a strong man, skilled in warfare, and did join the Roman legion in Gaul under General Aetius, where he progressed in his favour to the rank of tribune."

The boys now marched in Roman helmets, too big for their heads, with their swords out in front.

"Aurelius did return to Britannia with an army and engaged the tyrant Vortigern and his Saxon foederati in battle, winning a famous victory at Guloph Hill!

"The noble Aurelius did kneel before Bishop Germanicus to be anointed the true king of Britannia, after his father, Constantine. He was given the name Ambrosius - the Divine One - and charged with being God's champion in a holy war against the pagan Saxons. His strong and just arm did raise the sword Excalibur above his head and his followers did see him as Ambrosius, chosen by God to lead them."

This triumphant scene was met with noisy approval. Looks were shot at Artorius, who sat unmoved, except for a glance at a chortling Merlyn.

"But the matter was not yet sealed. The sly Vortigern had fled the field and was still king in the east. Ambrosius did pursue him across the land, gathering more men to his banner, and trapped him in his hall, burning it with a great fire which no one survived."

Merlyn leaned towards Artorius and whispered, "Not quite true. I did escape the flames as a youth barely older than you, and rescued Vortigern's youngest children, including Vortimer and Pascent. More on them later." He resumed his attentive posture and left Artorius with many images swirling in his head.

Gerwyn continued, "Ambrosius made his court at the legion town of Corinium, and founded with twelve true men the first order of knights in this land, the Knights of the Dragon and Bear."

Boys strutted before the tables with chests puffed and swords held high, and Gawain stood and bowed to a raucous reception.

"These knights did keep the enemy at bay and Ambrosius did rule over these lands in peace for many years. A pact was made with Triphun, King of Dyfed, on our western shore, whose daughter, Gwendolyn, Ambrosius received in marriage. She bore him three sons, royal princes who were yet boys when Ambrosius was poisoned at his feast by a Saxon spy."

Boos, hisses and general condemnation rang out as the boys enacted a scene where Ambrosius fell, clutching his throat. Artorius pushed his plate away and pulled a sour face. This amused some of his fellows, but drew a disapproving look from Merlyn, who had failed to prevent the sly assassination. Gawain was also curiously subdued, dwelling on fond memories of his secretive moments with Ambrosius.

"And so, the golden reign of the divine Ambrosius, sent by God to keep the Saxons, Picts and Scotti at bay, did come to an abrupt end. The nobles gathered and made the warrior Uther Pendragon, brother of the divine Ambrosius, their king. And so, Uther did take the battle to the rebellious Saxons. He chased them across the land, winning a victory over them at Badon Hill, where many of our own Coritani sons did join with our neighbours and fight bravely in that righteous slaughter of our enemy. Long live the Coritani!"

Gerwyn bowed low and stepped back, signalling that the tale was finished. The high table applauded the entertainers, who walked backwards, bowing as they took their leave, but then scrambled forwards to collect the coin and trinkets tossed to them by the guests. The feast continued and conversation filled the air as the happy revellers celebrated their glorious history whilst some brooded on their uncertain future. Maddox rose to his feet and at last hushed the drunken guests by banging his goblet on the table.

"My honoured guests, you do well to chew on the bold endeavours of our forebears. But Merlyn the healer craves that we hold our peace and give him a hearing."

Merlyn ignored the throat clearings and a rumble of conversations tailing off as his audience settled, and began. "I wish only to thank my lord Maddox and his household for their warm welcome and hospitality. Artorius here is indeed the one true son of Uther Pendragon, born to Queen Ygerne and taken by me to a place of safety to be raised by the family of a noble knight. His birthright has been wrenched from him by Morgana, Uther's first-born daughter, whose son, Mordred, now bears the title King, but whose tiny head cannot wear the crown." This last drew sniggers.

"Of the two sons of Vortigern, the eldest, Vortimer, fought bravely for Uther and gave his life defending him from Saxons led by his treacherous brother, Pascent. I have heard that this villain, Pascent, slayer of both his own brother and King Uther, is the lord of the Angles in their settlement on your coast, barely a day's ride from this hall." Angry shouts and mug-throwing broke out amongst the rowdy gathering.

"I therefore entreat of you, noble Maddox of the Coritani, that together we raise an army to find and kill the traitor Pascent, and drive the Angle invaders back into the sea whence they came!"

The wily Maddox took to his feet and quelled the boisterous hall with raised hands. This matter had been raised before the feast and he now judged the mood of the gathering to be favourable to Merlyn's proposal. "I am in agreement with Merlyn. It is our right and duty to rid our lands of these foreign settlers who take without asking. They occupy the settlement on the coast at the mouth of our River Glein and block our trade from the sea. Our battle-ready guests will lead our men and take back our port. Let the word go out to our villages to muster the men and prepare for war!"

THE GREY STONE walls and towers of Lundein stood intact before Velocatus as he led his troop of fifty riders at the head of his marching men. They emerged from the shade of trees onto a cleared space around the town that was clustered with crude huts of mud and thatch, and pens empty of animals. To their right there were cries and screams by the muddy river bank, where Saxon warriors chased fisherfolk who had been too slow to seek refuge behind the gates of the town. As many as eight longships were beached on the shingle or tied to the wooden pier built by Romans.

"Riders, announce our arrival by chasing off those Saxons by the riverside. Men, follow me to the gates," Velocatus commanded. They completed their march to the bridge over the ditch before the west gatehouse, and the gates were duly opened to admit them. Velocatus was led by the captain of the guard through well-kept streets of townhouses and livestock pens to the forum at the centre of the largest town in Britannia.

"You are most welcome," a town elder gushed, walking down the steps of an impressive imperial building to meet him. Velocatus dismounted and removed his helmet as his men stood in rows behind him. His black hair and beard hung in braids with silver ringlets swinging at the ends. The tattoo swirls on his cheeks gave him an appearance more in keeping with the barbarian savages outside than the cultured occupants of the town.

"You have kept your town in good order," he said, looking about him. "I am Velocatus of the Brigantes, father of King Mordred, he who sends me to rid you of these unwelcome raiders."

"Your coming is most timely, my lord Velocatus, as we have beseeched the king to send men to our aid for many weeks. Our guards have defended the walls of our town but we lack arrows and javelins, so now fire pebbles from sling shots at them. The settlement on the south side has been overrun by these foul barbarians and they now command the bridge. Our captain can take you to the south gatehouse and brief you on their numbers."

"They are a curse sent by the Devil himself," a grey-robed priest standing by his side added.

Velocatus grunted and mounted his black stallion, following the captain with his men. A scene of devastation greeted him from the stone parapet, with burnt and smashed huts and boats scattered across the foreshore. Saxons strolled around with grim purpose, some carrying their plunder, or leading strings of bound slaves, to their boats.

"How many?" Velocatus asked.

"There are close to five hundred of the brutes, a greater number than that of our guard."

"We chased three boats back downriver yesterday from Stanes. Are they here?"

"Yes, they returned the past evening and are included in our count."

"Good. Then let us eat and rest this night and be ready to fight in the morning," Velocatus said, fixing his black eyes on the smaller man and slapping his shoulder. "My warriors have already washed their blades on Saxon blood and are eager for more."

"I will show you to the barracks in the fort, my lord," the relieved captain replied.

Beneath them Saxon warriors shouted oaths in their guttural tongue, herding captives who were made to drag the carcasses of slaughtered livestock to campfires, their confident tones rising like a fearful curse to the ears of those manning the walls.

Chapter Five

WIPING SNOT FROM his nose with the back of his hand, a boy jostled with his mates to get a better view. Frustrated at his obscured position and the whoops of the crowd, he pushed between the baskets and woollen mantles of women come to market, opening the curtains to reveal a gladiatorial battle between two warriors. The younger man, his nutbrown hair contained by a leather band, was wielding a long sword, whose polished blade deflected shards of morning sunlight into the eyes of his gasping audience. The older man, a grizzled veteran, controlled the contest with deft movements and subtle parries, shouting breathless advice to his protégé.

"Be watchful, or you'll lose your head!" the tutor barked.

Frustrated, the younger man twirled his elegant sword above his head and lunged at his opponent. A body swerve and counter thrust had him rocking back on his heels. Shouts of encouragement from the crowd urged him on to another assault, this time a feint to the left, then slash to the right.

"Good. Better," Varden huffed, launching his own offensive.

Pushing his way through the sizeable crowd, Merlyn stood and watched for a moment, hands on hips. "This is good preparation, Artorius. Your sword arm will soon be tested in battle with the enemy. Come with me, both of you."

Working their way through the forum, now full of farm hands and townsfolk eager for battle, they climbed the steps of the hall and joined Gawain, Bedwyr and Maddox.

"This is my eldest son, Ambrose. I commend him to your care, Merlyn," Maddox said with pride. The shy youth stood straight under his father's stare.

"He shall be a companion for Artorius as they seem to be age mates. No doubt, you know your letters, Ambrose?"

"Yes, sir," he replied in a whisper to the imposing healer.

"Then you must ensure that Artorius does not forget his. But for now, our business is war." He turned to face the throng and silenced them with raised hands. "The day has come when we ride out to evict the unwelcome settlers from over the sea and reclaim your lands!"

The crowd of a thousand eager faces cheered in response. More were entering the forum, driven by Merlyn's loud and commanding tone, pushing forward from connecting streets. The muster had raised a sizable army of keen but unschooled men, their calloused hands gripping hoes and pitch forks, their weathered faces set in stoic determination to confront and fight those who coveted their land – the land of their ancestors.

A priest stepped forward and held his hands up to the throng as if giving a blessing. "Many of you know me. I am chaplain to the council of elders, Father Samson of the Order of Saint Augustine. I bestow the blessing of Our Lord Jesus the Christ on you all, in our holy and just war against the Saxons who defile our churches and bring their pagan gods to this land." He made the sign of the cross and declaimed his prayers in a high Roman tongue before the fidgeting Coritani.

When Father Samson fell silent, Merlyn bowed to him and stepped forward. "People of Linnius, you have come to defend your homes and way of life. This moment has not come by chance. It was foretold that a leader of noble birth would unite the people against the pagan invaders who enter this land like a plague and cruelly take what is not theirs."

He acknowledged the rowdy cheers and then beckoned Artorius to come forward. "I now give you Arthur, son of Uther and nephew of mighty Ambrosius!"

"Arthur?" Artorius whispered.

"'Arthur' declares that you belong to our island's future. It has the same meaning as your Roman name – as strong as a bear." Merlyn smiled and urged Arthur to draw Excalibur and lift it high. After a few moments, he turned to hush the crowd. "Arthur and his commanders, Gawain, Bedwyr and Varden, shall lead your army. You shall train in units, each with a commander. They will test your readiness for battle. Only then will we know when we shall be ready to march." With that, Merlyn moved back and nodded to Gawain and Bedwyr to organise the eager rabble into manageable units.

"Come Arthur and Ambrose, let us retire with the elders to make the plans that are necessary for an army marching to war."

"YOU CANNOT MARRY me off to a fat, illiterate oaf and exile me to a filthy hovel in the corner of this land!" Morgaise fumed, hands on hips, glaring at the impassive Lord Caradoc.

"It is the will of your king, my lady," Caradoc smirked, enjoying her discomfort.

"When shall we meet this Chief Geraint of the Dumnonii people?" Ygerne asked, laying a hand on her fretting daughter's shoulder.

"There will be a feast in his honour and to mark the occasion of the betrothal one week hence. He is a powerful ally to King Mordred and he commands a sizeable army. He also rules over the lands of your first husband, Gorlois of Cornubia, my lady queen," he said, with a mocking bow.

Ygerne glared at him. "Do not mock my family, Lord Caradoc. Gorlois is the father of Morgaise and in life a better man than you."

Caradoc smiled and moved to the door, turning to add, "Chief Geraint will be most pleased to see his fair prize. Make ready, Morgaise, for you shall be leaving with him."

Once alone, Ygerne hugged her two daughters and consoled the weeping Morgaise. "It was always going to be this way, my love. At least you will be near us, a little to the west. If he had married you to a rough northern chief like Velocatus, then I would weep with you. As the lady of Dumnonia you will have the company of priests and courtiers with manners. It is not the worst fate."

"If only Artorius would come to rescue us," Anne sighed.

"He will yet have a say in the happenings in this land," Ygerne replied dreamily. "I feel sure we shall see him again. Until then, we must continue to pray to Jesus and the Blessed Virgin Mary to keep him safe and for guidance and consolation."

A COMPROMISE OF three days was reached, when Merlyn asked the commanders how long they would need to get the men ready for war.

"A week is too long," Merlyn said, calculating in his head the cost of feeding the men, and ending the debate. "Any delay may lead to the enemy discovering our intentions. We march to the Angle settlement on the fourth morning from now." The town was alive with activity as blacksmiths pounded their anvils, cobblers worked and fitted leather boots, seamstresses sewed and donkeys trod their circular paths to grind the harvested wheat into flour. Workshops had been set up to make shields, armour and weapons.

"My men have captured these two loitering by the river," Varden said, interrupting a meeting by throwing two wretches onto the floor of the hall.

Merlyn regarded them with a mixture of alarm and disdain.

Maddox fired questions at them and noted their fearful denials. "They are locals. But even so, we cannot take the chance that they may be spies. We shall lock them up until after you have gone."

After the meeting, Merlyn asked Arthur to accompany him. He led them through the forum, into a side street, and to a blacksmith's yard. "Is it ready?" he demanded of a muscular, soot-blackened man in a leather apron. The smith nodded and went indoors, returning with a shining silver helmet. Merlyn took it in his hands and studied it, his bristling eyebrows rising and falling in silent appraisal.

"This is a fine job, my man," he declared, giving the helmet to Arthur and motioning him to put it on. Merlyn stood back and admired the customised cavalry helmet. New side flaps had been added and an emblem of a dragon had been welded on top, its wings spread and snout open in readiness to strike. Small openings had been carved at the sides for hearing. An ornate nose guard hung at the front and intricate symbols adorned the sides.

"Do you like it?" he asked the beaming youth.

"It is wondrous, and light to hold, Merlyn," Arthur replied, twirling it in his hands and placing it again on his head.

"And arm and shin guards," the blacksmith announced with pride, bringing the embellished items. Arthur tied them on with the fitted leather thongs.

"Yes, my friend," Merlyn said, inspecting the items, "you have fulfilled your brief. Here, six ounces of silver, as promised." Merlyn deftly cut six notches along his thin bar and handed the gleaming metal to the grateful man. With a nod, he pushed the items into a sack and led Arthur away by his arm. "And now for your new mount."

They walked further from the town centre to a row of animal pens that backed onto the high stone walls. "Ah, there she is," Merlyn said, pointing to a dappled grey mare. Arthur approached the sturdy and skittish creature, stroking its nose and then running a hand along its flank.

"She is beautiful," he murmured.

"Then you shall have her, and name her," Merlyn said triumphantly, beckoning the owner to approach. Removing his cap, the horse dealer shuffled forward, making small bobs of his head. Everyone in Lindum knew of Merlyn's commanding authority and natural leadership, that had galvanised and breathed confidence into their collective endeavours.

"I would willing give her to the young prince, but you know how times are hard, my lord…"

"Yes, yes," Merlyn tersely interrupted, loath to waste a moment. "We shall pay the agreed amount and take her." He haggled briefly with the fawning dealer to include the bit and bridle, and Arthur merrily led the horse away. "We need a fitting saddle and a breast piece, Arthur. Come, let us visit the saddler on our way to the stables."

Outside the town walls Gawain, Bedwyr and Varden were conducting military drills. The volunteers had been assessed and divided into four units – foot soldiers, cavalry, archers and non-combatant supporters. Gawain led the mounted soldiers in cavalry drills, whilst Bedwyr and his men took archery and sword fighting practice.

The majority were foot soldiers, and these were armed with long spears, short swords and sturdy rectangular shields with metal bosses, in the Roman legionary style. Varden drilled them in defensive and offensive manoeuvres, knowing in his heart that nothing could prepare the uninitiated for the full horrors of war.

"Keep a tight formation, shields touching the man next to you!" he yelled as he surveyed the awkward movements of the line as it advanced, spear tips bristling between shields. "I want the strongest men in the front line to take the first impact of the enemy. The second row will raise their shields over their heads and the heads of the men in the front line, protecting them from arrows and thrown objects." He had eight hundred men in his unit – less than the size of two Roman cohorts, and barely one fifth of a legion.

Merlyn appeared by his side, startling him further by reading his thoughts. "No Roman legion has taken the field on this island in a hundred years, Varden. A thousand men should be enough to see off a dozen ship-loads of raiders."

"A thousand experienced men, maybe," Varden replied sourly. "I have eight hundred farmers and assorted tradesmen."

"Are they ready?" Merlyn asked.

"No."

"Well, we march tomorrow anyway. Confine them to barracks this night, for they will not march well on sore heads."

ARTHUR WAS LESS than impressed with Merlyn's cosseting. After angry words, Merlyn finally relented and allowed Arthur to lead the cavalry procession with Gawain. The twin ranks of cavalry with their lances pointing to the sky and round shield bosses glinting in the morning sun took the cheers of the womenfolk and children as they led the procession out through Lindum's main gatehouse. Four hundred riders were followed by eight hundred marching men, then assorted archers and skirmishers who earned a living as hunters, some marching and some on ponies. Merlyn brought up the rear with the camp followers and cooks in oxen and donkey carts. They followed a well-worn dirt track that ran beside the river Glein, and crossed a bridge to its muddy tributary, the river Dubglas that conveyed dark, silted water to the coast.

The distance was not great – merely thirty miles over flat land – but two days was still needed by the slow convoy. They reached the coastal village, called Gleinmuth by the locals, as the sun touched the hills to the west. Salt in the air spurred on the tired travellers, but when the last creaking wagon wheels were finally still, word of what awaited them sped from the dismounted cavalry, through the ranks of dismayed foot soldiers, to the arthritic knife grinder at the rear.

The Angles were ready for them. They were arrayed in a line of conical helmets and oval shields that hung from sharpened stakes before the platform of a wooden fence. The fence enclosed the fishing village in a semi-circle. From a hilltop overlooking the estuary, the Briton army could count the masts of a dozen or more ships lined on the beached inlet behind the flimsy stockade that contained perhaps thirty dwellings. Gulls wheeled overhead, their squawks taken as a warning by the uneasy men.

Merlyn called the commanders to set their plans. Varden had wasted no time in lining his shield men up and rousing them to taunt the enemy by banging their shields and shouting threats.

Varden joined the others at a trot. "We have maybe one hour of light," he said, sniffing the autumn air and looking west, to red streaks below the sun.

Gawain replied, "Merlyn is for setting camp and waiting for the morning."

"They may take to ship in the night or at first light," Bedwyr commented, clearly itching for a fight.

Merlyn studied the faces of his experienced leaders, seeing their eagerness, and then asked Varden his opinion.

The old soldier paused before speaking. "We have the numbers on them and could breach their stockade with the Roman trick of making a bridge of shields – a variation of the tortoise that they have lightly practised. My gut feeling is to strike them now and gain entry to the stockade from where they cannot escape except to their boats."

"Then we must act swiftly," Gawain said.

Merlyn was doubtful. "Gaining swift entry to the stockade is vital, or we shall lose many men and our villagers will lose heart. Can you show them how to make a shield bridge in short time?"

"I know my men, a little," Varden replied, then adding, "they will learn it."

"If the three of you are in agreement," Merlyn sighed.

"A swift victory is what's needed, and the ground is firm and dry," Gawain added with a smile.

"Alright, then it's on you to lead the assault," Merlyn said, gripping Varden's arm.

Varden puffed his cheeks and cracked a smile. "Good. Then I shall brief my men and lead them down the slope to the front of the stockade. The enemy will concentrate their men there. Bedwyr should support us with his archers, but send some men around the sides of the stockade to gain access to the harbour and prevent them taking to their ships. Gawain's riders must fire arrows at the defenders and keep them thinly stretched along the walls."

"Gawain, will you give me the Jute, Herrig, as guard for Arthur?"

Gawain looked startled at this unexpected request. "Yes, of course. I shall send him."

With that the commanders strode away to make their preparations. Arthur and Ambrose had remained silent, hovering on the fringes of the meeting. "With me, you two," Merlyn commanded, striding with purpose of his own towards the rear of the army.

"When will I get to fight and dip Excalibur's blade in the blood of the enemy?" Arthur said, pulling at Merlyn's cloak.

"When the men have gained entrance to the stockade, we shall join the fray. Be patient, Arthur. Your moment will come. I would see Pascent captured, so you can have the honour of severing his treacherous head from his vile body." Noticing Ambrose's blanched face, he added, "But you and I, Ambrose, shall leave the fighting to those who are eager for it."

They were joined by Herrig, riding a solid farm horse, his broad shoulders and assured manner giving them comfort. "I would not ask you to kill your fellows, Herrig," Merlyn said, "unless in defence of our party here."

Herrig grinned and replied, "The Angles raided my village. They may be kinsmen, but they are also rivals for slender resources. I will fight and kill them if I have to."

Varden's purposeful strides towards his unit came to an abrupt halt at the unwelcome sight of dozens of men from the rear rank in the act of setting up camp, their shields and weapons lying on the ground. The front rank stood steady, but behind them men were chatting and dawdling. Just beyond the embryonic camp, Father Samson was blessing fifty or more soldiers kneeling before him. Eyes bulging with rage, Varden shouted for the horn blowers to come to him.

"Blow your horns until your lungs burst!" he raged. A deep booming noise shattered the relative calm of dusk, entering through the ears and into the guts of the startled soldiers, who instantly stopped what they were doing and re-formed the line. Their hopes for a night's rest before a dawn assault lay shattered. Varden called his four sub-commanders to him and delivered a swift briefing. In truth, it was a pleasant end to the day, with not a cloud in the blue sky.

Five minutes later, further horn blasts across the ridge signalled the advance of Varden's front line, followed by two hastily re-constituted rear ranks. They advanced downhill until positioning themselves thirty yards from the stockade. Varden noted the shallow dry ditch before the stockade, and a good eight yards of ground between ditch and wooden wall. It would be enough. He had briefed his four sub-commanders, who now gathered their units and barked out orders as a few arrows whistled through the air towards them, thudding into raised shields. As soon as Gawain's cavalry started their sweeps before the walls, hollering and firing arrows, Varden ordered the advance. With shields up in a tortoise formation, the four units advanced on their selected portions of the stockade. Behind them archers fired at the defenders on the walls, aiming to keep their heads down.

Rocks assailed them as they approached the wall and breached the ditch. Varden led one of the units and shouted instructions for the tallest men at the front, in a rank of ten abreast, to hold their shields high above their heads with upstretched arms. They tilted them backwards towards a second rank, who lifted their shields to join those in front, and then a third rank crouched under their upraised shields. The effect was to make a ramp reaching towards the top of the wooden stakes, up which their roaring comrades now ran, leaping onto the battlements, short swords at the ready to engage in hand-to-hand combat with the enraged defenders. The efforts of Gawain's cavalry had ensured that the defenders were thinly spread along the platform, allowing the raiders to get amongst them in sufficient numbers to overpower the Angles.

From on top of the ridge, Merlyn could see that two of the four ramps had proven successful, and Varden's men were now fighting on the battlements within the stockade. The cries of battle filled the air as he rallied the reserves and started a steady advance downhill towards the main gate, in expectation that those inside would fight their way there to lift the boom. As the gates were flung open, the soldiers outside flooded through with a roar of aggression. Merlyn rode beside Arthur and grabbed his reins, indicating they should hang back and wait. Arthur sat fuming as Gawain and his cavalry streamed through the gates, following the infantry to the bloody slaughter within.

After twenty minutes and in the growing gloom, Merlyn led the way through the gates. Inside was a scene of utter devastation, with burning thatched huts lighting up a muddy mess of dead and dying warriors and horses littering the ground. A guard of foot soldiers escorted them to the centre of the village, where an open space stood before a longhouse of mud bricks and thatch. Villagers were corralled in one corner, surrounded by guards as they cowered in the mud.

Merlyn barked out some orders above the din of cheering soldiers. "Ambrose, go and instruct the guards that the local fisherfolk should not be harmed. Arthur, come with me." He spurred his horse forward through the throng to where Varden and Gawain were holding prisoners. Herrig stayed close and kept his helmet on, not wishing his flaxen hair to be seen by the victorious Britons and be mistaken for the enemy.

"This one is Pascent," Gawain proclaimed, holding down a snarling man on his knees whose hands were tied behind his back. "And this is Saxon Sting, the sword of King Uther!" he held up a bloodied blade of white steel, with a bejewelled handle and cross-piece, to the cheers of the soldiers. Arthur marvelled at the tousled hair and bloodied face of his hero, eyes shining and mouth fixed in a cruel grimace of war.

"Indeed, you are a reliable witness, Gawain," Merlyn said as they joined the group. "Is the harbour secured?" Merlyn asked his commanders.

"There is still fighting there," Varden replied. "I have sent men to aid Bedwyr in securing the ships. We have taken many prisoners, held in cattle pens behind the hall."

"Good. Let there be no unnecessary killings," Merlyn said, looking about him. "Is there a village headman?"

An elderly man came forward from the shadow of the longhouse. "I am Hallam, the headman," he said in a frail and trembling voice.

"Your people will not be harmed, Hallam," Merlyn declared in a loud voice. "Let them help our men to remove the dead. Have the wounded brought to your hall where I may inspect and tend to them." With these calming words, the madness of battle ebbed away, as soldiers turned to tend to their comrades.

Merlyn approached Pascent and said, "We have captured you, son of Vortigern. You have travelled far from the boy I rescued from the flames of Genoreu. But you chose a different path from your brother, and sided with your mother's people."

Pascent spat blood and looked up with dark, hateful eyes. "I chose strength over weakness, Merlyn. The tide of Saxon warriors will continue to wash on these shores and claim this land..."

Gawain slapped the back of his head. "Enough of your lies. We shall defend our land from all pagan raiders."

Merlyn grunted. He knew there was little more to be said. Turning to Arthur he whispered, "Are you willing to kill this man?"

Arthur looked up with wild eyes, the excitement of witnessing battle still pumping in his veins. "Yes, I can and will."

"Then strike firmly and hard with Excalibur, for your destiny beckons."

Merlyn turned to face the sea of weary faces behind and declared, "This man, Pascent, son of Vortigern and Rowena the Saxon queen, slayer of King Uther and his own brother, Vortimer, is sentenced to death for his crimes. I call upon Arthur, leader of the Britons and son of Uther, to strike the blow!"

An eerily subdued crowd gathered around as Arthur drew his sword and stood beside the kneeling Pascent, who was accepting of his fate. None present challenged Merlyn's authority. Arthur looked at Gawain who grinned and nodded encouragement. Raising Excalibur, Arthur brought the sharp, flashing blade down onto Pascent's neck, severing his head with one swipe. Cheers rang out as Arthur stood, fascinated, as the dead man's body jerked and swayed briefly before toppling over, blood spurting from his severed arteries.

Gawain bent and lifted the head by its tangled light-brown hair, displaying it to the raucous crowd. "Behold the slayer of King Uther!"

Arthur stared at his gory blade and felt a sickness in the pit of his stomach as his bloodlust slowly dwindled.

Chapter Six

TWO LINES OF mounted soldiers approached the stone walls of Lindum, followed at some distance by weary foot soldiers. A sentry squinted in the afternoon sun at the banners in front, slightly confused by the unfamiliar symbols. He called the captain of the guard.

Stopping short of the stone gatehouse, Velocatus shouted up at the men lining the parapet, "Open the gates to the father of King Mordred!"

After a brief delay, the wooden boom was lifted and the gates swung open. Velocatus led his men into a familiar Roman setting, noting the clean streets and well-kept shop fronts. They progressed at a slow pace, past gawping women and children, to the central forum, where his soldiers arranged themselves in orderly lines.

Maddox and his fellow elders came down the steps of the hall to greet their visitors. "You are most welcome to our town of Lindum, noble sir. I am Maddox, leader of the town council of elders…"

"And I am Velocatus, chief of the Brigantes and father to King Mordred," he interrupted. "We are travelling north and ask for your hospitality."

"It is given, Lord Velocatus. I will arrange for space to be made in our barracks. You and your officers are welcome to our hall, where I shall order refreshment." He swept an arm upwards, indicating they should dismount and enter the hall. In passing his fellows, he shot warning glances and hoped they would have the guile to not mention the arrival of Merlyn and Arthur, whom he knew, from messengers recently arrived, to be fugitives from the king's justice. It was an awkward and delicate situation. He gave orders to an aide to have the possessions of their other visitors removed to storage, the beds prepared for new occupants, and the soldiers to be refreshed at the town's well.

Velocatus's mood lightened after supping the ale, made by monks, he was told, in their monastery by the river. "Ah, this fine ale has taken the dryness from my throat," he beamed, banging his goblet down on the table for a hovering maid to replenish. "Where are your men at arms?" he suddenly asked. "I count only a handful on your walls, and saw few men in the streets."

Maddox smiled and replied, "We have sent a force to the coast to repel a number of Angle raiders, my lord."

"That is good. This work is never done, Maddox. The king approves of his towns keeping a standing army in these uncertain times. Let me tell you of our victory over the devilish Saxons in Lundein only last week…"

Maddox listened patiently, whilst whispering the occasional instruction to attendants to make preparations for supper.

After an hour, Velocatus rose from his seat and stretched, belching loudly. "Pray, allow me to stretch my legs and walk to your riverside and see your well-kept lands. Will you give me a guide?"

"Indeed, my lord Velocatus. My priest and groundsman will show you where they grow the grapes for our sweet wine and the barley for our ale and gruel." The dusty riders withdrew from the hall, leaving Maddox to convene a hasty meeting of his elders to address the thorny issue of the imminent return of their army from the coast, with rebels at their head.

Outside, Velocatus breathed in the cool autumn air and allowed two priests and the portly groundsman to guide him and his commanders towards a side gate to the town.

"Your new king, Mordred, would be most pleased to see this town of purpose and fine manners," he declared, slapping the groundsman on the back as they emerged from the oak door and took in the vista before them. The river was alive with boatmen, while workers ploughed the fields, turning the stubble of the harvest back into the soil that would remain fallow for the winter months.

"A new king, my lord?" the rosy-cheeked gardener replied. "But we have our own king now – King Arthur of the Britons."

MERLYN SUPERVISED THE breaking of camp in the morning and set a slow procession on its way back to Lindum. Keeping Arthur, Ambrose and Herrig close, he paid a visit to the village headman, Hallam, with words of advice and encouragement. The commanders met in the village and it was decided to row the ships upriver as far as they would go, for use by the towns elders as they saw fit. Bedwyr and his men were delegated to take charge of the ships. A small unit of fifty men under a local commander was instructed to remain behind to help rebuild damaged huts and the stockade, and stay there until the first storms of winter would make the prospect of any further raids unlikely until the spring.

They joined the rear of the wagon train, Merlyn's mind still fully alive to the mission in hand. "Arthur, upon our arrival in Lindum, you should present Saxon Sting to Gawain – a famous blade for a gallant knight. And Ambrose, you shall record these events by the mouth of the River Glein, as Arthur's first battle."

Arthur did not reply. He was still subdued after his execution of Pascent. He had sought counsel from Father Samson in a quiet moment after the battle, the words of the priest still echoing in his head: "My son, it is only right that you should feel guilt and remorse for killing a man, for it is one of God's holy commandments that thou shalt not kill. It is an unnatural act. However, our Lord God will absolve you from killing your enemies in defence of His people. War is a terrible thing, but our war against vile and cruel invaders is a just war. Come, let us pray together and you shall receive God's absolution."

They stopped at the halfway marker to make camp for the night and Derward organised camp followers to fetch water, light fires and set about preparing a meal. Arthur avoided Merlyn and took Ambrose for a walk in the woods.

"You look troubled, my lord Arthur," Ambrose observed, kicking at fallen leaves under an oak tree.

"It is no easy thing to cut a man's head off, even if he is the murderer of your father. Do not call me 'lord' when we are alone, Ambrose. Arthur is sufficient."

"It takes courage to kill a man, Arthur. Is it your first?"

"Yes, although I fought for my life with my knife against an assassin sent to kill me in Glouvia. I wounded him on the arm, but Merlyn stepped in to slay him."

"You are much loved, Arthur, that I have seen. Merlyn and our noble commanders will look out for you." Ambrose picked up a twig and began fencing with Arthur. This lightened Arthur's mood and they chased each other with sticks for a while, briefly indulging in the games of youth, until an attendant summoned them.

They ate dinner and bedded down for the night. After the morning breakfast, they soon resumed their journey. An hour along the road, Varden rode back from the vanguard and came to Merlyn's side. "I have been sending scouts ahead to Lindum since first light, but none have returned," he grumbled.

"Would you expect them back so soon?" Merlyn asked.

"Perhaps not. But if they do not come soon, I will ride ahead with Gawain and a small company of his men."

"Your caution is an admirable quality, dear Varden," Merlyn laughed.

"It has kept me alive through many dangers, Merlyn," he replied, jabbing his heels into his horse and galloping ahead.

"What is it?" Arthur shouted to Merlyn's back.

Turning, he replied, "It's Varden's extra sense – that of a soldier. He imagines enemies behind every bush. But for that, we must be grateful."

THE SUN WAS at its highest when Gawain and Varden rounded a bend in the road and came face-to-face with a line of Briton warriors bristling with spears, steam rising to the clear sky from the nostrils of their horses. They pulled up their mounts and quickly conferred, barely fifty yards from those blocking their way.

"They are of a Briton tribe from the north, judging by their appearance," Varden said.

"We should try and talk to them and find out their purpose," Gawain replied.

Varden kneeled up on the back of his mount to try and see past them. "I don't like it. We do not know how many they are or who has sent them. To approach might prompt them to attack."

Gawain pondered the situation. "We have fifty riders. I'll send a man back for the remaining two hundred and fifty to come. We can sit here and face them, or edge towards them until close enough to shout our question."

"Alright," Varden agreed. "But if they charge us, I'm of a mind to turn and run until we join our forces."

Gawain sent his swiftest rider, and they sat for some minutes, regarding their silent and unmoving opponents. "Shall we edge forward and attempt to find out…" Gawain began, but stopped when he noticed their opponent's front rank moving at a walk towards them.

"Let's hold our nerve," Varden growled, tightly reining his restive mount. Six riders approached and stopped some thirty yards away.

"I am Ronan, captain of the guard of Chief Velocatus of the Brigantes. We are tasked with arresting the escaped renegades, Merlyn, Artorius, Gawain and Percival. If they are in your company, you would be wise to hand them over."

Varden leaned across and grabbed the reins of Gawain's horse. "Do not rise to their bait, Sir Gawain. They do not recognise you. Let me reply to them." Gawain's blood was up and Varden could see he was about to draw his sword. Their eyes met, and Gawain slowly calmed himself, assenting to his wiser comrade with a nod.

Varden moved his horse forward two lengths and responded, "We are guardsmen from Gleinmuth, come to report a victory over Saxon raiders. Will you let us pass?"

Ronan scoffed at this and replied, "We have your scouts in our custody, and they have talked of Arthur and his sword. You must lead us to them, or we shall display your heads above the gates of this town." His men joined in his mocking laughter.

Varden turned his horse and shouted, "Turn and flee, comrades!" He spurred his spirited mount into a full gallop and they fanned out across the flat grasslands that bordered the track, showing their flanks to their pursuers as they raced back to the caravan.

Gawain's scout had galloped for barely thirty minutes before reaching the main body of the army and delivering his news. Merlyn ordered all mounted warriors to ride with all haste to support Varden and Gawain. He instructed the eager Arthur to remain at his side and Herrig to stay close.

"You will see battle soon enough, Arthur, if my guess is correct. Now come with me to the head of the men and we shall lead them at a swift march. Ambrose, you stay with the wagons and take them on the next side track to nearby villages and disperse them. Derward will assist you."

THE BROAD FLAT lands of Linnius made for good pasture, but also allowed for a full cavalry charge. The two forces lined up, Gawain placing his riders in two ranks, each of one hundred and fifty men. They faced a force of a similar number, spread out across the width of the river meadow that was dissected by a narrow stream of black water.

"What is the name of this place?" Merlyn asked one of Varden's unit commanders.

"It is named for the stream that crosses it – the Dubglas, because of the black water flowing from a wild moor where no one lives," the gruff soldier replied.

"Hmmm, the Battle of the Black Water," Merlyn muttered.

At a trot, Gawain raised his green dragon pennant as the line moved forward, fording the shallow stream, allowing wind to moan through the mouths of the bronze dragon heads borne high on poles, an eerie sound in the desolate place. The

Brigantes trotted towards them on foot, before breaking into a full charge, yelling war cries and waving spears and swords in the air.

The galloping line of horsemen crashed through the ranks of warriors with a clash of metal and the cries of men and horses. Speared riders fell groaning to the earth as duels broke out across the meadow. Gawain and Varden slashed their swords at snarling opponents, raising their rounded shields to block counter blows. Wounded horses whinnied and pirouetted in terror, adding to the confusion of battle. Some men, dismounted or unhorsed, picked up weapons and clashed with their enemy. Varden's guard of a dozen hardened warriors formed a shield around their two commanders as desperate duels were fought and blood mingled with mud and grass.

From the south, Merlyn led the five hundred men who had survived the battle onto the meadow, where they lined up behind their Roman shields, facing the bitter conflict raging a hundred yards ahead. In the distance, behind the melee, a second army on foot was arriving from the direction of Lindum to reinforce the Brigantes. Mutterings broke out in the ranks behind Merlyn, so he turned his horse and raised his staff for silence.

"I have seen the banner of Velocatus of the Brigantes. They have come with an army to seize Arthur and his knights. They have taken your town, will be holding your elders as captives, and the fate of your scouts remains unknown. They have come to this field as our enemy, and we must fight them. What say you, men of Linnius!"

The cheers of support let Merlyn and Arthur know that the men were behind them, for there had clearly been some uncertainty about fighting fellow Britons.

"Let us march and join our comrades," Merlyn grimly intoned, drawing his sword and moving forward. "The time has come for you to face your enemy in battle, Arthur."

They waded across the stream and reached the massed brawl occupying the centre of the meadow before Velocatus's reinforcements, and Merlyn, Arthur and Herrig drove their mounts forward through battling men towards Gawain and Varden's group. The extra men swiftly overpowered remaining resistance from Ronan's cavalry, and a dozen horsemen turned and fled back to the main body of their army.

Arthur, Excalibur unsheathed in his hand, had not as yet used his sword for duelling, aside from vague slashes at the heads and shoulders of men who ducked out of the way as they met up with Gawain and Varden in the centre of the battle. Again, Arthur saw the grim grin of death on the blood-splattered faces of Varden and Gawain, now recognising it for the bloodlust of war. Their excited horses pawed the muddy earth as Merlyn discussed tactics with his two commanders, the cries of battle slowly subsiding around them.

"We have destroyed their cavalry," Gawain shouted, "and now must take on their foot soldiers."

Merlyn looked about and saw the expectant faces of soldiers waiting for instruction. "This is a bad business, and wholly unexpected," he groaned. "What say you, Varden?"

The grizzled veteran had been counting the enemy heads and now turned to his comrades. "We have the numbers on them, and should strike whilst our men have the heart for battle."

Merlyn was swayed by their steely determination. "Then sound the advance."

This time, the advance was led by two ranks of foot soldiers, their shields locked in a wall. Varden and his guards rode to the sides, shouting instructions and egging them on. Gawain followed behind with his remaining cavalry, still numbering close to two hundred. He rode beside Arthur and shouted some words of encouragement to him.

"In the noise of battle, stay close to me, Merlyn and Herrig. Remember your lessons from Varden and you will prevail."

They closed the gap to within fifty yards of the chanting Brigantes, who banged their spears and swords on their shields in defiance. The decision to charge was taken from them when their opponents broke ranks and ran at them, hurling themselves onto the shield wall, slashing with little effect at the unflinching barrier of raised shields before them.

Varden's loud voice carried on the winds. "Hold fast!"

The second rank had been instructed to thrust their spears between the shields of the men in front of them, whose main purpose was to use their strength to keep the wall intact. The cries of wounded men falling filled the air as a deadlock of pushing held sway. Gawain seized the moment to send his riders in two evenly-matched groups to left and right, rounding the melee and slashing at enemy soldiers on the fringes and behind. Velocatus and his twenty or so riders also committed themselves to the fight.

Arthur found himself hemmed in by Herrig on one side and Merlyn on the other, unable to pick out an opponent to duel with. He spurred his horse forward, straight into a Brigante warrior who lunged at him with a lance. Arthur blocked the blow with his shield and made a wild slash with Excalibur at his opponent. This was easily deflected by the raised shield of the older warrior, whose eyes then widened at the prospect of a famous kill. He spurred his black horse towards Arthur's grey mare until the beasts bumped shoulders, but he had misjudged and found himself too close to Arthur to use his lance. Arthur drew his sword arm back and thrust Excalibur at the burly warrior's midriff, finding a gap below his chainmail. The blade sliced into him, and he rocked backwards with a groan. Withdrawing the blade, Arthur hacked at the man's neck, knocking him from his horse.

This had not gone unnoticed by Velocatus who spurred his burly warhorse towards Arthur, barging past all in his way. Arthur was static and unsure what to do as the huge warrior bore down on him. Herrig had seen what was happening and guided his horse between the two, taking the full force of Velocatus's charge. With a loud whinny of pain, Herrig's horse buckled under the impact and fell, unseating his rider into the mud. An enraged Arthur moved forward and took a swing at Velocatus, who smirked as he raised his shield. Others arrived on the scene, with Gawain and Merlyn forcing their horses towards the chief of the Brigantes and his guards.

"I will have your head, boy," Velocatus shouted above the din, edging closer to Arthur, leaning forward and jabbing with his sword. The force of his jabs dented Arthur's shield and rocked him back in his saddle, his arm aching from the blows. Arthur found his war cry from somewhere deep in his throat and leaned forwards as he brought Excalibur crashing down, sending sparks flying to the air as the blade sliced through the metal rim, wedging in the wood of his enemy's shield.

Velocatus laughed as he freed his arm from his shield's straps, raising his sword with two hands for the killing blow. Arthur was static, Excalibur stuck in the cleft shield of his enemy. He could do no more than raise his own battered shield as he looked in horror at the gleaming eyes of the Brigante chief. Velocatus edged forward, positioning himself for the death blow. Arthur's eyes widened, sensing his final moments, unable to move.

A flash of movement to Arthur's right broke the spell. With a loud snort, the head of Gawain's horse came between Arthur and his tormentor, and in that instant, Gawain's lance entered Velocatus's ribs, exposed by his raised arms, and his gloating look turned to a grimace of pain. Letting go of the lance, Gawain swiftly drew his sword and moved in for the kill, swiping at the big man's neck. Velocatus rocked with the blows and slowly toppled over, his horse bolting from his falling body.

All around them the din of battle raged as Arthur struggled to free his sword from the dead man's damaged shield. Gawain merely nodded at him and looked for his next victim. The battle began to thin as the Brigantes were overpowered. Word ran through their ranks that Velocatus was dead, and they soon lost heart and threw down their weapons.

"We have won," Merlyn puffed to a dazed Arthur. "And you have fought bravely."

Chapter Seven

GIRLS DRESSED IN finely woven bleached linen, their heads wreathed with holly, threw dried rose petals before the wedding procession as it passed from the church to the great hall in Venta Bulgarum. Morgaise was tall and elegant in a flowing gown and mantle of ruby silk edged with gold thread. She held the hand of her shorter, rotund husband, Geraint, who bowed to townsfolk jubilant at the prospect of food and ale awaiting them in the forum.

"My love, this is a wondrous and holy day," Geraint beamed, his brown eyes glinting at the prospect of bedding his beautiful prize.

"Indeed it is, my lord," she replied curtly through a fixed smile, nodding over his balding head at familiar faces in the crowd. They mounted the steps to the hall and turned to face the joyous gathering, with their family and supporters filing onto the porch behind them.

Caradoc leaned over her shoulder and whispered, "You look lovely, my dear – your late father would be so proud of you."

Morgaise turned and shot him a withering look, that delighted Caradoc but drew a disapproving glance from her mother, Ygerne. Geraint clumsily pulled her towards him by the arm and leaned up to plant a kiss on her cheek. The crowd roared their approval, and some wedding night advice was shouted by the bawdier elements.

"Let us retire inside," Morgana said, turning to lead the way with her fidgeting son, King Mordred. "There will be jugglers and tumblers to entertain you, my king," she said, keeping firm hold of his arm.

Anne dutifully picked up the lace train of the bride's gown as the wedding party took their seats in the hall for feasting and entertainment.

"You are doing well, my sister," she whispered in Morgaise's ear as Geraint conversed with Caradoc. "Eat and be merry."

"You may be merry, for you will lie in your own bed tonight."

Anne squeezed her sister's hand and distracted Morgaise from her impending ordeal by poking fun at the pompous line of invited nobility, as Geraint and Caradoc ignored them to discuss matters of regional security.

THE BODY OF Velocatus was conveyed to Lindum, together with lines of prisoners. Maddox and his fellow elders had been held hostage by a handful of Brigante guards, but were quickly released on news of the death of Velocatus. The slain chief's cavalry commander, Ronan, now stood before the victorious commanders on the steps of the great hall.

"We cannot free you, Ronan, nor do we wish to take you and your men with us," Merlyn said, searching for a solution.

Gawain leapt in. "If you swear fealty to Arthur then you may join us…"

Ronan scoffed at the suggestion. "My chief died fighting for his own son who is king over this land. I shall not betray my own people and the oath I took to King Mordred. You are rebels and must do what you will with us."

Varden responded to a questioning look from Merlyn. "I do not believe in killing Briton hostages – it is different with Saxons. But to move through this land fighting against fellow Britons will see our own numbers dwindle like dying stars before dawn. We are no longer the slaves of Rome and must find a way of living together."

Arthur's eyes widened to draw in more of this wisdom, and Merlyn nodded encouragement for him to share his thoughts. "I believe Varden is right," Arthur began. "But if we set these Brigantes free they will find us again on the field of battle. I know not how to solve this, unless they remain in Lindum as slaves."

Maddox then had his say. "We do not want to keep the king's men as slaves. It will be our ruin."

"Then cut off their sword hands and send them on their way," Gawain proposed.

Merlyn turned to Ronan and said, "You have listened to our debate, Ronan. Arthur will continue to rally men to his banner, but wants only to fight invaders to this land, not the followers of Morgana and Mordred."

"But that fight will find you, wherever you may be in this land," he replied. "Do with us what you will, but we shall not follow you."

"Then we shall sleep on it and decide your fate in the morning," Merlyn concluded. "Master Maddox, we will detain these men in the barracks, and I note that it is against your will. In the morning we shall make our plans and assist with burying and honouring the dead."

An uneasy truce held sway. Varden and Gawain instructed their own men to take the sixty Brigante prisoners to the barracks and lock them in one of the blocks, under close guard. Maddox was keen to talk to Merlyn about the fate of his son, Ambrose, who had not returned.

"I instructed Ambrose and our cook, Derward, to take the camp followers and wounded on a track to the villages and hide themselves. In the morning we shall send riders out to scour the countryside. Fear not, the fighting did not reach them – we shall find them all safe, my friend, I swear by the gods of our fathers."

Maddox had aged considerably in the past two days, his hair seemed whiter and the lines more ingrained on his thin face. The rage of Velocatus, who had ranted at him for harbouring enemies of the king and then threatened to execute the elders and burn the town, was still ringing in his ears. He disclosed this to Merlyn and added, "You are rebels from the king and have now killed the king's father! You have brought ruin on our people."

"This is what happens when there are two kings in a land," Merlyn mournfully replied. "Let us go inside and share a drink. I do not wish us to part as enemies, Maddox, so we must come to an understanding over this situation." The two old men walked slowly into the great hall, dwarfed by the high doors and taunted by the imperial magnificence of the interior – the gaiety of the feast and grandeur of the bard's tale now a distant memory.

They were served the honeyed mead of the monks and seed cakes, assuaging the tension between them.

Soon Maddox spoke. "You cannot call Arthur 'king'. He is more what the Romans would call a 'dux bellorum' – a landless noble who looks for a cause to espouse. Sadly, I fear you are doomed to be rebels in this land, hunted down and…"

Merlyn interrupted his woeful forecast. "For now, he is a rebel, set against an unjustly appointed king. How can a grandson succeed when the son is alive? I have seen in my visions that it is Arthur who can unite the Britons and secure this land, as did Ambrosius. Things will only get worse under a weak leadership, and a divided land will be ripe for plunder by our enemies."

Maddox took a sip and nibbled at a cake. "I think this is your vision and your cause, Merlyn. Arthur is a young man – much like my son, Ambrose, his head is no doubt full of romantic notions. Be careful you do not lead him to his destruction. Politics is a dangerous game to play."

"You chide me, Maddox, like no other. I thank you for your honesty and for sharing your thoughts. I have a father's love for Arthur and would give my life to protect him." He took a sip of the sweet brew and wiped his mouth. "My life's work is the preservation of the Briton way of life – our bond with the nature of this island, our culture and beliefs. Arthur is the symbol of that and can bind our people in a tight knot of unity that will withstand outside influence and interference. We have survived being part of the Roman world, but our new-found freedom is fragile."

"This is a grand scheme, Merlyn – some might say a folly. My concern is what will happen to us here in Linnius. We cannot run away and will surely face the wrath of Mordred's followers, who will seek revenge."

Merlyn leaned forward and gripped his arm. "I have an idea. We shall ride north and meet with your neighbour, the chief of Deira, Morcant, I believe?"

"Morcant the Unifier is dead, Merlyn. His son, Colgrin, now calls himself King of Deira. Morcant emboldened several squabbling northern tribes to drive the Angles back to the coast. He came here on two occasions to ask for men. We could spare none. After that, we heard no more from them until reports of his death some two years past."

"What welcome do you think we shall be afforded there?"

Maddox looked over the rim of his goblet and replied. "Coming from Linnius, I expect you will have a cold reception. I know not what they think of King Mordred, but you must know their rivals in the north are the Brigantes. King Colgrin may be pleased at the news of the death of Velocatus."

"So, they have the Brigantes on one side and the Angles on the other. At least you have not attacked them from the south?"

"No, we have kept to our lands and looked to our own defence. I can send you with our warmest greetings and a gift for the new king, perhaps…" Maddox searched the murals on the ceiling for inspiration.

"And fifty of your men, for our protection?" Merlyn asked.

"This I am reluctant to do, Merlyn, for then we side with rebels over King Mordred, who will surely send Caradoc with soldiers."

"Then send the body of Velocatus to Venta. Report there was a clash between the Brigantes and Arthur's rebel group on your lands, but you had no part in it. Swear fealty to King Mordred if you must, but we shall return in time for your support, and expect it, if we succeed in growing our numbers in the north. That might do."

"And what of the Brigante prisoners?" Maddox asked.

"I think we shall take them north with us and hand them over to King Colgrin as a goodwill gesture. Then their fate will pass to him."

Maddox leaned forward and his face brightened. "That may be a good thing, Merlyn. He could well make use of their lives as a bargaining tool. That would solve our problem." The two men drank to a solution that was far from secure, but gave a glimmer of hope for all concerned.

Merlyn stood to leave and clasped forearms with his host. "We shall find Ambrose and the others in the morning, and take the Brigante prisoners to collect and bury the dead from the field at Dubglas. We will leave you with your own trained and blooded fighting men. You must continue to look to your defences in these troubled times, dear friend. My advice is to keep a standing army."

"Velocatus gave me the same advice," the elder dryly replied.

THE TOWN WAS a bustle of activity in the morning, as groups were formed for burial duty and to search for Ambrose and the missing camp followers. Varden and his men marched the Brigantes to the battlefield with shovels to dig a burial pit, whilst Merlyn busied himself sourcing supplies, loading the wagon and recruiting guides, including a Deiran trader who was willing to take them to his chief.

Arthur insisted on joining the search and Merlyn agreed, asking him to have a special care for finding Ambrose and members of their own group, including Derward their cook. Arthur led a dozen riders to the villages south of Lindum, and they soon found some of the wounded soldiers being cared for by villagers, with their oxen grazing in a field and the carts lying empty.

"Where are Ambrose and Derward?" Arthur demanded of a soldier.

"They went on to the next village, my lord."

Arthur left three men to escort them back to Lindum and continued along the track to the next village. They followed the rutted track for a mile as it wound beside a stream, and, rounding a bend, they saw a disconsolate boy sat by the barley stubble, hugging his dog.

"What ails thee boy?" Arthur asked.

"Bandits did raid us in the night, sir. There was fighting and much noise. I ran away with my dog…"

"Were there visitors staying in your village?"

"Aye, sir, and they did fight with the bandits. I know not what happened for my mam told me to run to the fields."

"Then come with us back to your village. We shall see what has happened." Arthur dug his heels into the flanks of his mare and whispered, "Come on Venus, let us make haste."

Crows sat in silence on denuded branches as the searchers approached a wooden stockade of weathered sticks, a gate hanging on one hinge creaking and swinging in the breeze. A faint hint of wood smoke hung in the air as Arthur passed through the unguarded opening, hearing little but the howl of a dog. He jumped from his horse, then edged forward with hand on sword hilt, his men at his back, to the central space. Whatever had happened was past. Wounded men lay outside huts, being tended to by villagers. He saw Derward and strode up to him.

"Derward, I'm pleased to see you, although I see you are wounded."

"Yes, my lord. My arm and side are bruised. They came in the night. Maybe as many as a dozen of them, looking for plunder. They made off with our ox and some of the village's livestock. We were roused by the noise, and those of us who were able took up arms. After a struggle, we chased them off."

"And where is Ambrose?" Arthur asked, his tightened chest raising his voice to a squeak.

Derward shifted to a sitting position and slowly replied, "He is in that next hut, my lord – alive but hurt. We lost two of our own, dead." Derward lifted a painful arm and pointed. Arthur hurried over and lifted the sackcloth awning, entering into a gloomy space that reeked of unwashed bodies.

"Ambrose!" he cried, seeing his new friend lying under an animal skin, his eyes closed beneath a bandaged head. A woman rocked back on her knees from bathing him. Arthur knelt beside him as his eye lids fluttered and half-opened.

"Ah, Arthur... you have come... good," he whispered through cracked lips.

"I am happy to see you alive, Ambrose. How are you hurt?"

He laboured to raise himself onto one elbow before replying. "Thieves... in the night. I ran out with the others. I grappled with a man. He pushed me over... and knocked my head with his club. And I woke here."

"You are lucky to have survived, dear friend. I shall take you to your father's house and Merlyn shall tend to you. It seems the raiders were repelled and the others are alive, bar two. Rest a moment and eat some broth. I'll rouse the others and make ready to return to Lindum."

The wounded were carried to their cart, now hitched to the horse of one of Arthur's riders. Arthur led the slow procession back to the first village and onwards to Lindum, relieved that both Ambrose and Derward had survived the attack by a band of notorious outlaws known to the villagers, who lived in the forest.

THE LEAVING OF Lindum was celebrated by the townsfolk. Despite the loss of many men, they were glad to have rid the coast of the Angle settlers, who had been there for too long and whose presence had hung in the air like storm clouds that never break.

"I am pleased to be reunited with my son," Maddox said, resting a hand on Merlyn's shoulder, "although we are concerned about what will happen now our Coritani men have fought and defeated the Brigantes, killing Mordred's father."

"You son's head wound will heal. The arrival of Velocatus was unforeseen by me, my friend," Merlyn replied. "I am sorry it came to pass. The Brigante prisoners have revealed that they were expecting to fight only Saxons on their way north to their lands."

"Then you do not see everything, Merlyn," he replied with a sigh. "We wish you well with marching the captives north – and convey our gift and our desire for friendship to King Colgrin. On the other matter, our council have agreed to act on your advice and send the body of Velocatus to Venta with a messenger giving our account of what happened. I hope that is an end to the matter."

The sixty Brigante prisoners were marched through the streets, hands tied behind their backs and joined to the man in front by rope tied around their waists, to the boos of the crowd, marshalled by Varden's twenty guards. Maddox masked his disapproval at the sight of some local men who had chosen to join Arthur's army, now bidding farewell to their friends and family before passing through the gates. He had given his assent to a Coritani guard of fifty accompanying them northwards to the boundary of their lands. Bringing up the rear, with the cooks and followers, was the wagon of Gerwyn and his troupe, on their way to try their luck in entertaining the court of King Colgrin.

Arthur rode at the head of the procession with Merlyn, Varden, Bedwyr and Gawain, pleased to be heading to another adventure, secure in their company. "I shall miss my friend, Ambrose," Arthur said, turning back to see the walls recede. Behind them rode Father Samson, who had asked to accompany them.

"I am hopeful that we shall return here when we are stronger in number. Then we will ask the Coritani to join us," Merlyn replied.

"We have made a powerful ally in the Coritani," Gawain added, "and have defeated the army of Mordred's father and closest supporter. When we are ready, we shall meet Caradoc in battle and clear the way to the throne of Britannia for you, Arthur."

Chapter Eight

MORGAISE HAD BEGUILED and tormented her new husband until he agreed to petition Caradoc to allow her sister and mother to accompany them to his hall at Isca Dumnoniorum. Caradoc had consented, and preparations were made for them to leave together.

"You must not make eyes at the captain of the guard, Morgaise," Ygerne cautioned quietly as they sorted linen. "Others will notice. You husband is one of the most powerful lords in this land, and we are indebted to him. I feared we would never again set foot beyond these walls, and be spied on for the rest of our days."

"Oh mother, you misjudge me. I am aware that men look at me, and a smile or kind word wins favour where I may need it. It is not so different for us women as it is for our men – we must also build alliances and be watchful of our enemies."

They had been gone a week when news reached Venta of the death of Velocatus, shortly followed by the arrival of his body. It was delivered by a grovelling messenger from Lindum, cleaned and wrapped tightly in layers of linen and sack cloth. The late chief's widow sat alone with the bundle in his chamber for a day and a night. Her servants tiptoed along passages, leaving platters of food and wine and then later replenishing them. She was stoking a furnace. They listened briefly to her unintelligible mutterings and then scurried away, lest a roar of heat scorch their heels. In the event, Caradoc met the blast in the great hall the following day.

"My husband slain by Merlyn and his rebels!" Morgana raged, clutching her son's hand so tightly he cried out and pulled away. "I will have my revenge on that cheap conjuror and the pale youth, Artorius. If Ygerne and her serpent-eyed daughters were here I would have their heads! Caradoc – send men after them to bring them back here to face my wrath!"

Caradoc blanched at the fury of her words and hesitated before speaking. "I would not offend our good ally, King Geraint of the Dumnoni, by executing his wife and mother-in-law. And so soon after the wedding," he stuttered.

"I order them to be killed!" Mordred yelled, kicking the thick oak leg of his throne and regretting it with a howl of pain. He then threw himself onto it, red-faced and teary.

Caradoc knew there would be no peace until the rebels were caught or killed in battle. "I shall raise an army and follow Merlyn northwards, my lady," he said, bowing to the lone mother and the boy-king.

"Yes, you shall, my lord Caradoc. Do not return until King Mordred's will is done. For now, Geraint can keep his wife, but when our paths cross again, there will be no mercy for the remnants of my father's second family."

ARTHUR AND HIS COMPANIONS had travelled north on Ermine Street from Lindum. At the end of the second day, the weary commanders drew their men to a halt on a hilltop overlooking a wide estuary. The sea was in view away to their right, blending into a barely visible horizon that merged with the grey blanket above them. But their focus was on the stone heads and wooden span of a bridge standing where the river narrowed below them. Guards were posted at each end, where huts and the people moving between them were illuminated by the light of their smoking fires.

Gawain called forward the captain of the Coritani guard and asked, "Are they your men on this side of the bridge?"

He leaned forward in his saddle and shook his head. "No, my lord. They are Parisi, neighbours of the Deirans on the north bank."

"Are the two tribes at peace?" Merlyn asked.

"The Deiran king rules over the Parisi, my lord," the captain replied. Their Deiran guide had joined them and nodded his agreement.

"Then we must negotiate with them to pass," Varden said. "You will both join me to speak with them and assure them of our peaceful intent," he instructed the Coritani captain and Deiran guide.

"I shall remain here with Arthur and the men," Merlyn said. "Take Father Samson and Bedwyr with you, Varden – tell them we are travelling to the court of King Colgrin. Blow your horn to signal when it is safe for us to join you."

Merlyn and Arthur dismounted and allowed their horses to nibble at the lush green grass. Others followed their lead. Arthur saw an opening to press Merlyn on his mysterious information gathering.

"Merlyn, I have seen that you scrutinise the symbols on carved stones we encounter and talk with druids in the forests. You huddled with the elders in the remote places we passed through. What do you search for?"

Merlyn removed his riding cap and scratched at his unruly grey hair. Taking Arthur's arm, he guided them away from the others. "I search for the wisdom of the ancients, Arthur – those who ruled this land before the coming of the Romans. I drink from the cup of their knowledge of the world around us – of the wind, rain, stars, rivers, and the animals who roam the forests. We elders often share a thirst to understand how all things are connected, to know better the creators who watch over us. For our knowledge of the divine powers of nature can teach us what may come to pass. And I seek out tales of tempest-tossed gods, to learn how I might steer us Britons through stormy waters to a hopeful future, Arthur."

"Is the leaving of the Romans an omen of ill fortune for us?" Arthur asked, kicking at toadstools.

"Not at all. After many generations here, they have gone, but we remain. We are the people of this island, and must forge our own destiny. It is my purpose to prepare you, Arthur, for the great task of leading our people to a safer future, free of conflict and free of rule by outsiders."

"You have great faith in me, Merlyn," Arthur mumbled.

He beamed at his protégé and replied, "Yes, for I see greatness in you. Your wisdom will grow with experience, and your sword arm will strengthen through combat. You have your father's strong will and your mother's forbearance – and you will need both. Be patient and stay alive, Arthur. That is my advice for now."

Spying some plants of medicinal interest, he broke off from their discourse to wander along the fringe of a forest lined with thick bushy plants, occasionally kneeling to pull at leaves and berries, or dig for roots. Arthur walked to the edge of the escarpment and looked out over the grey and empty sea.

The distant sound of a horn floated to them on the wind and they returned to their horses. Merlyn led the band downwards, following a well-maintained road, to the crude settlement that had grown around the bridgehead.

"For a few coins from my purse, we may pass," Varden growled. He led the way across the bridge, giving no thought to the engineering skill that had made this wide span. Merlyn and Arthur bade farewell to the Coritani guards and followed their wagon train across the sturdy bridge.

"I thank the gods for each passing from one tribal land to another without a fight," Merlyn quipped, enjoying the view of the widening estuary and the fishing vessels bobbing at anchor in the murky waters.

"I HAVE A mind to change the name of our great town to something shorter," Geraint announced from his horse as he halted the string of wagons and riders. He paused on this last hilltop to admire the captivating view of the walled town, which was perched on the junction of the rocky coast and a widening, white-capped river estuary. Their journey from the king's court at Venta had taken three days. Small farms dotted the opposite side of the valley, disappearing inland along the winding river valley.

Morgaise humoured him and asked, "And what would that be, my lord?"

"The Romans named the town for our tribe, calling it Isca Dumnoniorum, 'the place of the Dumnonians by the flowing waters'. It is too long. Also, it is a growing custom, I have noticed, to change place names that sound Roman."

"What is the name of this river?" Anne asked Geraint.

"Ah, a good question, my sister. It is Exe, mercifully brief. Perhaps we have a solution here. How does 'Exisca' sound?"

"Better. Much shorter," Morgaise agreed, rewarding her husband's praise of her sister.

Their horses slowly picked their way down a steep path towards a bridge, where the white waters of the Exe rushed to meet the sea in a crash of waves beside a high black cliff. The far bank was populated with round thatched huts that overlooked a sandy beach, on which dozens of fishing boats sat idling in the weak autumnal sun. Purposeful fisherfolk attended to endless lines of fishing nets held up on poles to dry, or carried wicker baskets of fish or whelks to be sorted.

"This is a merry town," Morgaise muttered to her mother and sister, holding up the shade that hung on the side of their wagon.

"Our new home," Ygerne smiled, looking up at the circling gulls. "It is not far from Tintagel where you were born, my dear," she added.

"Perhaps my husband will allow us to visit what was once my father's castle," Morgaise replied.

"Perhaps..." Ygerne echoed.

Geraint rode beside them and boasted, "Our town is a centre of trade, with the old Roman road connecting us to the North and West. Sea traders come from Gaul and beyond, bringing cloth, wines, farming implements and jewels to be traded in our marketplace for livestock, pelts, pottery and metal ingots from our mines. My people are not lazy and we have grown in power and influence as a result."

"Tintagel is also a place of trade," Ygerne said. "And you are their lord now."

Geraint laughed, his belly wobbling in his saddle. "Yes, I am the lord of the south-west corner of this island, including the lands of your first husband. Gorlois of Cornubia was a leader well respected in these lands. You will be accorded the love and respect of my people, Queen Ygerne." He bowed in as dignified a manner as he could muster and rode ahead, shouting to the guards to open the gates.

AFTER A DAY'S ride, Arthur's band decided to stop by a junction where a track led to a farm. It was marked by clusters of huts where animated women and children held up baskets of farm produce to the riders, shouting the names of their wares and hoping to catch an eye. Varden and Merlyn agreed it was as good a place as any in the flat lands they were passing through to make their camp. Fresh vegetables and meat for their pots would be welcome, as would any news of passers-by. Derward soon busied himself negotiating for farm produce for their evening meal.

The straight road had been raised up on a stony base by Roman engineers and paved, keeping the surface well-drained and affording vulnerable travellers clear views in all directions. They made an early start, leading their horses onto the road before mounting, wrapping their cloaks tightly against the chill. A low mist blanketed the wetlands and an eerie silence hung over the land – the smell of sea salt mixed with the air. A lone kestrel hovered over a hillock that stood above the mist, the occasional tree being the only other sight across the flats that seemed to go on for miles towards the coast away to their right.

After some hours, Varden returned to the group from a forward foray, giving his gruff report. "We shall see the walls of Eboracum in one hour. There is nothing but farms, wetlands and forest, and the silence of the graveyard, between here and there. Our guide tells me that the Angles did reach this road earlier this year, raiding farms before being chased back to their coastal dwellings. The people are wary and hide away from strangers, in the forest."

"There is unease along this eastern coast," Merlyn added. "They are the lands these Saxon and Angle settlers crave and stubbornly cling to with their ever-increasing numbers. Maddox called it 'the lost lands of Lloegyr'."

The hour passed in quiet reflection until they were met by a dozen warriors on horseback, blocking the road.

"Escort, or guard dogs?" Merlyn asked Arthur, to test his reasoning.

"Guard dogs bark," Arthur replied, passing the test.

Varden, Gawain and the scouts trotted forward, returning after a minute.

"We are welcomed by King Colgrin and invited to follow his guards through the town gates," Varden said, leading them onwards.

Entering through the high stone gatehouse, Merlyn turned to Arthur and said, "Behold the great northern town of Eboracum, probably called something else by the locals now. It was once the base from which Rome conquered and pacified the northern tribes. As Maddox has told us, it has a place in Roman history as the town where an Emperor died, and one was proclaimed – the mighty Constantine who ruled over much of the world."

Merlyn patted the neck of his horse as the shouts of traders reached their ears. "Oh, and remember what I said about keeping Excalibur wrapped and hidden at all times. It is far too valuable to lose."

Arthur nodded as they passed out of the shade of the towering gatehouse and into an open cobbled square lined with market stalls and pens, the peace of the countryside replaced by lively chatter and the grunts and squawks of livestock. They followed the guards to the forum at the town's centre, dismounting in front of a familiar-looking imperial hall.

"The Romans lacked imagination in the design of their towns," Arthur observed.

Gawain laughed and replied, "They are built for a military purpose and are replicated across their empire with a consistency that speaks of success."

"But perhaps less useful once the need to dominate and suppress the local tribes has gone," Merlyn added. "They are built on open land, often by a river or stream, whereas our people built their forts on higher ground."

"That is a more natural place to defend yourself from enemies, who can be seen approaching and must fight uphill," Arthur said, defending them.

"That did not stop the Romans when they first came," Varden dryly observed.

They waited at the foot of the steps for the customary welcome, and finally the great oak doors of the hall were pushed open and a line of warriors, clad mostly in animal furs and leather, arrayed themselves above them.

A barrel-chested warrior with silver ringlets in his brown beard demanded, "Who has come to Ebrauc to seek a welcome from the mighty King Colgrin of the Deiran people?"

Merlyn stepped forward. "I am Merlyn, once healer and adviser to King Uther, and this is Gawain, a noble knight whose deeds are spoken of across this land. We are travelling northwards to the Great Wall, and have come to ask for King Colgrin's welcome and hospitality. We have brought with us sixty Brigante warriors, who are our captives taken in battle in the lands of the Coritani. We would make a gift of these warriors to King Colgrin."

"Our king will give his reply soon," Colgrin's spokesman said, sending a messenger into the hall.

Two minutes passed as the two bodies of men surveyed each other, whilst the voices of townsfolk massed behind the visitors grew in volume. The messenger then reappeared and the spokesman announced, "You are welcome, Merlyn and Gawain, and your companions. You may enter. Our guards will take your horses to the stables and show your men to the barracks."

Inside the hall's gloomy interior, their eyes slowly adjusted. Light filtered from openings high up and also pooled beneath the standing lamps set at intervals by the stone columns supporting the roof's wooden beams. Wood smoke stung their eyes as they made their way across the straw-strewn stone flags to a raised dais on which sat the king.

"Welcome to my hall, Merlyn and Gawain. Your names are known to us, and we look forward to hearing of your journey and of your battle with our pestilent neighbours, the Brigantes." Colgrin leaned forward and narrowed his eyes beneath thick black brows to inspect them. He wore a band of twisted gold threads around his head and his beard swayed under the weight of silver ringlets. Copper bands adorned his thick forearms, and his fingers, displaying jewelled rings, rested on knees covered by a long crimson robe.

Merlyn bowed and replied, "We thank you for your hospitality, King Colgrin, and shall willingly share our tale with you."

They had agreed that Arthur would be kept in the background and, if asked, be introduced as the squire to Gawain. Merlyn had argued that his true identity should be withheld until they had got the measure of their hosts. They were directed to sit along one side of a banqueting table, facing Deiran nobles, with Colgrin on a throne at the head. Next to Varden sat Bedwyr, then Father Samson, the leader of the Coritani contingent and, finally, Arthur.

"This is a merry bunch of travellers," Colgrin noted jovially, regarding each of them through eyes of glittering coal, whilst indicating with a flick of the hand that ale should be served. Turning to Merlyn he asked, "I believe you have been here before, Merlyn the Healer, and knew my father, Morcant?"

"Indeed, I have visited before, with King Uther, when your father ruled these lands. He did swear allegiance to Uther and together they drove Votadani invaders back beyond the Wall."

Colgrin chuckled. "I remember that as a boy. Much has happened since then, and we are troubled not only by the northern tribes but by the cursed Angles who swarm like a hive of angry bees on our coast. Now, tell me of your adventures, Merlyn, and how you come to be in our fair town?"

Merlyn delivered a rehearsed account, ending on greetings sent by the elders of Lindum. "The Leader of the Elders of Lindum, Maddox, has sent you a gift contained in this trunk and his wishes for peace and friendship between your peoples." He motioned to a Coritani guard to bring a small chest forward and lay it beside Colgrin's throne. Colgrin nodded to an attendant to open the lid and inspect the contents. This was done, and the findings conveyed in a whisper.

Colgrin took a sip of ale and cleared his throat to speak. "We had heard that you are fugitives from the new king, Mordred, and that now presents us with a difficult choice to make: whether to hold you hostage and win favour with our king, or aid you in your escape."

He eyed the stony faces before him and then continued. "However, the fact that we have a feud with our Brigante neighbours, whom you have fought in battle, slaying their chief, Velocatus, and have delivered captives to us, makes me more inclined to embrace you as friends and allies. You say you march to the Great Wall. But for what purpose?"

Merlyn exhaled, smiled and replied, "We thank you for your wise summation of events, my lord king. We intend to occupy one of the forts on the Great Wall, using it for a base to harry the Angle and northern invaders. This quest puts great distance between ourselves and the remains of Mordred's army. In truth, without Velocatus's warriors, they are weakened. If I were Morgana, I would be content with ruling in the southern lands." He laughed. "Did I say Morgana? Come what may, we will aid you in your war against the pestilence from across the Saxon Sea, my lord." Merlyn bowed and took a sip of ale.

Colgrin drummed his fingers on the table, his bejewelled rings flashing in the lamp light, his black eyes moving from one face to another and settling on Arthur. "We have also heard that you have a young prince in your midst, a claimant to the throne of Uther. Let him show himself and tell us of his claim."

A silence fell across the hall broken only by the low growls from dogs chewing bones under the table. As Merlyn deliberated on the safest response, a chair scraped on a stone slab and Arthur stood. All eyes were on him as he bowed hesitantly to the king. "I am Arthur Pendragon, son of Uther, my lord."

Colgrin leaned forward and glared down the table. "Come forward, Arthur, so I might see you more clearly." Arthur walked behind the row of stiff backs of his seated comrades and stood next to Colgrin's throne, like a pupil before his teacher. "So, you are the son of Uther. How is it that no one has ever heard of Uther having a son?"

Merlyn jumped to his feet to answer but Colgrin held up a hand to silence him. "Speak, Arthur Pendragon."

A ripple of barely suppressed guffaws ran along the line of Colgrin's nobles, causing Arthur to gulp before replying. "Your Majesty, I am the one true son of Uther, born to Queen Ygerne some eighteen summers past. For my safety from assassins, I was taken to a haven and given over to the family of a noble knight, there to be raised in secrecy, until such a time as..." His words trailed off and Colgrin's laughter triggered more from his courtiers. But they were indulgent, rather than scornful.

"This tale raises more questions than gives answers, young Arthur. We have much to talk on. I think that a king's place is with another king, not hiding out in Roman forts on a windswept wall. I invite you to remain with me here in Ebrauc, whilst your friends go northwards with my warriors to raid the Brigantes and capture one of the many forts on the wall. Once the strength of the Brigantes has been sapped and our primacy over them established, then we shall jointly turn our attention to making war on the Angles."

This was not the outcome Merlyn expected or wanted, but he felt he should not challenge the king of Deira in his own hall. Instead he stood and bowed. "As you wish, Your Majesty."

Colgrin waved them away, but indicated that Arthur should stay, sitting close to him. His roving eye settled on the bard, Gerwyn, loitering in the shadows but hoping to be noticed. "And you, minstrel. Prepare to entertain my table this eve."

Gerwyn bowed and shuffled off in the direction of the kitchen, keen to keep a distance from any trouble that might erupt between Merlyn's group and the brooding king. He was startled, therefore, on walking into Merlyn as he left the hall.

"Ah, Merlyn, I did not expect to meet you…"

"Clearly not, Gerwyn. I wish you no ill will." Merlyn took the portly bard by his arm and walked him away for the building and any prying ears, to sit on a stone bench. "I ask you, in the name of friendship, to keep watch on Arthur, that no harm may come to him. If you feel he is in danger, then try your best to spirit him away with your troupe when you leave. And when you do come to leave, my guess is that you will travel south to earn your keep in the halls of chiefs and kings?"

Gerwyn nodded between furtive glances over the kitchen garden.

"Then know, in confidence, that we travel northwards, to a place as yet unknown. You will find out where we are when you next return to this town. I ask you to be my eyes and ears, in particular at the great hall in Venta Bulgarum. It would please me to know all, every time Morgana buries a crow at a crossroads, every time Caradoc oils his saddle and rides out, but I shall make do with such nuggets as you stumble on."

Gerwyn frowned, so Merlyn smiled, putting his hand lightly on the bard's shoulder.

"I know, as well as you, Gerwyn, the soft music of your harp floats from your shadowy corner of a hall after supper. Ale flows, the player is forgotten, and tongues run away with themselves. In the yard, you pluck your strings invisibly, with the sun behind you, and maids gossip as they pluck their master's capons. Discover from them the fate of our former queen, Ygerne, and her daughters, Morgaise and Anne."

"I never knew we were such good friends, Merlyn. I sang, you pressed coin on me and I stuffed it in my scrip. It was the way in Lindum and many times on Ermine Street."

Merlyn 's hand hovered over the dagger at his waist as he continued.

"On your return northwards, I would ask that you gather news from our mutual friend, Maddox. Use fair words, friend Gerwyn, to tempt his son, Ambrose, to leave with you. He is the loyal friend Arthur needs by him." Merlyn produced a thin bar of silver and briefly showed it to the gawping entertainer, before cutting a slice from it and holding it out. "The rest of this bar of silver I shall keep for you, should you bring me useful information and arrive with Ambrose in a year's time."

He fixed Gerwyn with an intense, searching stare. "Do we have an understanding?"

"Erm, yes, of course Merlyn. I shall listen, observe and then find you, perhaps the year after next, in the spring?"

"So be it. Then I shall bid you farewell, Gerwyn the storyteller. But one more thing..."

Gerwyn looked up cautiously. Merlyn smiled and continued, "Do not forget the feats of King Uther in your telling of the tale of our island. His victory at Mount Badon stands in importance with that of Ambrosius at Maisbeli in keeping the Saxon threat at bay... at least for a while. Good day."

Merlyn swept his cloak about him in a theatrical manner and stalked away, leaving the rotund bard to waddle away to his quarters.

IN THE DISPENSARY at Venta Bulgarum where Merlyn had once mixed his potions, Morgana now railed at her own healer, Alicia, whom some called a witch.

"I want to put a curse on that aloof wench, Morgaise. Can it be done?" she demanded of the old woman who shuffled with downcast head, muttering, from one jar to another. Morgana's mood had soured further over the days following the news of her husband's death. She had known that Morgaise's status had dramatically improved through marriage to Geraint, but he now commanded an army to rival that of the depleted forces of Mordred and Caradoc combined. The possibility that Morgaise might influence her husband to stand against them was too much to bear.

"It can be done, my lady," Alicia croaked, measuring out some dried leaves and placing them in her mortar. "I will summon the spirit of Queen Mab at the full moon and curse her womb so that she will bear no children..."

"That is not enough!" Morgana shrieked. "I want her dead! Prepare a poison that is odourless and can be hidden in food. I shall think of a way to administer it." Morgana turned her back and exited the room that held mixed memories – where she had flirted with Merlyn in her youth and begged him to teach her his knowledge of remedies and poisons. He had taught her selectively, she felt, keeping the depths of his knowledge hidden from her. She banged the door shut on the old woman, leaving her muttering darkly as she ground a potion with firm presses of her pestle.

Chapter Nine

"WE CANNOT LEAVE Arthur behind!" Gawain shouted, gripping the sheath of Saxon Sting in a show of defiance.

Arthur had given him his father's sword on the eve of their departure from Lindum, and Gawain had wept. He had shed tears of relief as a burden of guilt was lifted. This very particular honour had been bestowed on him, the knight who reluctantly followed Uther's noble orders to abandon him to certain death. Saving Arthur from Velocatus had redeemed him, or maybe there was only ever his own regret, and perhaps, after all, no grudge had ever been held against him.

"We cannot confront King Colgrin in his hall – he is surrounded by guards who outnumber us ten to one," Merlyn tetchily replied. "For now, we must leave Arthur here and I shall return for him once we have subdued the Brigantes and found ourselves a base for the winter. That is our best plan, would you agree, Varden?"

Merlyn noticed the aging warrior cupping his weaker arthritic hand in the other, wearing a look that feared the onset of winter.

"Uther did not allow Colgrin's father to call himself 'king'," Varden grumbled, his rheumy eyes finally settling on his leader. "All the nobles who bent their knee to King Uther knew they could only bear the title 'chief', or face Uther's wrath. Now everyone is a king in this unruly land. Yes, Merlyn, your plan is the only one that stands a chance of success. However, if Colgrin refuses to release the boy..."

"We shall deal with that if it happens," Merlyn interrupted. "Let us prepare to leave with Colgrin's warriors and confront the Brigantes. It is possible they have not yet heard of the death of Velotacus and the destruction of his army."

"Their chief and no doubt the best of their warriors," Gawain said. "The news should dishearten them…"

"Or enrage them," Varden added.

A knock on the door ended their discussion and they were instructed by the captain of the Deiran guard to make ready to leave. Their unit consisted of Varden and Gawain's thirty assorted cavalry and Bedwyr's dozen men, with Merlyn and Derward marshalling the various cooks and helpers in two wagons. Herrig and two others had been detailed to remain with Arthur as his squire and bodyguards.

Their road from the barracks took them through the forum, where a large and boisterous crowd had gathered.

"Are they here to see us off?" Gawain joked.

"I think not," Varden replied, pointing to the sixty Brigante captives, who knelt with their hands tied to their ankles before the steps of the great hall. They halted their horses and wagons behind the crowd and formed a line. At the front of the hall, between high columns, King Colgrin, with Arthur to one side, raised his hands for silence.

"My people," he began, "for too long we have been chased off our farms by our greedy neighbours, the Brigantes." A few jeers and growls didn't halt him. They would hear him out. "In recent days our outpost was attacked by Brigante warriors, and many of our men were slain. Now, our warriors are ready to ride out, with our new allies from the south, to reclaim our lost lands."

He paused to allow the crowd to turn and cheer the warriors at their backs who were ready to depart. The crowd then returned their attention to the hall, altering their shouts to rude hostilities, thrusting knives and makeshift weapons into the air, and edging forward.

Colgrin pointed to the helpless captives below him and raised his voice further. "The widows and children of our dead comrades shall avenge our fallen warriors who have gone to the netherworld!"

Merlyn noted the look of horror on the face of Arthur as shrieking women and children flung themselves on the screaming Brigante captives, slashing, stabbing and bludgeoning them with whatever objects they held. The men in the crowd roared them on with shouts of encouragement. The Britons, with Gawain at their head, turned their back on the savagery and walked their snorting and uneasy steeds through the gates and away from the massacre. Arthur was at last ushered into the hall by Colgrin, the hand of the king lightly rested on his shoulder, for all the world, a favoured nephew.

"I shall report this unholy deed to the bishop," Father Samson sourly remarked to Merlyn, adding, "and the use of pagan language by the king."

Merlyn did not dignify the priest's cold sanctimony with a response. He cursed under his breath before muttering an apology to the corpses being dragged away by the guards. "You deserved to die as warriors or serve a master. May the gods smile on your kin and pardon me my poor judgement." And then he raised his voice to the riders ahead. "Let us leave this place without further delay. We have witnessed the fate of Colgrin's enemies. Now let us search out the rest!"

THE RIVER TAMESIS at Readingham, some eight miles north of Calleva, was alive with the shouts of boatmen, some waiting in the steady flow for their turn to dock. Trade downriver as far as Lundein had been restored after the Saxon raiders had been defeated by Velocatus and his warriors. Caradoc looked out over the scene below him from the tower window of his hall, the purposeful activity of townsfolk and traders doing little to assuage his foul temper.

"Send out my orders to the village headmen to send me half of their able-bodied men for my army. And take stock of the grain, livestock and available horses. Go!"

His attendants were sent scurrying, relieved to be out of his brooding presence. He was now committed to pursuing the fugitives in the dangerous and unpredictable north, but was equally sensitive to the threat of another Saxon incursion coming up river, or from the south coast.

Reading his thoughts, his chancellor crooned, "It is unlikely the Saxons will return before the spring, my lord. That affords you time to hunt down the fugitives and return to the king's favour."

Caradoc glared at him, but elected to slowly exhale and calm himself. "Yes, you are right in your calculation. But a winter campaign in the north was not exactly my first choice of endeavour. I shall leave a small force here under the command of my captain of the guard to deal with any unforeseen problems that may arise. After one week of preparations, I shall march north to Lindum and pick up the trail of the fugitives. Only with their death or capture will my life become bearable again."

STURDY PONIES WITH long shaggy manes bore the troop of three hundred Deiran cavalry northwards, following a Roman road for some miles before exiting onto a single track that crossed a boggy moorland. Behind, Merlyn's band of fifty followed, unsure of what part they would play in the confrontation that lay ahead at the main village of the Brigantes.

"Has your path brought you to this northerly part of our island before, Merlyn?" Father Samson asked, taking the reins of their shared wagon from the dozing older man.

"Aye, I have been to the great Roman wall and seen its might," Merlyn replied, suddenly awake and attentive. "It is marked every mile with a tower or fort where soldiers from across the Roman world were once barracked, guarding their most northerly frontier. The organisation of the Romans and their collective will to dominate and rule over the people they encountered has always impressed me."

"They brought with them the one true God, our Lord Jesus Christ," Samson added, smiling with a certainty Merlyn had come to recognise in priests.

"Christianity is but one of many faiths the Romans brought to our island, adding to the ancient beliefs of our people," Merlyn replied, provoking the priest out of boredom.

"But since the conversion of Constantine the Great, whom you correctly pointed out was made Emperor in Ebrauc and travelled these same roads, the Christian faith has supplanted all others, as the truth of God's teachings reaches out to all mankind..."

"You are on a mission from your bishop, are you not, Father Samson," Merlyn asked, tersely interrupting what would have developed into a sermon. "What exactly do you hope to find out in these wild lands?"

Samson glanced at him and whipped the horse onwards over the lumpy sods that lined the track. "My bishop is keen to make these northern lands into a new diocese. I am to assess how far the Word of God has spread amongst the folk who live by the wall, and look for those priests who have previously travelled to these lands..."

"Ah, so you have ambition to be a bishop?"

"If that is the will of the Council."

"A Council of Bishops. There's a frightening thought," Merlyn muttered. The riders ahead of them had slowed to walking pace, and soon stopped. Marsh birds trilled their annoyance as camp followers spilled into the marshes to drop their breeches or lift their skirts.

Varden rode up to Merlyn's wagon to brief them. "The scouts have reported that we are close to the fortress of the Brigantes. The wagons are to wait in yonder wood and our warriors are to join with them to advance on the stockade."

Merlyn nodded and Varden turned his horse to move up the line. Soon they were moving again and the non-combatants left the road for the shelter of the copse. Merlyn instructed Derward and his attendants to make a fire and boil up a broth.

"We shall wait for news of the outcome," Merlyn said to the priest who followed him closely. "Let us hope it is not too bloody, otherwise a feud will rage between these peoples that will see them both destroyed."

"Yes, I shall pray for a peaceful resolution," Father Samson echoed.

ARTHUR HAD BEEN taken to a villa in an enclosure for senior figures in the Deiran establishment that was adjacent to one side of the hall. His three followers were shown to servants' quarters close by. Colgrin had detailed the family of one of his kinsmen to provide a room for Arthur and to keep a close watch on him. Arthur had prudently given his sword and prized possessions to Herrig for safekeeping, knowing that he would have little privacy. He was a captive and knew he must do what he could to keep on Colgrin's good side. His room had a window that looked out onto a herb and flower garden, with a fountain splashing water into a trough. His thoughts drifted to his home at the farm of Hector and Gayle, the only parents he had known during his early years, and he wondered if they were alive and safe.

"I shall pray for them," he whispered. Yes, he would ask for a Christian priest to visit him in the morning, hoping that he might open up a means of communication to Father Samson and Merlyn.

A knock on the door interrupted his thoughts and a servant brought in some clothing and sandals for him. He was instructed to rest in his room and prepare for the evening meal after sundown.

Arthur knew he must stay alert and be positive, and not dwell on the gloomy thoughts that crowded his mind. He felt powerless and at the mercy of Merlyn's plans for him. How does one become a king? By birth or by conquest. But if others competed for the ultimate position of power then it would lead to conflict. Uther had succeeded his brother, and had in turn been succeeded by his grandson. The nobles would follow whoever they believed to be the strongest – except that a boy was now on the throne. They had been beguiled by the strong will of Morgana and intimidated by Velocatus and Caradoc. Things are never as straightforward as they might seem. Having met Anne briefly on their escape, and looked into her eyes, he now firmly believed that she was his sister and they were the offspring of Uther and Ygerne, as Merlyn insisted. He would also pray for the safety of his mother and sister, and hoped he would meet with them some day.

AS EVENING SETTLED over the camp, Merlyn rose from his wooden stool at the sound of horses approaching. He swiftly moved to the wagon and found his sword, pulling the blade from its scabbard. His followers picked up sticks and stood behind him as the shadow of approaching horsemen entered their clearing.

"Stay your blade, Merlyn," Gawain's voice commanded. "We have come to share your camp." He dismounted and took Merlyn by the arm, leading him away from the group.

"What has happened?" Merlyn impatiently asked.

"There was a brief fight, but once we gained entry to their stockade, they threw down their weapons. Varden and I succeeded in preventing any wanton slaughter of the Brigante villagers and their headman submitted to the Deiran commander."

"That is a relief," Merlyn muttered. "What now?"

Gawain removed his helmet, shook his curls and replied in a low voice, "The Deirans and most of our men will camp there for the night, and we shall join them in the morning to see what shall be resolved. You may yet have a say in how an uneasy peace is set between these people. Now, let us make our beds and share some victuals by the fire."

The first rays of dawn through the trees saw Gawain, Merlyn and the remaining soldiers leave camp. In short time they arrived at the damaged stockade of the Brigantes and passed by a tented village of Deiran warriors, busying themselves with breakfast as their hobbled horses grazing contentedly close by. They continued onto a bridge over a dry ditch, through an unguarded space lined with a pair of shattered gates, into the centre of the village. At the longhouse of the chief they dismounted, and joined Varden, Bedwyr and the Deiran leaders, sitting in a semi-circle facing the Brigantes across a steaming caldron over a fire. A ring of armed Deiran warriors lined the open space.

"They have been told of the battle near Lindum and the death of Velocatus," Varden whispered to Merlyn, "but the

Deirans have followed your advice to say nothing of the butchering of their captives at Ebrauc. We are waiting for you."

The Brigante leader, who looked like a younger version of Velocatus, stared at Merlyn and spoke. "Merlyn the Healer. We know of you, and we know that my brother, Velocatus, did hunt for you after your escape from Venta where my nephew, King Mordred, did imprison you. I am Venutius, brother of Velocatus, now chief of the Brigantes."

Merlyn bowed and said nothing. The young chief did not have the look of a warrior to Merlyn's eyes. After a brief pause, Venutius continued. "We have been rudely attacked by our Deiran neighbours, who now hold us as hostages. Now we shall hear what fate is to befall us." He sat back and folded his arms, his beard rings clicking on his bronze arm guards.

The captain of the Deiran guard, a tall thin man of few words named Grime, motioned to Merlyn and his commanders to walk a few paces away. They huddled in a ring and waited to hear Grime's thoughts. "They will never submit to us. They see themselves as being superior to our tribe," he said, spitting onto the compacted earth.

"We cannot slaughter them because they are an inconvenience," Merlyn said. "Nor should we evict them from their lands. This tribe has been here since long before the Romans first came and their queen, Cartimandua, made peace terms for all the northern people with them that lasted many generations."

"That is why they think they are better than us," Grime grumbled.

"Our aim is to take over one of the forts to the north of their lands, so we shall also become their neighbours," Merlyn said. "We must make peace with them. Varden, what are your thoughts on the matter?"

Stroking his white beard, he replied, "This Venutius, named after Cartimandua's husband, I believe, and perhaps of their line, is the new chief following his brother's death. He would want to feel secure in his position. That is the way to gain his friendship. If the Deirans agree to withdraw and respect the border between their lands, and the Brigantes agree to tolerate us as their northern neighbours, then perhaps there can be peace. The alternative is more war that weakens all of us, and plays to the hands of the Angles who will surely return on the spring tides."

"We have won a victory over them and shall not run away as if defeated!" Grime shouted, causing others to look at the group. Merlyn looked to Gawain to say something.

Gawain cleared his throat and said, "You have the opportunity to show your strength by withdrawing and seeking an alliance against a common enemy. Varden is right. The Angles will be back, and it is the land of Deira that will first be overrun. Your king needs to start building alliances. We shall come to your aid when attacked, and we must gain such an undertaking from the new chief of the Brigantes. Add to this our friends from Linnius to the south and you have a powerful alliance."

"Well said, Gawain," Merlyn added. "We have travelled the length and breadth of this country and know where the real danger lies. You have also been troubled by the Angles. Grime, captain of the guard, you can win a powerful alliance here for your king, and receive his praise. Varden is right – Venutius has been given his chance to be chief of his people and may be contented by the news that his brother died bravely in battle. What say you?"

Grime was far from convinced. "You are travellers through these lands with your own plans. I can see how what you propose benefits you. My king expects me to destroy their villages, slay their warriors, and bring back slaves. Anything less would put my head on a spike."

Merlyn patted his arm and replied, "And Venutius, sitting there amongst his kin, expects the same. And he may do the same if the positions were reversed. That is why you can offer him a way out, a way to save his people from more torment, by pledging his loyalty to King Colgrin. You have already proved you are the stronger force in this land. They know they have been weakened by Velocatus taking their best warriors south and not returning. Try it. If they refuse, then do what you will."

Grime studied the three earnest faces before him through narrow eyes. He turned and stalked back to the campfire and took his seat across from Venutius. Merlyn, Varden and Gawain followed.

Grime glanced at his comrades and spoke. "We have discussed the matter and... on behalf of King Colgrin of Deira, we are prepared to spare you any further bloodshed and misery, knowing you are mourning the loss of your brother and his warriors – a loss that has severely weakened you – and allow you to remain in your lands without interference if you swear an oath of allegiance to our king."

Venutius's eyes widened and his mouth hung open for a moment. "This is... unexpected. We thank you for you offer of peace and I ask if I may discuss the matter with my elders?"

"You may," Grime growled through gritted teeth. Venutius turned and huddled with half a dozen elders who were sitting behind him.

After barely five minutes, Venutius turned around and addressed his tormentors. "You have come upon us in a time of weakness, as you say. My brother did take our best warriors and they have not returned. We have treated you rudely in the past, and now feel the lash of your retribution. We will accept the peace that you offer. I, Venutius of the Brigante, will swear an oath of allegiance to King Colgrin, and shall honour the peace between our peoples."

"Then you shall come with us to the hall of King Colgrin and tell him yourself," Grime replied. He turned to Merlyn and added, "And you shall come too, Merlyn, and explain this to my king." He stood and rejoined his men, shouting orders to make ready to leave.

"This could get tricky," Varden whispered to Merlyn. "When Venutius finds out about the massacre of the Brigante captives by Colgrin, he might change his mind."

"One problem at a time, dear friend. The other possibility is that Colgrin will kill him too. It seems we are all returning to Ebrauc, but this time, hopefully, leaving with new friends and with Arthur by our side."

Chapter Ten

SNOW FLURRIES BLURRED Varden's vision and his gloved hands gripped his reins tightly as he leaned forward, squinting, to keep the tail of his scout's horse in sight. A ridge of snow would build up on the visor of his helmet and periodically fall onto his face, causing him to curse as he brushed it from his equally white beard. One cycle of the moon had passed since Colgrin had seen fit to allow them all to leave Ebrauc, and their way now led north to a Roman fort of good size – and an uncertain reception.

The scout had stopped and Varden drew level with him. "How much further?" he shouted into the cold wind.

"We are here, my lord. Below us is the village of Vindolanda, and beyond stand the fortress and the Roman Wall."

"Then move on and we shall seek lodgings in the village and escape this foul storm." The rocky path led downwards from a ridge to the plain below, an expanse of snowy hillocks with the occasional lonely tree stubbornly protruding. He knew the others would see the approach to the village and take heart, for the cold had increased with distance from Ebrauc, and the snow now tormented the unhappy travellers who had made slow progress from one Brigante village to another over three days of travel.

The first building they encountered was a small stone temple, then lines of stone tombs standing out of the snow, carved with the names of officers and wealthy citizens who could afford them. Modest wooden markers topped with snow stood behind them in uneven rows. At the end of the burial ground was a wooden stockade that surrounded a village.

Their approach had been noticed and two guards with long spears came out through the stockade gate to challenge them.

"We are travellers from Ebrauc, seeking a meeting with your town elder," Varden replied.

The guards looked along the line of riders to the wagons behind, clearly assessing their number, before one of them stabbed a thick finger at Varden and the scout.

"You two may enter and see our headman. The others must wait."

This message was conveyed along the line, and Varden entered with their local guide from Ebrauc. Horses snorted and shook the snow from their manes, stamping on the hard ground for the ten minutes it took for Varden to return. The gates were opened and he waved at them to enter. Crude wattle and daub thatched huts were interspersed with livestock pens and lean-to shelters for the animals to huddle in. As they followed the pathway to the centre of the settlement, the houses were better kept and made of Roman stone blocks. They stopped before a longhouse standing in the shadow of the fortress wall.

Varden dismounted and waited to be joined by Gawain, Bedwyr, Merlyn and Arthur. "The headman of the village is called Cardew. We are invited to enter and explain ourselves to him."

The warmth of the interior was welcome to the travellers, but wood smoke stung their eyes as they adjusted to the gloom. A series of fires lined the middle of the space, that was lacking in furniture, save for a long table at the far end where the headman and a dozen men now waited for them.

Merlyn stepped forward and made introductions, again not mentioning Arthur's heritage.

Cardew, the headman, showed the whites of his bony knuckles as he gripped his staff and leaned forward, grinning through his white beard at the introduction of Gawain. "Ah! Another knight from the order of Ambrosius! Sir Gawain, you will be pleased to hear that one of your fellow knights lives in the fort behind us, and is the commander of the garrison."

Raised eyebrows greeted this wholly unexpected revelation. Gawain asked, "Pray tell us, good sir, what is the name of this knight?"

The headman chuckled before replying. "He is Sir Bors. A veteran of the armies of Ambrosius and Uther, as he keeps telling us. He is my age-mate and the passage of time has not been kind to him – he is crippled in one leg and hops about on a crutch. But his mind is still alive and he is a shrewd military leader, keeping a peace of sorts along our stretch of the wall."

"This is wondrous news!" Gawain gushed, his memories of battles fought rousing him to high spirits. "I must meet with my old friend. Can you show us the way?"

Cardew smiled and bowed. "It is indeed a blessed day that brings two noble knights together at our fortress. My son shall show you to the commander's office when you are ready to leave."

"Let us not rush," Merlyn said, pushing forward to ask more questions. "Can you tell us more about this place? It is bigger than we expected."

"We have been fortunate in maintaining a busy and prosperous village that continues to grow in numbers, spreading outwards, since the fort was re-occupied."

"And it would appear there is more than one tribe here. Am I right?"

"Many who live here are the descendants of legionaries, giving our community differing looks that range from the black-haired and dark-eyed to the fair-skinned, green or blue-eyed sort. You will find pale-skinned and dark-skinned folk side by side, as was the way in Roman times. Farming and trading. When the new moon rises, our neighbours from north and south of the wall know to bring their goods and livestock to our marketplace."

"You open the gates to tribes north of the wall?" Gawain asked.

"Oh yes, they come in peace to trade with us, sharing news and enjoying our fine victuals. All people are the same at a market," he said, laughing. "Cold, and hungry."

"And we all have a liking for the look of a familiar hearth," Varden added.

"Indeed. We have adapted the town since Roman times, and many have chosen to take stones from what were once square dwellings or storerooms to make their own roundhouses. We have used Roman building materials to fashion our own dwellings in our traditional manner."

"And what of the famed temple to the water goddess, Coventina, that I have heard tell of on my travels?" Merlyn asked, fixing the headman with a keen stare.

"It is still there, and well-maintained, a half mile to the east on a well-worn track. It remains popular with our people and many go to make craven supplication to the goddess and throw offerings into a sacred well, although our priest frowns on it."

"Indeed, he would," Samson muttered.

Satisfied, they made ready to leave. Father Samson hung back and approached Cardew. "I see you wear the Christian Chi Rho symbol. Is there a priest here and a church where I might pray?"

"There is, Father. We are Christians in this household, as are most of the villagers and soldiers. Our priest is Father Ninian. My youngest son shall guide you to our humble church. You are most welcome, Father...?"

"Samson. My last parish was at Lindum, and I was schooled in Christ's ministry in Dyfed, away to the south and west of this place. I thank you for your kind welcome, Master Cardew, and am pleased to hear there is a thriving congregation here."

Gawain, Bedwyr, Varden, Merlyn and Arthur followed their guide through the back door of the longhouse and along a gravel path towards the high stone wall of the fortress and an oak door set into it. The unguarded door creaked open on obstinate hinges when their guide pushed it. Varden glanced back before passing through the door, noting that the wooden fence that enclosed the village was three-sided, as it backed onto the sturdy wall of the fortress.

Once through the door, they saw they were in a familiar Roman fort of the larger variety, built to house an entire legion. Its cobbled streets were well-kept. They passed the whitewashed walls of a granary to their right, and rows of barrack blocks to their left, as they marched to the central square in front of the commanding officer's headquarters. The buildings were all built of block-stone, with roof tiles of red baked clay covered with a thin layer of snow. What few soldiers they encountered went about their business in Roman wear of warm woollen garments overlaid with leather jerkins, stout boots and red cloaks against the cold. From somewhere, a cheer and laughter told them there was activity out of their sight.

They mounted a flight of worn stone steps where a guard held open the door to an officers briefing room, dominated by a large table at its centre. To their left was an alcove that appeared to be a shrine; once to the gods of the legion, now containing some carved figures on shelves but dominated by a wooden crucifix. Two doors to ante-rooms were on the opposite wall, and to their right, was an ornately carved door to the office of the commanding officer. On the walls hung oddly assorted tapestries – some locally fashioned animals in the forest, others remnants of the Roman legions who had been garrisoned here, including a legion banner in red with the words 'Legio XX' embroidered across it.

"Someone left in a hurry, to leave their legion banner behind," Varden gruffly remarked as they spread out around the room.

The commanding officer's door opened, and a rotund, neatly bearded balding man balanced on a crutch filled the doorway, his black eyes flickering over the faces of the visitors and resting on one he knew. Gawain stepped forward and confirmed the identity of his former comrade with a cry. He walked towards Bors with open arms and hugged the confounded commander.

It was a lot for Bors to take in. "But... Gawain, how could this be? We heard you had been imprisoned in Venta Bulgarum."

"It is true. I was imprisoned, along with young Arthur, here, and our good friend, Percival." He motioned Arthur to come forward. "Percival is alive but we left him nursing his injuries with some friends of Bedwyr here." Bedwyr bowed. "And this is Varden, our other commander, and Merlyn, whom you know."

"Ah, Merlyn!" the old knight croaked. "It has been long since we sat around Uther's round table. You are all most welcome!" He guided them to his more modest table and they all sat. An attendant appeared and Bors ordered wine and cakes be brought.

Their host waited until their goblets had been filled and raised his in salute. "May all the gods be praised – those of the old world and the new." They sipped the sweet wine and smacked their lips in appreciation.

"It is my last barrel," Bors said, his deep booming voice filling the room. "I knew a fitting time would come when it could be drunk, and now that time is here. Old friends and new, you are most welcome to Vindolanda, the last outpost of the civilised world!"

"My old friend, Bors, tell us how you came to be here?" Gawain asked as he grabbed an oatcake.

"The news of Uther's death came to me when I was fighting Saxons in the southeast. It was a blow to our morale, sure enough. I sent a scout to Venta for more information, but remained vexed by the enemy and was implored by the people to stay and finish the job of chasing Saxons back to their boats. After a week my scout returned with the news that you had been imprisoned for opposing the appointment of Uther's grandson, Mordred, as king. I was set to ride west to confront those who had done this, when I received a new injury, to add to my old ones, in a skirmish." He patted his stiff leg and continued, "My men were against us going there, where we would be declared enemies of the new king, and so they loaded me onto a cart and we headed north."

"How come you command Vindolanda, sir, and in whose name do you serve?" Merlyn asked.

Bors laughed and quaffed his drink, wiping red wine from his lips with the back of his hand. "We avoided Velocatus and his roving bands of Brigante warriors. When we came here, the place was occupied by a handful of rogues who terrorised the local people. They were little more than Gododdin bandits. We fought them and chased those we did not kill to north of the wall. I had thirty men in my command at that time, and we were accepted by Cardew, to be the protectors of the village. My rank of knight stood me in good stead, and we soon attracted new men who helped to repair the walls and gates and man this stretch of the great wall as far as mile towers in both directions."

He indicated to his attendants that they should refresh their goblets. "As for your second question, I have no lord, but a partner in Cardew. Numbers have grown here since word spread that we have improved Vindolanda's security and do not harass the locals, except for some of their women!"

They laughed and shared stories of their adventures, until Bors looked at Arthur and said, "And tell me your story, young man. In truth, you remind me of…"

"Uther?" Gawain suggested.

"Yes – he has Uther's eyes and bearing," Bors replied, popping a piece of cake into his mouth.

"I am told I am the son of Uther and Ygerne," Arthur said, "and have come to believe it."

Bors' eyes widened. "This is indeed a day full of surprises. The son of Uther?"

Merlyn leaned forward and recounted the story of Arthur's upbringing in the house of retired knight, Hector.

"Hector, my old sparring mate? Well, this is some story, Merlyn, and raises the question, why would Uther allow his only son to be taken away and raised in secrecy?"

This was a question that had also been lying without satisfactory answer in Arthur's mind. He turned to look at Merlyn.

Merlyn coughed and shot a glance at the expectant faces around him before choosing his words. "There are reasons. The most potent one being that Uther was afraid for the baby's safety. I proposed a solution and he agreed. In time, Uther and Ygerne had another child – a girl named Anne. Uther directed me to bring the boy to court, but I refused, still sensing danger, thereby frustrating his wishes, and I feared for my own safety if I remained at court. I sent Varden to be the boy's bodyguard and teach him the ways of sword fighting."

"So, Hector did not keep his charge. Is he infirm now?"

Merlyn nodded head at the commander's question, smiling. These knights would be forever competing, one against the other.

"I took Arthur to my farmstead after the Saxon threat had been curtailed by Uther's army at Badon Hill. A reunion between father and son was prevented by Uther's untimely death, and when I produced Arthur to claim his birthright, he was arrested and imprisoned by Morgana. She and her faithful hound, Caradoc. Indeed, it was Morgana who had sent assassins to find the boy and kill him. She had her own plans for Uther's succession."

Arthur huffed, noting Merlyn's opening statement. What other reasons?

They chattered merrily for some time until the food and drink had been finished.

"These are wondrous and dangerous times we live in," Bors concluded, draining his goblet. "Come, my friends, I'll show you to your quarters in our barracks and let you rest. We shall talk further this evening. You may avail yourselves of our fine bath house in the morning, situated outside the east wall."

IN THE SHELTERED bay dominated by the walled town of Exisca, on Britannia's rocky southern shore, Queen Morgaise of the Dumnoni walked on the sands with her sister, Anne, and mother, Ygerne, enjoying the cool breeze and steady rhythm of waves breaking on the beach. Behind them walked another aging knight, Sir Tristan, and his wife, Iseult. Ygerne had wept with joy at finding them living a modest existence in the town on their arrival. King Geraint barely tolerated their presence, as Iseult was the daughter of King Mark, whom he had defeated and evicted from the town after a bloody siege. Tristan, however, had once been a favourite of Uther's, and had made for a prestigious trinket to parade before Geraint's invited guests.

"Sir Tristan," Morgaise called, summoning the gentle knight forward, "I would hear your thoughts on your fellow knights, Gawain and Percival, being imprisoned by my husband's friend and ally, Caradoc." She smiled mischievously at him.

"Do not torment him," Ygerne chided.

"I do not mind, my lady," Tristan replied, sweeping a strand of greying hair from his worn but handsome face. "I was deeply vexed at the news, knowing of the good character of those gallant knights. We fought many battles against the enemies of King Uther, your husband, my lady." He bowed to Ygerne and continued. "But with the succession undeclared by him, there was always room for mischief. I was not surprised that Morgana had a plan of her own, and now her son, Mordred, is king. I suppose we must give our pledge of loyalty to the king, and pray for our dear friends."

Morgaise clapped. "A truly diplomatic and noble response, dear knight."

Tristan smiled and added, "I know of the misery of imprisonment, my ladies, for I was imprisoned here for a year by King Mark, until Iseult helped us both to escape." A look of love flickered between the elegant couple.

Morgaise smiled and said, "A sweet tale, indeed." She paused. "What if I were to tell you that Uther had a secret son, named Artorius, who has a stronger claim to the throne?"

"This rumour has circulated through the town, my queen, but few believe it to be true."

Anne replied with a flash of anger. "And what if we told you it IS true?"

"Hush, my child," Ygerne soothed. "Such talk can get us all in trouble with our lord and master. Let us be thankful for our liberty, but mindful of the vengeful spirit of Morgana."

Morgaise announced, "My husband tells me that Caradoc has taken his army northwards, to hunt for the fugitives."

"At least he will not be visiting us soon," Anne said, laughing as she slipped her arm around her sister's waist. "Let us hope he finds nothing but shadows and goblins."

They walked on towards the bustling port as the low winter sun cast long shadows, the coarse language of sailors and traders growing louder. Ygerne took Tristan by the arm and whispered, "We shall be pleased to take you into our confidence, Sir Tristan, and keep company with the lady Iseult. I shall speak to the king about having you housed next to our quarters."

Arthur, Dux Bellorum

PART TWO

Chapter One

A STOUT BLACK beetle marched across the table top, its antlers an imitation of the king of the upland moors, seemingly emboldening it with the belief that it could defend itself from all challengers or attackers. Arthur allowed it to run onto the blade of his dagger, marvelling at nature's creation.

"How is it possible, Merlyn, for a beetle that lives on dung to imitate the noble stag of the forest?" He was bored, waiting his turn for Merlyn's attention in the dispensary at the former Roman fortress of Vindolanda, in the shadow of the Great Wall.

Merlyn finished applying a poultice of crushed herbs and plant juice to the blade wound of a soldier, who groaned as he tied a bandage around it. "There. Keep that on for one week and come back to see me. I expect it to still be in place, even if it causes you to itch." The soldier stood and bowed to the healer before shuffling out through the door.

"Ah, Arthur. The beetle who thinks he is a stag. Yes, a curious creature. Now, let me see the growth that is troubling you on your back. Take your tunic off." Merlyn inspected the lump and squeezed it gently, seeing that there was fluid within. "It is just a boil, Arthur, not witchcraft or any bad fortune. I shall pierce it, then wash it and apply a poultice. This may hurt, but after that you'll be much relieved."

Pryderi attended on Merlyn with her usual quiet efficiency, bringing a scalpel and towel and organising Ulla to stand by with a basin of water. Merlyn had sent for them, and Percival, to join the rebel group at Vindolanda after the first winter had passed.

Arthur yelped as the boil was lanced, but then pulled a face at Ulla in jest, causing them both to laugh. He was no longer a slim youth, but now a man of twenty, broad shouldered and as strong as any other. With three experienced military leaders to learn from in Varden, Gawain and Bors, Arthur's knowledge of tactics and his confidence when leading patrols north of the wall were improving, to the point that his opinion was sought when they met together.

Merlyn could not be more content. His family had joined him; he had a dispensary stocked with all manner of plants and pickled creatures; and he was satisfied that he had led Arthur to a place of safety, where he could mature to manhood and develop the skills required to lead and one day be king of the Britons. He had made a secret friend in the shy druid who administered the sacred well of the goddess Coventina, a short walk from his dispensary, opening a covert line of communication to the world of the old beliefs.

Two knights had become three, with the arrival of Percival, still limping, and their reputations had helped swell the numbers at Vindolanda. Their army had multiplied to five hundred cavalry and three hundred guards, trading for horses with their neighbours, the Rheged. They could now rival any chieftain's in the region, north or south of the wall.

Such an army and their families required feeding and housing. Farming activity had increased, as had husbandry of cows, sheep, goats and fowl. The Romans had bequeathed them a fortress that could sleep up to five thousand, and granaries for the storage of wheat and barley. A bakery produced bread and cakes for the population, and the area was well served by freshwater streams. The absence of timber was compensated for by the cutting and drying of peat to stoke their fires. Contact with neighbouring tribes strengthened ties, and Merlyn insisted on frequent diplomatic missions as far as the great northern town of Ebrauc, for news and trade.

Merlyn accompanied Arthur from the dispensary and hospital block to the headquarters for a meeting of the council of leaders. Their second winter had passed at Vindolanda, and Arthur now looked up with smiling face at the warming sun above them. Birds squabbled over a nest in the eaves above the entrance to the building as they joined those waiting for them within.

At the head of the large oak table sat the fort commander, Sir Bors, his big hands spread over a parchment map as he waited for the group to assemble. To his right and left sat his fellow knights, Gawain and Percival. Then sat Varden, Merlyn, Bedwyr and Arthur. It was a military committee that ruled the fortress, a two-mile stretch of the Great Wall, and watched over the village, whose civil matters were administered by the headman, Cardew.

Bors began by briefing them on his intelligence. "Our western tower reports a build-up of Rheged warriors at their fort. Shall we send a patrol to uncover their intent?"

The weathered warriors looked at each other, then turned to Merlyn. He was wont to pick holes in the answers they gave so they had learned to let him speak first.

Merlyn smiled and placed his clasped hands on the table. "Yes. We should always seek to understand the reasons behind the activities of our neighbours. Perhaps they prepare for a foray northward, or have news of an impending attack? Let us send a knight, perhaps accompanied by Arthur, to enquire politely of their commander."

Bors grunted. They were always challenged to come up with counter proposals to Merlyn's wisdom. This time he could find none. "My thoughts exactly, Merlyn. We have no quarrel with the Rheged and we cover each other's flanks." He looked at Percival and then Gawain, waiting for a volunteer.

"I'll go," Percival said. "The weather improves, and I must make more of an effort to leave the safety of the fort."

"It would do you good to get back in the saddle, brother. Gather a patrol and leave after the men have fed and made ready." Bors looked at the map spread before him and moved his finger across it. "The scouts also report a build-up of Angles on the east coast, some fifty miles south of the last wall fort. About ten ships have been seen on a beach, and no doubt nearby settlements have fled at the news. I suggest we also need to know if our neighbours are aware and prepared for war with these wretches." He looked up at the stern faces around the table.

"Indeed, we must know," Gawain agreed, lolling back in his armchair and signalling to an attendant to pour him a drink.

"This was always coming," Merlyn added. "I will ride to the Brigante village and speak with the chief, Venutius, then on to Ebrauc to see King Colgrin and test the fragile alliance between the fractious neighbours. I shall urge them both to raise an army, and say that we are ready to take the north flank in a confrontation with the invaders."

"Each ship might carry fifty warriors, so we can estimate their numbers at about five hundred," Bors said. "In that case, Merlyn, advise our allies that they should each put no less than four hundred men to the cause. We shall match that number. It is time that we tested whether a northern alliance can act together to defend our lands from our enemies, whether coming from the sea or north of the wall."

"I can ride with Merlyn," Gawain offered, between sips of his honeyed water.

"Perhaps it would be prudent," Merlyn said, "if Percival and Arthur did not mention to our rough neighbours that an Angle army is on our east coast. They may get ideas to take advantage if they think our fort is lightly guarded."

"You are wise to be cautious, Merlyn," Bors concluded. "I shall prepare our men here. Bedwyr can be my legs. Let us make ready."

WAGON WHEELS TRUNDLED along deep, rutted grooves in the dirt road over an open moor, their groans accompanied by the cries of grouse and the caws of crows. Gerwyn the bard and his troupe of performers broke into cheerful chatter, adding to that of birds overhead, now that the rain clouds had passed to reveal a pleasant vista of green heather patterned with white blossoms, and colourful meadow flowers reaching for the sun between rocky crags. The two wagons, each pulled by four oxen, were accompanied by two horsemen, one a soldier and one a scholar.

The scholar, Ambrose, drew his horse beside the first wagon and spoke to the driver. "How much further to Vindolanda?"

Gerwyn flipped the reins to encourage more speed from his sturdy beasts. "Since we left the cobbled road our progress has slowed. I hope we see the Roman wall before the sun dips behind those western hills, putting us in darkness. Send your guard ahead to look for signs of a settlement. We will need to stop somewhere in two hours."

Ambrose rode ahead to the guard his father had provided, an experienced soldier named Sheridan, and told him to scout ahead, looking for a suitable place for them to camp if the fort was not yet in sight. He galloped on, dipping before them and soon reappearing as a dot in the distance on the track that carved a line across the undulating moors.

The sun was turning orange when Sheridan returned. "We are close to Vindolanda. I have told their guards to expect us with the last light of the day."

News reached Merlyn in his dispensary that two wagons accompanied by two horsemen were approaching from the south. His curiosity was piqued and he strode to the stables, asking a stable boy to saddle a horse for him and two guards. They rode out through the west gate and bypassed the village, joining the south road and heading for the first hill. From there, illuminated by the last golden rays of sunlight, they saw the travellers approaching. Merlyn and his guards rode towards them, squinting to see if he might recognise them. The two riders who approached carried no banners or pennants.

A young man on a white horse removed his helmet and shook long blond locks. His bigger companion, riding a large brown horse, was clearly a soldier, holding a short lance and with a sword by his side. Merlyn squinted in the half-light and then shouted, "Is that you, Ambrose?"

"Yes Merlyn, it is I. My father finally gave his permission for me to accompany Gerwyn, after much entreaty. I am looking forward to seeing Arthur again. But where is he?"

"Arthur has ridden out this morning with a patrol, but you will meet him in a few days. I am most pleased to see you, Ambrose, and see that you are recovered from your wounds. We can certainly do with more scholars able to read and write. Come with me. My guards shall stay and guide Gerwyn's wagons to the fort. Come." They spurred their horses and galloped back to the fort to make preparations for the new arrivals.

The arrival of a troupe of entertainers caused great excitement in the village and the barracks, and soon Gerwyn was pressed into agreeing to perform a play devised by Cardew and Bors. Accommodation was found for them in an unoccupied barrack block.

"Give us two days to rest and prepare," Gerwyn huffed as he supervised the offloading of their baggage from the wagons. Night had descended but the fort was lit by oil lamps positioned strategically on walls along the two main thoroughfares that met at the central square.

"Let us speak some more over our meal, Gerwyn. I shall return for you in one hour. This must be done tonight, as I ride out in the morning and am eager for your news," Merlyn said, scrutinising the weary traveller.

Gerwyn nodded and Merlyn promptly turned and walked away, reminding the bard of how their previous meeting had ended. "Much has happened since then," he whispered as he took charge of his personal items and carried them into the warm barrack block, seeking out the privacy of the optio's quarters at the far end.

PERCIVAL LAUGHED AT the sight of two hares, one chasing the other across a patch of grass between rocky outcrops, on rolling hills upon which the Great Wall sat like a huge, silent grey snake, slithering across the island from east coast to west. Arthur had pointed them out to him, breaking his moody reflection, and had been cheered at the response of the troubled knight, who had aged visibly since his ordeal at the hands of Caradoc. His broken leg had mended, but he would forever walk painfully, with a heavy limp that caused him shame and worry. Although pleased to be reunited with his two fellow knights, he was conscious that his age-mate, Gawain, still had the bearing of a powerful warrior, whereas himself and Bors carried the marks of injuries that would never let them forget. Since his arrival, he had rarely ventured out on patrol.

"Yonder is Birdoswald, fortress of our neighbours, the Rheged," Arthur said, pointing. Their patrol of fifteen stayed their horses on a hilltop looking down on a fort similar to their own at Vindolanda. It was busy with warriors and camp followers, and dirty smoke trails from peat fires rose to the clear, mid-morning sky.

"Do you know these people?" Percival asked.

"Yes, we trade with them for horses, pots, furs and the like," Arthur replied. "They see us as allies when our guards meet on the wall or on patrol, and we have not fought them, at least in the two years since I have been here. Their leader is Meirchion Gul, a tall, thin, but formidable man. He is lord over a huge territory and spends much of his time in the saddle. Let us ride down and see if he is here." He led them down a sheep trail and his sure-footed mare, Venus, hopped across a stream, heading for the open gates on the eastern wall.

They gave their horses over to young boys who came running from the stables and mounted the stairs to the command centre, noting the large numbers of warriors about the place. The smell of roasting meat hung in the air as they approached a guard with conical helmet and drooping moustache, who inclined his head to Arthur as he opened the door. Inside they interrupted a meeting of four men standing over a map laid out on a table.

"Ah, Arthur, welcome," an unsmiling man with silver beads hanging from his forked beard said, standing tall at the end of the table. "And your friend... come in and share with us your news."

Arthur bowed and replied, "Chief Meirchion, my thanks for your welcome. I have come with a noble knight, once in the service of Ambrosius and Uther, Sir Percival."

Percival, as tall as the Rheged chief, bowed and said, "My honour to meet you, Meirchion Gul of the Rheged. I am Percival of Pellinore, once a Knight of the Bear and Dragon, an order initiated by King Ambrosius of the Britons."

"And now a proud warrior who bears his wounds with grace. We have heard of you, Sir Percival. Come and drink at my table." Meirchion barked some orders and attendants were sent scurrying. Soon pewter mugs were placed before the assembled group and ale poured from a long-necked flagon. "Our own ale, brewed by priests at our western settlement," he said, raising his mug in a welcome gesture.

They tasted the ale and nodded their approval. Meirchion continued, "Your feats of valour in fighting the enemies of our kings are sung of by minstrels who travel this land, Sir Percival. What brings you to our fort?"

Percival glanced at Arthur and took on the seniority demanded by his position. "I bring you the greetings of Commander Bors, and our fellow knight, Sir Gawain. We have brought our patrol to meet with you and enquire after the reason for the rallying of your warriors in large numbers. We are mindful of the delicate security of this wall from those who seek to invade our lands."

Meirchion held his stare and replied evenly, "Your scouts have done their job. We have a situation that needs our attention. We received reports of Scotti warriors on the coast north of our end of the wall. They have come by the boatful from their island of Hibernia, bringing their families, goats and possessions, as if they mean to settle. We expect the chief of the Clyde, Ceredig, to march south and confront them. He may try to bargain with them to leave his lands."

He took a sip from his mug and continued. "That could lead either to conflict, or most likely, to the prospect that they travel south to the wall. We intend to show them by the size of our army that they will not be welcome in our lands."

Percival looked to Arthur, more familiar with the politics of the region, to reply. "We wish you well in this endeavour," Arthur said. "Furthermore, we shall keep watch over your situation and should battle ensue, send men to your aid."

"That is pleasing to hear, Arthur," Meirchion replied. "We have many more warriors than the Scotti, but might need help should they form an alliance with the wily Ceredig. He can command an army that more than matches ours.

"But tell us more of your own growing army of the three knights that we hear about. Where is your threat coming from?" He eyed the visitors keenly.

Percival replied, "Our immediate threat is from the Gododdin to our north. They have the numbers to trouble us, and they have made alliances in the past with the Angles who raid our coast from time to time. We are ever watchful."

"And what of our mutual neighbours, the Brigantes?"

Arthur replied, "As we speak, Merlyn is undertaking an expedition to meet with Chief Venutius, to test our friendship. We know the importance of alliances between tribes south of the wall in these uncertain times."

Meirchion grunted. "We know too well that battling sea-borne invaders, or those blue-painted savages from the north, can leave our backs exposed to incursions from the Brigantes, amongst others. But we are grateful for the peace and stability brought by Commander Bors in recent years. It is my earnest wish that our alliance remains strong."

He raised his mug in a toast to their informal treaty and stood, indicating the meeting was at an end. Arthur and

Percival bowed and took their leave, finding their patrol lolling about amiably with the Rheged neighbours known to them from their time patrolling the wall.

"To horse!" Percival shouted. "Let us ride!"

MERLYN COLLECTED AMBROSE and Gerwyn from their quarters as evening gave way to night, and led them to the commander's office where a table had been laid. He introduced the newcomers to Bors, and they were reacquainted with Gawain, Varden and Bedwyr.

"Please sit," Bors said, indicating their places. "I believe Merlyn wishes to garner news from you both ahead of his journey to visit our neighbours tomorrow."

"Indeed, I am anxious for news," Merlyn added. They sat and drinks were served.

Gerwyn drank thirstily, draining his goblet and smacking his lips. "This is good ale, my lord. Well, I was directed by Merlyn to travel the land and bring news of what our lords and masters are up to." He gave a smirk of familiarity to Merlyn who bridled in annoyance.

"Pray, tell us what you have heard, Master Gerwyn," Merlyn tetchily replied.

The rotund bard was used to having an audience hanging on his words, and now looked at the faces around the table to ensure he had their attention. "I did travel south to the court of King Mordred at Venta Bulgarum – they now call it something else – Dunbelgar, I believe. We performed our history play to the boy-king and his brooding mother, Morgana. They were a poor audience, and the king kept throwing food at my lads…"

"Yes, yes, get on with your news of courtly matters," Merlyn chided.

"Indeed. I found out that Caradoc had returned to his capital at Readingum to raise an army to hunt you down. But the king's mother, Morgana, vented her irritation that he had made slow progress."

"How far has he travelled with his army?"

Ambrose spoke up for the first time. "They are camped at Lindum and are wearing my father's patience thin as they have sat out the winter months, leaning heavily on his hospitality."

"Then they should be moving soon?" Gawain asked.

"I expect so," Ambrose replied. "They were making ready to leave, and so we departed very early one morning as the town slept."

"How many soldiers does Caradoc command?" Varden asked.

"I would say about eight hundred. Half mounted," Ambrose answered.

"A sizeable force," Bors said, blowing out his cheeks. "They will most likely make their way to Ebrauc and demand Colgrin's allegiance. That could cause us a problem."

"Is there a chance we could draw Colgrin onto the field of battle against the Angles before Caradoc reaches him?" Gawain asked.

"An army marches slowly," Merlyn mused. "It is possible. With swift horses we could reach Ebrauc in two days. I would have to convince Colgrin that the Angle threat is serious, and imminent, and that we have combined forces with Venutius…"

"...but time is against us," Bors interrupted, "unless we send someone to Venutius at the same time as your mission to Colgrin, and gain his agreement to raise his warriors instantly."

Varden pushed himself to his feet to give gravitas to his summation. "Do you suppose that if we form a combined army with our neighbours, we could swiftly defeat the Angles and then persuade our allies to join us to fight the king's army? I think you assume too much. The alternative is that we flee before the oncoming Caradoc and live to fight another day."

"Until Arthur and Percival return, we do not know the reason for the build-up of Rheged warriors to the west," Bors said. "If we march the bulk of our men out for battle with the Angles without knowing this, we could leave ourselves open to attack."

Varden sat and the group lapsed into silence, taking little interest in the platters of food laid before them.

Merlyn broke the silence. "If we do nothing and allow Caradoc to join forces with Colgrin, then we are doomed. I believe that Arthur's time has come to assert his claim to be King of the Britons and lead a united army against Caradoc, who has been drawn further northwards than he would care to be..."

"It is a dream, Merlyn," Bors grumbled. "With our small numbers and potential enemies all about us, we have little time or room for forming alliances."

"Riding through the gates of Ebrauc would be inviting Colgrin to seize you and I as nice hostages to offer to Caradoc as a token of goodwill," Gawain muttered. "We must be realistic, Merlyn."

Gerwyn had started to fill his platter with cold meats and vegetables, prompting the others to also eat.

Merlyn decided on one more attempt to gain a consensus for action. "I feel the threats from Caradoc and the Angle army will not go away. If we do nothing then trouble will find us. If those of us who are outlaws flee, then Bors will still have to deal with hostile forces without us."

"What would you have us do, Merlyn?" Varden asked.

"I feel that we should wait for Arthur and Percival's return, and if there is no threat from the Rheged, then we should march to Venutius. We should recruit him and his Brigante warriors to fight the Angles, having persuaded him they are an imminent threat to his lands. Once our army has swelled to a sizeable number, then we send representation to Colgrin to urge him to join us and rebuff Caradoc. In reality, Caradoc has little to offer him, and King Mordred is the son of Colgrin's recently vanquished enemy. Now, if word was to reach Mordred that Colgrin had sixty Brigante warriors executed…"

"You are ever the conspirator, Merlyn," Bors said, tearing a strip of meat off a bone with his teeth.

They ate in silence until Merlyn had a thought and turned to Gerwyn. "I had forgotten to ask you what you know of Queen Ygerne and her daughters?"

Gerwyn chewed and swallowed before replying. "The queen's eldest daughter, Morgaise, has been married to King Geraint of Dumnonia. They were fortunate enough to leave Venta before the body of the king's father, Velocatus, was brought there, and Morgana spilled her rage on those around her. Despite the passing of several months, I found an oppressive atmosphere at court, and was keen not to tarry. But I have heard that the ladies reside under Geraint's protection at his capital far to the south-west."

"And who arranged this marriage?" Merlyn asked.

"I believe it was Caradoc, acting for the king, with a view to strengthening ties with the influential and powerful Geraint. We did visit them in the town they now call Exisca to perform our play. They seem happy and content, and have found a new friend in another one of your knights – Tristan. I think they are safe for now, with Caradoc being otherwise engaged in the north."

"Arthur will be relieved to hear his mother and sisters are safe," Ambrose added, his brow furrowed.

"I am pleased to hear that my old friend Tristan is alive and well," Gawain laughed.

"That makes four of us old knights!" Bors chortled, downing his ale.

Gerwyn leaned towards Merlyn and whispered, "I have brought with me a gift for Arthur from his mother. I look forward to giving it to the young prince, when all debts are settled."

"Don't make threats to me, you scoundrel!" Merlyn blurted, getting the attention of the table. He quickly composed himself and smiled, adding, "All is well between us. Just a personal matter that we shall attend to after this excellent supper."

The matter between Merlyn and Gerwyn didn't distract them. They lingered on the happy news that Queen Ygerne and her daughters, who had played their part in aiding the escape from Morgana's dungeon, were in a place of relative safety. Then talk returned to the more important matter in hand, and it was finally agreed that should the report from Arthur and Percival be favourable, then they would execute Merlyn's revised plan. Sitting and waiting to be found by their enemies was no one's preferred option.

Chapter Two

A BLACK BOAR'S head rippled on the king's banner at the head of a procession of riders and wagons that approached the fortress town of Exisca on Britannia's southwest coast. King Mordred, now a sturdy boy of ten, leaned out of the royal carriage to watch gulls diving and circling in a noisy skirmish.

"The air tastes of salt, mama," he exclaimed, pulling a face.

"It is the seed of the great sea gods that surrounds your kingdom, my dear," Morgana replied, gripping the wooden sill as the great wheels of the carriage rolled over a stone.

"It is God's bounty to his people, my lord," a sour-faced priest sitting opposite corrected. Mordred was not listening. Next to him, Morgana's healer, Alicia, cackled to herself as she pointed out a stone circle to the bored king.

A scout pulled up beside the coach in a shower of dust and stones. "The town is ahead, my lord and lady," he reported. "In half an hour we shall be there."

Morgana's lips twitched at the prospect of a reunion with the dowager queen, Ygerne, and her impudent daughters. "Ride ahead and announce the arrival of the king," she shouted back at the scout.

Word quickly spread around the town and soon a boisterous crowd lined the main thoroughfare between the imposing granite gatehouse and the forum. Mordred laughed at the commotion their arrival had caused, and waved back to dirty-faced children who leaned over balcony railings of the two-storey townhouses they passed.

"Welcome to Exisca, King Mordred and Lady Morgana!" Geraint gushed, coming down the steps of his hall to greet them as they stretched after alighting from the coach.

"We thank you for your welcome, Geraint," Morgana purred, looking past him at the distant figure of Morgaise standing alone at the top of the steps. Ygerne and Anne had decided to stay out of sight, feigning illness.

"Come to my hall to refresh yourselves," Geraint said with a smile, indicating his attendants should help unload their baggage. "We have prepared your rooms in our royal enclosure to the back. King Mordred, you are growing tall and strong like your father..." his words trailed away at the mention of Mordred's deceased parent.

Morgaise grabbed the distracted boy by the hand and marched up the steps. "He is indeed growing taller and stronger by the day. Come, let us be welcomed by your lovely wife, the lady Morgaise."

ARTHUR AND PERCIVAL'S return the following afternoon was eagerly anticipated by the council of leaders at Vindolanda. They were swiftly conveyed from the stables to the commander's briefing room and Merlyn sent for Gerwyn and Ambrose to join them.

"Ambrose, my brother! It is so good to see you again," Arthur cried, hugging his smiling friend. Arthur held his shoulders at arms' length and inspected him, as if appraising a painting. "You are fit and healthy, Ambrose – much recovered from when we parted."

"Indeed, I am recovered, Arthur, and pleased to see you so well and much broader of shoulder. You are now a fine, manly figure." They laughed again and Ambrose stood aside. "I have travelled here with Gerwyn the bard, who has news for you."

Gerwyn had his arms full of unseen objects under a blanket. He wobbled forward and placed his load onto the table. "Arthur, I am happy to find that you survived your enforced stay with King Colgrin in Ebrauc. I bring gifts from Exisca."

The group gathered around, intrigued by the prospect of the hidden objects being revealed. Gerwyn theatrically pulled the blanket aside to reveal an oval shield, rimmed and bossed with steel, on whose golden field was painted a picture of the Virgin Mary holding the infant Jesus. Next, he unfolded a lance pennant of yellow cloth that bore the red dragon emblem of King Uther. The third item was a skilfully crafted silver brooch on which was carved the Christian Chi Rho symbol.

Arthur gasped at these riches and fitted the shield to his arm, adjusting the leather straps.

Merlyn was also taken with the striking objects and when he spoke it was with solemn certainty. "Your mother, Queen Ygerne, has sent you the most powerful message, Arthur. She has confirmed your identity as Uther's son by sending his battle pennant, and desires you to lead the Christian faithful against our pagan enemies. Your destiny is unfolding before you."

"Were there any words from my mother that came with these gifts?" Arthur asked.

Gerwyn cleared his throat as if about to give a speech, glancing with annoyance at Merlyn for pre-empting his words. "The dowager Queen Ygerne, resplendent in a gown of gold, her beauty defying her years, did instruct me in a most royal and elegant manner to deliver her words to you, Arthur."

"My beloved Arthur, a mother's love is never misplaced. I know that you are the infant taken from me only hours after your birth. My husband, your father, never spoke of our loss, nor the substance of the devilish bargain struck with Merlyn, and so I have lived in ignorance of you and your upbringing. But dear Anne has described you as a fine youth with the bearing and look of Uther, a youth who must by now be a powerful grown man. She claims you as a brother."

When Gerwyn paused, Arthur gestured impatiently for the performer to pick up his pace.

"These are her very words: 'It is your birthright and mission, dear son, to continue the work of your father, King Uther, in securing the safety of the Britons against the pestilence that endangers us from all directions. Perhaps it is a punishment for our wicked ways, as some priests do preach, but I know in my heart that you are God's instrument in driving the heathen hosts back to the dark lands from which they have come. Take this shield I have had crafted, so that God's people may rally to your side, and lead them with pride under Uther's royal pennant – for you are his true heir.'" Gerwyn smiled and bowed to Arthur, his hand in front of him in a theatrical flourish, as if expecting a reward.

"I shall see to Gerwyn's reward," Merlyn hastily concluded, bundling the bard towards the door. He was eager to avoid Arthur's inevitable question concerning 'the devilish bargain' part of Gerwyn's recital. "I shall return forthwith to participate in the discussion of our most urgent business." With that he pushed Gerwyn through the door and closed it behind him, leaving Bors to convene the meeting.

A MODEST FISHING port, sheltered from the storms of the Germanic Sea in a cove on Britannia's bleak and lonely northeast coast, was alive with axe-carrying warriors whose broad shoulders were draped with wolf and bear skins. From dragon-headed ships that lined the shingle shore, some silently carried barrels and bundles of supplies to their temporary homes in the abandoned huts of absent Britons. A horn blast from a sentry high on the cliff drew them to assemble outside the chief's longhouse for instruction.

The Angle king, Icel, distinguished from his deputies by a black eye patch over a hollow left eye socket, exited the longhouse and stood before his men. His one dark eye flitted over the faces of hundreds of warriors amassed before him, seeing more than most men saw with two. "The sentry has announced the arrival of an army from beyond the Great Wall, they who wish to join us in carving out a new kingdom. I will talk with their leaders here, and our cooks shall offer some fish soup to the warriors. The rest of you make ready for the night, as we shall march in search of a fight in the morning."

The Angles hooted and howled their approval, raising their axes in the air as a line of horsemen snaked down the track from higher ground into the estuary settlement.

Icel waited with his kinsmen to greet his visitor, King Lot of the Gododdin. The short, stocky red-cloaked king jumped from his horse, rattling the bronze and silver adornments around his neck and arms. Standing by to fill the shortfall between their differing strands of the Celtic tongue was a captive from a previous coastal raid, whose survival depended on her usefulness to Icel.

"Welcome, King Lot. You and your warriors are most welcome to our temporary home," Icel said in a thick, Germanic accent through his interpreter, who altered some of the inflections.

"I am pleased to meet with the King of the Angles, descendant of mighty Woden. Your enemies are also mine – the tribes who inhabit these lands south of the Wall. We have been in conflict since before the time of the Romans, who kept us apart. But now, this land is ripe for the taking." He bared teeth like desecrated tomb stones in a grin, peering up at Icel from under bushy brows.

Icel had no intention of trusting this man, merely using his local knowledge and his warriors to make up a stronger army and clear away all resistance before them. He planned for the Angles to carve out a kingdom and then send for their wives and children, to form a new colony. He would deal with King Lot in due course.

"Come into my longhouse and let us share food and drink," Icel said, grinning back and pointing the way into the dim, smoky interior.

Once settled, the two leaders exchanged awkward small talk. The interpreter could hardly keep her gaze from the loaded platters when the choicest victuals were served to Icel and his guest without delay. Icel then asked the question he had in his mind. "What opposition will we meet when we march inland?"

Lot tore a strip of meat from a bone, chewed and answered. "The local tribe is the Brigantes. They have recently been weakened. Their best warriors marched south and were vanquished in battle, along with their chief," he said, dribbling warm fat from the meat onto his quilted jerkin as he gave a throat-cutting gesture with his free hand at the fate of Velocatus. "Now they are ruled by that chief's younger brother. He is barely weaned, by all accounts, and no warrior."

Icel raised his eyebrows in admiration of his new ally's terse report. He exchanged looks with his followers and nodded. "Then our coming has been guided by Woden and Thor. The time is good for us to find a new homeland. We shall make sacrifices this night before marching tomorrow."

Lot grunted and washed down his meat with ale. "We will march inland some twenty miles to an old Roman fort now called Guinnion. There will be livestock traders there and some Brigante warriors, I expect. It will make a good base. We shall seize more of the land around there, much of which is good for farming and settlement."

Icel nodded and grinned his gap-toothed pleasure at this plan. "Then you shall lead us there."

"THEY ARE COMING for you, Venutius, to slaughter your people and take your land," Merlyn said, staring intently at the unsure Brigante chief.

"We are not ready for war, Merlyn," he groaned, looking about him for support or guidance from his followers.

"But war will find you, and soon," Varden said, puffing out his chainmail vest, his hand on his sword hilt.

"You must make ready, my neighbour," Bors added, stepping forward, leaning on a staff, and slapping the younger man's shoulder in a friendly gesture.

"I know it takes a matter of great importance for you to leave your fort, Bors," Venutius groaned. "We thank you for coming and offering your aid, but..." His words trailed off.

An older relative approached the young chief and spoke in his ear. Venutius nodded and faced his visitors.

"We cannot avoid conflict with these devils from across the Saxon Sea who have come for our land. Many of our people have come to us from the coast, their homes burnt or occupied. Their crops left unharvested in the fields, their lives bent to the whims of those who came on the ebb tides. What they learned from their forefathers no longer serves them. They are now robbed of their way of life, and of the familiar beauty that they never thought to leave."

Bors nodded. "It is true that if any man following Arthur did not know before the rugged splendour of our island, they surely must know it now. The north's winter frosts shrivel more than I care to think of, but even then, such grandeur humbles the spirit. We shall not be dispossessed of it."

"We shall raise our men and face them with your army of wall-watchers, Bors. If only we could persuade Colgrin to join us." Venutius was not too green to know his was a flimsy force.

"That will come later," Merlyn assured. "Once we have won a victory, then Colgrin will be impressed and more malleable to our entreaties for a defensive alliance. I think we all know that this scourge cannot be ignored and must be met before it can be defeated."

"And we have the Christian God on our side," Varden added, pointing at Arthur, who sat behind them on his horse, his golden shield of the Virgin Mary already attracting an admiring crowd. "Our priests have been calling the men between here and the Wall to join our holy war against the pagans who would loot and burn their churches. Already our militia has swelled by over two hundred. Add to this our two hundred-strong cavalry, and we are ready for a fight."

"Then we shall rally our men and be ready to march with you at dawn," Venutius concluded, barking out a series of orders to his followers.

IN THE GREAT hall at Exisca, King Geraint stood to toast his royal guests. "Your Majesty, King Mordred, and the lady Morgana. You are most welcome to my hall. May your reign be long and you sire many sons." He had given up his throne to the boy-king, whose feet swung under the broad seat, not quite reaching the stone flags. Behind the throne stood the king's champion, a huge, menacing hulk of a man. Geraint took his seat to Mordred's left, at the top of a long banqueting table. Beside him sat his wife, Morgaise, and opposite, the king's mother, Morgana.

"I thank you for your welcome, Chief Geraint," the king replied in a slow, practised manner. His mother had instructed him to call no other 'king' in his kingdom, as had been the way with her father, King Uther. He turned dutifully to prompt his mother to take up the conversation.

"You are to be complimented, Chief Geraint. Your town is well provisioned," Morgana began, "and I congratulate you on the child that grows in your wife's belly." Geraint gasped in wonder and turned to his wife, wide-eyed. She instinctively placed a hand on her still-flat stomach. Morgana smiled and took a sip of wine that coloured her lips dark red. "Mothers have a way of knowing," she purred.

Morgaise squirmed under Morgana's dark gaze, as if sitting on hot coals, and Ygerne reached over to grip her arm. Their eyes met briefly, long enough for Morgaise to have her mother confirm her deepest unease and sense of foreboding. Food was served but the women continued to eye each other across the table, saying little as the volume of conversation and merry-making around them intensified.

"You had not told me you are with child," Geraint whispered to Morgaise.

"I had only suspected a quickening this very morning, my lord," she breathed. "My mother did confirm it and I intended to share the news with you when we were alone together."

"Well, Morgana has spoiled the surprise," he replied, planting a kiss on her brow.

Morgaise gripped his arm and stared into his eyes. "My husband, I fear that Morgana wishes me harm and may…"

"Hush, hush, my dear," Geraint interrupted. "Do not get upset or give our guests cause to question our loyalty. They rule this kingdom and we must show ourselves to be loyal and true subjects. Come on, be merry and smile." He pushed his chair back and stood, raising his goblet. "A toast! To my beautiful lady, Morgaise, and our child whom she carries in her womb!"

Thunderous applause filled the hall, accompanied by stamping and clashing of cups as Geraint stood proud and smiling, bowing to his nobles. Morgaise tried to avert her eyes away from Morgana's stare, wondering how, when and where the threat to her and her unborn baby would come.

As the platters were cleared away and a troupe of minstrels prepared to perform, Morgaise whispered to Geraint, pleading the need to be excused. She allayed his anxiety and then left the hall with her mother and sister, the three of them hurrying to their chambers.

"My wife is tired and must rest," Geraint explained to his guests, "but now, my king, my minstrels will play and our visiting troubadours from Gaul will tumble for your amusement."

Morgana smiled at her son's laughter and wild applause at the tumblers, pleased that he was entertained, although her eye kept wandering to the corridor down which her prey had escaped. As soon as the performance was ended, she thanked her host for a pleasant evening and guided the young king by his arm to their quarters. Once Mordred was put to bed, she wrapped a black cloak about her, lit a torch from the fireplace, and went in search of Alicia.

"Alicia," she hissed into a dark room, "come quickly." The old woman mumbled and groaned as she got dressed and followed her mistress by the light of the glowing torch along the corridor to the kitchen. Sleeping dogs briefly looked up but soon lost interest in the intruders and returned to sleep.

"Let us search for our final ingredients and honey to sweeten our remedy," Morgana whispered, pointing to a line of pots on a shelf. Alicia lifted the lids and sniffed at the contents, selecting some plants and placing them in her flask, then returned the jars to their places. She found a pot of honey and dribbled some into her flask, before they crept to Morgana's chamber. Once they were secreted there, behind Geraint's solid walls and heavy tapestries, designed to protect his household, Morgana lit an oil lamp on the table and they set to work mixing a potion.

Chapter Three

"IT IS AN old Roman fort they called Vinovium, but we now call Guinnion," Venutius explained to his fellow commanders. They sat on horseback atop a sparse ridge and looked down on a clearing littered with empty animal pens and the smouldering ruins of herders' huts that had been torched by the Angles. The invaders now occupied the dilapidated fort at its centre.

"The Romans would have cut this clearing and kept it clear of scrub and settlement," Varden growled, pulling the fur on his cloak tightly around his troublesome throat. At the sight of the line of horsemen, those Angles who had been milling about now entered the fort and busied themselves propping up the shattered gates and blocking the two gatehouses with crude barricades. The walls of the fort, where intact, were the height of two men and stood behind a ditch and a bank. It was a small fort that could accommodate no more than five hundred men, with two main gates, north and south. In places the stone walls were denuded, where locals had taken blocks for their own dwellings, signs of defensive weakness that were noted by the commanders.

"This was a thriving cattle market," Venutius moaned. "Now they have killed or driven off our people and stolen our livestock." Between smoke columns they could see the shapes of the unhappy dead, carelessly littering the trodden grass and filthy animal pens.

"We should make a head count," Varden said, turning to Gawain. The fair-haired knight nodded, knowing his part. "As Gawain's cavalry rides around the fort, they will take to the battlements and we shall count them and make our plan for an advance. Venutius, have your men cut some trees as we shall need thick logs for battering rams and others to prop up against the walls." The old warrior still commanded the respect of his comrades and they set about their tasks.

Merlyn took Arthur and Father Samson to the rear where the foot soldiers were amassed. "Now is the time to evoke the will of your God, Father Samson, and for Arthur to make a rousing speech. They will follow you into battle, Arthur, but hold back until the time is right."

Ambrose had taken on the role of Arthur's squire and trotted dutifully behind him. Close behind came Arthur's personal guard, Herrig, and Ambrose's guard, Sheridan. Merlyn smiled, knowing the young men were well-protected and rode off into the forest on his own quest, accompanied by his adopted son, Ulla, now a youth able to ride a pony.

It had been agreed that the horsemen would ride under the command of Gawain and Bedwyr, and the foot soldiers be split into two units – Bors approaching from the north and Venutius leading his Brigantes from the south. Varden and, much to his annoyance, Arthur, would remain on the ridge with a small mounted reserve. Percival's absence was keenly noted – he had been left in command of Vindolanda, where he fretted and applied Pryderi's salve to the raw and itching skin on his body, the newest evidence of his frailty.

As the wood cutting commenced, so did the circling of the fort by Gawain's mounted archers, who whooped as they peppered the battlements with arrows, causing angry defenders to return fire with only a few arrows and stones from slings. The two groups of foot soldiers, each numbering about two hundred, took up their positions facing the south and north gates, banging on their shields and shouting crude threats at their enemy.

After thirty minutes, Gawain called his riders off and they returned to the ridge. He removed his helmet and asked Varden, "So friend, what are we facing?"

"There are cone-headed Angles there, about four hundred, and others, I'm guessing, from a Briton tribe. I'd say, at least three hundred of them, giving a total of about seven hundred."

"Who are their Briton allies?" Gawain asked.

Varden shrugged. "Maybe Venutius can tell from their banners. Inform all our commanders that we estimate their force to be seven hundred, a mix of Angles and Britons. Our numbers are almost matched – this will be no easy fight."

Gawain nodded and instructed his sub-commanders to ride to the north and south and brief their comrades.

The early morning mist had lifted by noon, and a warm spring sun lit what flowers remained on the meadow. After three hours of chopping down trees, denuding them of branches, and mounting logs onto wagons for battering rams, they were ready. The commanders had met and set their strategy. Horn blasts rang around the clearing and the two shield walls edged closer to the south and north gates. The cavalry was divided between east and west walls, ready to harass the defenders with arrows and javelins.

The strongest men set their shoulders against the battering rams and trundled them forwards, protected by comrades holding their shields up to deflect stones and arrows. The bulk of the armies followed behind, crouched behind shields. Groups of thirty or so broke off in a hastily rehearsed drill and carried improvised ramps to the side walls, where there were jagged gaps where stones had been plundered.

On a second horn blast, the attack on the fort began from all sides. Men screamed war cries and banged their shields as they moved forward, noting the defiant riposte of the defenders as they got close and crossed the ditch. The Angles had few objects to throw and only axes and swords for fighting at close quarters. King Lot's horsemen were armed with lances, which they now thrust at the men trying to breach the damaged walls with their crudely constructed ramps.

The defenders, ill-equipped to withstand a determined assault, could not stop their attackers from barging past their barricades in each gatehouse and breaching the walls. Soon, men were clambering over the rams and jumping through the gaps in the walls from their ramps, onto their enraged enemies. Fighting fanned out inside the fort as swords and axes were deployed by both sides. Once a large enough gap had been made through the gates, cavalry started to ride in, hunting down men in the spaces between barrack blocks, spearing them with lances or slashing with short swords to their left and right.

With the battlements secured and the enemy being pushed back towards the centre of the fort, Bors deemed the time was right to signal to Varden and Arthur to lead the reserves – and they joined the fray with much noise. Many were farmers with hoes and forks, eager to fight for their families, farmland and God. Fathers Samson and Ninian, and two other priests followed the men into battle, cheering them on. Men on both sides were hacked down, with the screams of wounded and dying men and horses, and terrified livestock in pens, adding to the cacophony. The commanders drove their horses into the melee, shouting encouragement to keep their men moving forwards.

The Angles and Northmen were fearsome opponents who fought like cornered animals, snarling and shouting oaths as they defended themselves with axe and sword. But the experience of Varden, Gawain and Bors, allied to the youthful exuberance of Venutius, Bedwyr and Arthur, kept their men at fever-pitch, their bloodlust overcoming any reticence and driving them onwards into the killing zone, immune to fear as bodies were falling all about them. The tide of attackers crammed into the alleyways between buildings and were pushed forward by those behind. It was the only way – for if they paused to consider the fearsome build and warlike manner of the Angles, or the wild blue-painted faces of the Northmen, they might have quaked and doubted themselves. As it was, momentum won the day, and the attackers drove the defenders back until they could retreat no more. Dozens threw down their weapons when they saw their champions killed.

Arthur, for the second time, had bloodied Excalibur in battle. This time he was stronger, more skilled and confident. The victorious commanders took the cheers of their men as they disarmed King Lot of the Gododdin and King Icel of Anglia. Arthur noted how Icel fumed, his one eye glowing with anger.

As if reading his mind, Bedwyr said, "The Angles and Saxons are at their best when jumping from their ships, rushing upon unprepared settlements and overcoming patchy resistance. The tables have been turned, and they found themselves penned in, unready and unable to fight off our spirited attack."

Ambrose rode to Arthur's other side and commented, "Your third battle is another success, Arthur."

Their horses came together and Arthur laughed before replying. "Indeed, it has been a victory, although I am still being protected by my betters – and Herrig guards my back." He turned to nod his appreciation to the muscular Jute who had become his shadow.

"They are preparing you to lead, my lord," Ambrose added. "And Merlyn has charged me with recording your victories.

May they keep coming, and may your enemies quake before your mighty sword, Excalibur!"

"Then you keep writing, Ambrose, and I'll keep swinging my sword!"

Bors, standing with Venutius, held his hands up to quieten the boisterous victors. His deep voice commanded attention. "My friends, we have bettered both the Angles who have come from across the Saxon Sea, and the notorious raiders from north of the Wall, the Gododdin!"

Huge cheers greeted this as more men crowded into the square. "The Angles came to seize your land, and we have killed many and captured their king, Icel. We have also discovered a damnable plot between the Angle invaders and the Gododdin. But we have poured water on their fire!" More cheers and banging on shields.

"But this is not the end of our troubles. We must remain vigilant and be wise to those who eye our lands with envy and would seek to pour scorn on our God. To this end, the commanders here assembled have agreed that we must keep this army together and march to Ebrauc, where we shall challenge King Colgrin to join us in an alliance to protect our lands for years to come!"

When the noise died down, Bors added, "But first, let us take the prisoners to dig pits and then honour and bury our dead. The day is drawing to an end and we shall camp on the high ground, away from the smell of death. Report to your commanders for your duties, but first, bow your heads for a blessing from Father Samson – for Jesus Christ and the Virgin Mary, whose image was borne into battle on Arthur's shield, have smiled on us this day."

As the meeting broke up, Gawain approached Bors and Varden. "I'm of a mind to take the cavalry to the coast where the Angles will have left some men to guard their ships."

"It would send a strong message, to burn their ships," Varden agreed. "But leave Arthur here with us, and be quick to join us before the gates of Ebrauc." Bors nodded, and Gawain took Bedwyr by the arm to make ready for their expedition.

THREE WOMEN SAT huddled together for warmth by a hearth in the small hall next to the kitchens of King Geraint's castle in Exisca. One wore the royal colours of the queen of Dumnonia, her gown and the wimple covering her hair being blue bordered with yellow. Alicia, dressed in the drab and anonymous woollens of the lowliest servants, approached them with care, carrying a tray bearing three bowls of steaming broth. Morgana watched from the kitchen doorway as she placed the bowls before each of the three women, then placed a platter of flatbread in the centre of the table, bowed and withdrew.

Morgaise carefully stirred her broth, and then lifted a spoonful towards her lips to blow gently. Morgana narrowed her eyes and gripped the open door, her knuckles white in anticipation, but the queen hesitated before taking the spoon to her lips. She elected instead to lower it below the table and allow a small dog to lick it. She then placed her spoon on the table and waited, listening to whispered comments from her companions, none of whom tasted their broth.

Alicia, hunched with old age, joined her mistress at the door.

"How long does it take?" Morgana whispered.

"Just a mouthful will have the victim writhing in agony within a moment," Alicia croaked.

The meal-time conversations were suddenly interrupted by a pitiful howl. The three women pushed back their bench seat to reveal the dog rolling on the stone floor as it whimpered in agony.

Morgaise yelled, "Guards! Seize that woman!" She was pointing directly at Alicia, who stood quaking in the kitchen doorway. The old sorceress turned to her mistress, but Morgana was gone. Two stout men appeared from the kitchen and seized the shocked woman by her scrawny arms.

Ygerne stood and held her hands up to their fellow diners, shouting, "Do not eat the broth – it is poisoned!" Below the table, the little dog convulsed, spewing white foam flecked with barley pearls from its mouth, then lay still.

Alicia was bundled away to the dungeons as Morgaise restored calm to the room. She stopped her maid removing her bowl of poisoned broth. "Bring a flask with a firm stopper. I wish to keep this poisoned broth and make those who prepared it taste it."

Her sister, Anne, came to her side and added her own instruction to the waiting maids. "The other bowls and their contents should be buried in a pit – so that no other innocent creatures suffer this fate." She was looking down mournfully at her dead pet under the table, whilst gripping her sister's arm.

"We have had a narrow escape from certain death," Ygerne added, guiding her two daughters through the door and towards their chambers.

Morgaise's eyes burned like coals. "I must tell my husband that Morgana sent her sorceress to kill me – all of us – with her poison!"

Ygerne guided her away from the throne room where Geraint conducted his business and down the corridor to their quarters. "I shall send for him, my dear. Then we shall discuss privately what can be done. She is the king's mother and we must tread carefully..."

"She is the devil!" Morgaise blurted. "I shall make her drink her poison!" She pulled an arm free from her sister and touched her belly where she felt a movement, conscious that her unborn child was also a target.

"Not so hasty, dear sister," Anne soothed. "Let us wait for your husband."

They did not wait long. Guards had already alerted King Geraint to the commotion in the kitchen, and he came running to his wife's chamber. "My love, what has happened?"

Morgaise flew into his arms and wept, looking down on her husband's bald pate with teary eyes. "It is Morgana. She sent her sorceress to poison our broth. Were it not for the words of caution from my mother, I would be dead, and your unborn child!"

Geraint held her at arms-length, his eyes wide. "But can you be sure it was Morgana's doing?"

Ygerne stepped forward and replied, "We recognised her creature, Alicia, whom she brought with her from Venta. She awaits your justice in the dungeon."

"But how did you survive the poison?" he asked, incredulous.

Anne replied, "We had seen the hag, and Morgaise fed the soup to my poor little Cherub, scarcely believing Morgana would really harm us. He died, writhing in agony!"

Her surviving pup looked up at her with questioning eyes, as well he might, Anne thought, fighting back the urge to punish her sister.

Geraint scratched his head, searching for words. "This is a bad business indeed. They have seized this poisoner you say? Then we shall confront Morgana with her in the throne room."

"She will deny any involvement, of course," Ygerne said.

Geraint looked unhappily at the three women. Then he nodded and backed to the door. "Stay here. My guards are outside. I shall send for you when the meeting is arranged." With that he left them to console each other and wait.

After one hour there was a knock at their door. Morgaise answered and Sir Tristan and his wife, Iseult, entered. The ladies hugged each other as Tristan stood uncomfortably in the background.

"You seem uneasy, Sir Tristan – what tidings do you bring?" Ygerne asked.

"I bring you news… that King Geraint has bid farewell to King Mordred and the lady Morgana. They have left with their followers." He bowed awkwardly at delivering news he knew would disappoint.

Morgaise cried out and ran towards the door. Tristan stepped away, not wanting to lay hands on his queen. But Anne ran after her and pulled her back by her arm. "Do not have angry words with your husband, my sister – he has had to make a hard choice."

"A hard choice!" Morgaise yelled. "He has allowed the woman who tried to murder his wife and unborn baby to get away!" The sisters struggled by the door until Ygerne stepped in and pulled them both back.

"Be still, my daughter," Ygerne said to Morgaise, holding her gaze, her face gentle but her tone emphatic. "We have much to be thankful for in Geraint. For we have no power of our own and must not oppose him. The most important thing is that you are safe, and your enemy has gone. Let us be comforted with that."

Chapter Four

THE WALLS AND towers of Ebrauc stood silhouetted in pale moonlight on the far side of a meadow. The wide field was pock-marked with a series of dark lumps separated by smouldering campfires that confirmed the presence of an army. The combined armies of Arthur and Bors, allied with the Brigantes led by Venutius, had taken three days to march south to the great northern town where Colgrin, the Deiran king, was based. The soldiers of the army of northern allies hid further back, at a clearing in the wood, whilst Arthur, Venutius and six scouts tried to estimate the size of Caradoc's army camped before them.

Merlyn's forceful presence was missing, so the case for a first strike to degrade Caradoc and King Mordred's army was made by Arthur. "We must attack under cover of darkness and kill as many of Caradoc's men as possible, thus halting his northern advance," he whispered to his agemate, Venutius. The steep slope that separated the forest's edge where they stood from the bulk of their army had deterred the veterans Varden and Bors, who had elected to stay in camp.

"They have more men than us – it would be madness. Our cavalry is yet to join us. I say we wait for Gawain and his horsemen to get here," Venutius cautioned. "Their horses will have been rested after the ride to burn Icel's longships, and they will not be far behind us. Besides, we have not yet spoken with Colgrin to try and turn him to our cause."

Venutius kept his deep sense of unease at being part of a rebel army to himself. Secretly, he was alarmed at the idea of staging an unprovoked attack on the forces of King Mordred, led by Chief Caradoc. The boy-king was, after all, his nephew.

After a pause, Arthur turned to Venutius. "Half of our army is yours, Venutius. Have your say, friend. What action do you think we should take?"

Venutius thought for a while and replied, "I cannot lead my Brigante warriors in an unprovoked attack on Caradoc, who is the guest of Colgrin. We are watchful of Colgrin, who was our enemy for many years. He would welcome an opportunity to declare us rebels and try to seize our lands. And we would be easy prey for him if we had lost warriors to Caradoc on the battlefield. I say we wait for Gawain to join us and swell our numbers before pressing Colgrin from a position of strength. We should not lose sight of our purpose, Arthur. We need to forge a northern alliance that can withstand invasion from without. Our victory at Guinnion was just the start."

Arthur, keen as he was to extinguish the personal threat of Caradoc, knew they could do nothing without the backing of Gawain's cavalry and the Brigante foot soldiers. Venutius had spoken well, with more sound reasoning and firm intent than he had expected.

"Then we wait," Arthur said. "We must hope Gawain and Bedwyr join us tomorrow. There are many fires. How many warriors lie in wait for us?"

Venutius conferred briefly with his scouts. After he had instructed them to remain and keep watch on the enemy camp, he turned back to Arthur. He indicated that he should lead the way up a slick, mulch-carpeted track, moving deeper into the forest where their men were camped. "We estimate almost two thousand men," he said to Arthur's back as they started their careful accent up a slippery path. "At least three times our number," he added under his breath.

Arthur stopped walking and glanced back at his companion, who met his concerned look with a nod that confirmed he had heard right. He let out the breath he had been holding and they continued. Shafts of silver moonlight filtered through branches and lighted their way along a tree-lined trail. An owl hooted above them and in the far distance a wolf or dog howled.

Arthur, holding his leather scabbard in his right hand to stop it slapping against his thigh, glanced to his left at the sound of a small animal or bird scuffling in the scrub and instinctively crouched, reminded in that instance of his boyhood hunting expeditions in the woods. The land levelled off and, in the distance, he could hear voices and see the red glow of campfires beyond the shaggy fringe of gorse.

Varden was waiting for them as they emerged from the cover of overhanging trees and Arthur clasped forearms with his old sword master. They stood together for a while, waiting for Venutius to reach them, listening to the chirping of insects and the croaking of frogs, breathing in the fresh smell of pine needles. Arthur opened his mouth to speak but his words were curtailed by cries and shouts away to their left, followed by the clash of steel. The faint glow of burning brands held by men could be seen approaching them.

"To arms!" Varden shouted, pushing the two young men, whose eyes were darting amongst the dark trees, along the track towards their camp. "A defensive line. Quick. Run ahead you two and give the orders," he puffed, shuffling behind them on painfully swollen feet.

The camp was alive with men pulling on chainmail vests, fixing sword belts, grabbing spears and fastening helmets. Arthur and Venutius brayed out orders for a line of shield men to form, facing the bobbing torches that fast approached. Once satisfied, they joined the rear ranks, continuing to encourage and goad.

Arthur found Ambrose by a line of wagons, close to their cook, Derward. "Secure the horses between those wagons,"

Arthur shouted, stirring Ambrose into action. He gripped his friend by the shoulders. "Dear Ambrose, tonight I must fight. But you stay here with your guard, Sheridan, and Derward, and have our horses saddled and ready for flight." He grinned at his anxious friend and rushed off to join the men.

Arthur found Varden and Bors, who had marched their two ranks of shield men forward out of the camp to a clearing. Now they could see a line of warriors standing on the edge of the forest, burning brands in hand, waiting for the order to advance. They did not wait long. A shout from a mounted commander began the moonlit advance across heather and bracken, trampling and hacking the brush from their path. The commanders, joined by Venutius in battle dress, quickly conferred.

"I shall lead the front rank," Varden said, taking charge. "Arthur and Venutius, either end of the second rank, and Bors, the reserves."

The four men placed gloved hands on top of their neighbour's before dispersing to lead their men against the onrushing, howling enemy. Was it Colgrin or Caradoc who was attacking them? They did not know, even as they barked out words of encouragement into the darkness and confusion to the lines of Brigante and assorted northern warriors.

Bors called for his horse and was helped on, giving him an elevated position to see ahead. The only others mounted were the two priests, who rode up and down behind the lines shouting out blessings and encouragement to the men.

"Spears ready!" Varden yelled at the front rank, as the screaming attackers fell onto the spear points bristling between the shields.

Arthur yelled at the second rank to push up to their comrades and stab at the enemy in any gaps that opened up.

He thrust the point of Excalibur at a screaming warrior, who had forced his way between two shield men, then continued to jab, slash and hack.

The attackers soon broke through the thin line, and a muddy ruck of desperate struggle covered the clearing. The screams of the wounded and dying filled the night air, and the confusion increased when the moon slipped behind clouds, plunging them into darkness. Arthur was not sure who he was fighting as the two armies of Briton warriors were similar in looks and dress. Arthur's painted shield and distinctive helmet with the dragon emblem atop made it easier for Varden to find him in the melee.

"Arthur, we must fall back in a group between our two campfires, for we cannot see who are fighting," Varden yelled.

They stood together and edged backwards, yelling to their men to follow them. Their opponents seemed to outnumber them, and they were driven forward by half a dozen mounted leaders whose indistinct outlines could be seen in the gloom.

Bors had seen an attempted flanking movement, and rallied thirty men to follow him to block their progress. He was aware of the dangers of being outflanked and surrounded that would almost certainly spell their doom. He shouted orders for the camp followers to flee.

Arthur and Varden found themselves in the centre of a reconvened line of Brigante warriors, who brandished battered cow hide shields lined and bossed with iron. Arthur grinned at his bodyguard, Herrig, who had muscled into the line to his right. For the first time they were showered with arrows, as their attackers brought up archers to their rear ranks. The yells and screams of men pierced by arrows filled the night as shields were hastily raised above heads. Some men screamed their pain and ducked too late under their shields when the arrows pierced them.

"Rear ranks cover the front rank!" Varden shouted above the din. Whilst the enemy paused to reorganise their front line, Varden sent soldiers to build up the fires to cover their left rank from attack. Bors, he knew, was busy holding their right flank.

Arthur looked to the east, over the heads of their opponents, where the first signs of dawn were creeping upwards from behind the screen of trees. Would they survive the next onslaught? He kept his thoughts to himself and turned around to see if Ambrose was within sight. All he could see were campfires burning low and the line of wagons slowly departing to the rear.

"They are coming on!" Varden shouted, jerking Arthur's attention back to face the enemy who now rushed towards them, screaming their war cries. As the light improved, Arthur noticed the colours and banners of both Caradoc and Colgrin, and thought he recognised the face of the Deiran captain, Grime, twisted in rage and hate, coming straight at him. Arthur raised his shield to take the impact and thrust at Grime's ribs with Excalibur. He leaned forward with all his might to hold the screaming warrior on his shield in check, whilst trying to jab between his shield and the man next to him. The hot breath and oaths of warriors rose to the sky as both sides hacked and slashed at each other.

The defenders were being driven back by weight of numbers pushing against their shields. Men were falling as they were speared, stabbed with sword or knife, or hacked with axe. The wounded went underfoot, to be finished off by spearmen to the rear. Arthur, Varden and Herrig fought shoulder to shoulder, knowing they must stay standing. There was no chance to give out any orders, even if they could think of any. Some of their conscripted Christian farmers threw down their weapons and ran towards the wagons that were now leaving the clearing.

Grime's face was between shields and he twisted his body to bring his left arm up, holding a short sword, towards Arthur's face. Arthur rocked backwards, but not fast enough to avoid the blade cutting his chin strap and slicing into his cheek. Arthur cried out in pain as his blood wet the blade of his tormentor. He was hemmed in with little room to move and his sword arm, clutching Excalibur, was on the wrong side. He could do little but push upwards with his tired shield arm and try to force his gloating enemy away. Arthur could smell the sour ale on Grime's breath as the man was pushed forward by those behind, cackling in anticipation of a kill. In desperation, Arthur drove the point of his sword downwards towards Grime's feet. With a howl of pain, Grime jerked backwards, taking his weight off Arthur's shield. In that moment, Arthur twisted, pulled his sword arm back and thrust forward, driving Excalibur into Grime's belly below his chainmail vest. Grime groaned and fell as Arthur withdrew the blade.

"Apologies, my lord," he heard Herrig say in a rasping voice. "I am wounded in the fight," he groaned, clutching his side. Arthur's eyes widened as blood oozed between Herrig's fingers. The loyal Jute had discarded his shattered shield and now stood swaying beside Arthur, barely able to lift up his sword.

The remaining Brigante and Vindolanda warriors had been forced backwards into a semi-circle, their backs to the campfires and retreating wagons. The first rays of dawn peeped over the trees as their attackers pushed on, sensing they were close to victory. Bors rode in behind Varden and Arthur and yelled words they could not hear above the din of battle. Arthur glanced back to him between blows and saw he was pointing with his spear away to their right – to the north.

Grime's body was underfoot and Arthur was now fighting another determined warrior, motivated to kill the princely figure in fine armour with distinctive shield and helmet. He staggered backwards under a rain of blows from an axe, feeling the earth tremble under his unsteady feet. To his right he could hear the shouts of men growing louder and more urgent. Herrig, although unsteady on his feet, was covering his commander's right side with defensive blocks of his sword. Arthur checked to his left and saw that Varden was still there, flaying about with determined but slow movements. But then he too staggered backwards as two warriors rained blows down on his shield and sword – he could do little else but parry them.

"Horsemen approach!" a voice shouted in a brief lull in the commotion of battle.

The cheers seemed to come from their own side, giving heart to the unsighted men in the thick of battle as the shaking of the ground started to make sense. Arthur turned and craned his neck, seeing bobbing helmets coming towards their right flank. Friend or foe? It would be the end of them if they were Caradoc's cavalry. A blow to his deformed shield dragged his attention to his front.

Arthur's blood had dripped onto his shoulder piece and the sting of the open wound focussed his mind on pushing his tired body in the fight for survival. To his left he heard Varden cry out and fall heavily on his back close by. Arthur yelled in anger and brought Excalibur down on the head of his attacker, slicing through his tin helmet and embedding the blade in the man's skull. The dying man crumpled before him as he worked his blade free. He turned to his left just at the moment Varden was impaled on the ground with a spear driven with great force through his mail into the centre of his broad chest.

"Varden!" Arthur screamed, staggering backwards.

The enemy were emboldened by the death of a fearsome warrior and leader, striking a ghoulish cheer and briefly raising their weapons with tired arms. Arthur looked about him, shocked, his arms down, snatching a moment of rest. Horsemen had joined the fray, raising the noise with their fresh cries. Arthur searched for a friendly face and saw Herrig, staggering under a rain of blows. Arthur stepped to his side and hacked off the arm of his bodyguard's tormentor. The man dropped to his knees, clutching his gushing stump, and Herrig finished him off with a chop to his neck. A warrior rushed at Arthur with a gurgling war cry, alerting him to raise his shield to take the blow. Their line had broken and his fellows were falling back in disarray.

"Arthur!" a voice he recognised shouted from somewhere behind him. It was Gawain.

Arthur, invigorated, batted away another blow with his shield and parried an axe swing with the solid steel of Excalibur. Gawain's chestnut stallion appeared beside him and his enemy was speared on the rider's lance.

Doubt now appeared in the faces of their enemies who started to fall back as hundreds of riders drove their well-schooled war horses into the battle. Arthur and Herrig stood swaying behind the rumps of their mounted comrades, who forced back their enemy and laid terrible slaughter on their tired bodies. The tide of the battle had changed and now Caradoc and Colgrin's men broke ranks, turned and fled.

Arthur watched as Gawain, Bedwyr and their men whooped as they thrust their lances at the backs of stumbling men. He looked around him at the desolation of their campsite with bodies of the dead and wounded strewn across the trampled grass. To his relief, he saw Bors still upright on his mount. The wagons had gone and, he hoped, had conveyed Ambrose and Derward to safety.

Herrig sheathed his sword and took Arthur by the arm, leading him to a command post at the rear where Bors sat on his horse, shouting out instructions.

"Arthur, I am glad to see you alive," Bors boomed at the staggering men. "But where is Varden?"

Arthur removed his helmet, made eye contact with Bors and shook his head before sinking to the ground, his legs finally giving way.

Across the meadow, Gawain blew his horn, signalling his riders to end their pursuit and fall back. Their enemy had fled into the trees, still numbering many hundreds.

"It is done," Bors said. "Our cavalry has saved us from certain slaughter. It is a sad day when Britons fight each other. Cousins have killed cousins, and many mother's sons have died on this field."

MERLYN WAS WAITING for them, two days later, in the fortified village of the Brigantes. The remains of the Brigante and Vindolanda army, now reduced to barely two hundred cavalry and two hundred-foot soldiers – the latter, weary and with heads downcast, trudged through their gates to be welcomed by their thankful families.

In contrast, Gawain and Bedwyr's cavalry had experienced nothing but success – firstly against the Angles they had chased to their boats on the coast, and then in saving the day against the combined forces of Colgrin and Caradoc. But the triumph of their return soon soured when Gawain delivered the unwelcome news that Venutius, their youthful chief, had been killed.

"But where is Varden?" Merlyn asked, after warmly welcoming Arthur and Ambrose.

Arthur's glum looks hinted at his response. "He fought bravely at my side, as ever Merlyn, but fell. I am sorry for the loss of your friend. Only moments later, Gawain's cavalry joined the battle and drove our attackers away. We have brought his body on our wagon to be honoured and buried."

The Brigante women wailed as they lifted the body of their young chief from the wagon and carried him away, wrapped in a blanket. Merlyn shook his head in sorrow and, perhaps, regret, prompting Arthur to ask, "We did miss you in our action, Merlyn. Where did you go?"

Merlyn turned his sorrowful eyes to his young protégé. "I accompanied a friend to a forest grove where druids once met. There we talked and I gained much insight into matters that greatly concern me. But I am deeply vexed at the death of my guardian and friend. I did recruit him as my guard, but he became much more, assisting me greatly and also looking out for you when you were a boy, Arthur. I will miss him. The death of Venutius is also a blow to our alliance."

Arthur's face clouded in anger. "You are a vain and foolish man, Merlyn! You disappear on a whim to meet with old druids whilst we battle our enemies – and we were nearly all slaughtered!" His hands were clenched in fists, and his face had reddened.

Merlyn could see his anger and frustration as he realised the difference his mentor's wise counsel might have made. "I did not foresee these events, Arthur. Forgive me. I left you on the eve of battle with the Angles, but did not think you would move so quickly to Ebrauc and a confrontation with Caradoc and Colgrin. You are all lucky to escape with your lives..."

"Yes! Luck, fate or God's grace – and the late arrival of our cavalry. I am angry and mournful... this wasn't meant to be..." His words tailed away and he looked to the sky. Ambrose stepped forward to put a comforting arm around his shoulder.

Merlyn fidgeted with his hands in the sleeves of his long robe, suddenly feeling the weight of sixty winters on his bony shoulders. "Yes Arthur, I was careless to abandon you. Henceforth, I shall endeavour to remain by your side to offer guidance."

They walked in slow procession behind the body of Varden, carried by six warriors to a hut behind the church. Merlyn was left reflecting on how their escape from Morgana's prison had led them on a perilous journey that had delivered them to the relative safety of Vindolanda, and two years of rest and consolidation. Arthur had grown to be a strong man, and recent events had thrust on him the necessity to test himself with the challenges of leadership. He now had an idea that would involve seeking out the Brigante leaders.

The priests bowed their tonsured heads to the Brigante and Vindolanda warriors assembled at the edge of the burial ground, following the burials of those notable warriors who had been spared the battlefield pit. Arthur noticed the lines of shackled slaves outside the burial ground, their yellowish hair and unusual body tattoos indicating that they were Angles captured in battle. He wondered at the fate of their one-eyed king, Icel.

Father Samson, who had seniority, eulogised the fallen with dry eyes. To love one's enemies, as Jesus preached, was the duty of a Christian, but war was justified by Almighty God in defence from hostile attacks. In this regard, their warriors had died well and would be at peace with God. He led a chant of words familiar to the congregation.

Merlyn followed the Brigante elders and entered their longhouse. Arthur and Ambrose met with Bors, Gawain and Bedwyr to discuss their next move. After a brief discussion, they agreed the best course of action was to start out for Vindolanda in the morning. They concluded that the battle had damaged both sides, and felt that Caradoc would be less inclined to pursue them north. He had seen their might and resolve. The mission to persuade Colgrin into a defensive alliance was now thwarted, as the Brigantes would not be reconciled with their neighbouring Deirans.

"But where is Merlyn?" Bors asked, keen to get his thoughts to their proposal.

"He went to speak with the Brigante elders," Arthur replied, pointing to the longhouse where smoke trails rose from vents in the thatched roof. They busied themselves with visiting the wounded and making preparations to leave.

After one hour, the elders and Merlyn emerged from the longhouse, and an attendant faced the open square outside it and piped a summons on a horn. The villagers, and some from the fields without, congregated in the space before the longhouse. They had left their tasks and made their way, but some dragged their feet, anxious. Nobody runs to meet bad news. The Vindolanda contingent milled about at the back, curious.

A white-haired father of the tribe held his hands up for silence. "Dear friends, we have lost the last two brothers from the House of Cartimandua. Both Velocatus and Venutius have died in battle, with no male issue save for the boy-king, Mordred, who rules far away to the south. He is a stranger to us and we do not know his mind."

Some murmuring rippled through the crowd. He continued, "It is the right and duty of the council of elders to appoint a new chief to lead our people. A bloodline is not as important in choosing a chief as a willingness and ability to protect our people. This is the quality of a great chief. With this in mind, we name Arthur Pendragon, son of Uther, as our new chief."

Stunned silence greeted this unexpected announcement. After a moment, clapping and cautious whoops of assent spread through the crowd, growing in volume. The equally surprised Vindolanda warriors added their voices to the growing clamour with loud cheers, and slaps on the back of a stunned Arthur.

"Go forward, Arthur," Gawain said, pushing him gently. The crowd parted as Arthur ambled to the front. He was motioned by the elders to come to them, and a holly wreath was placed on his head. The elder who had spoken then invited Arthur to tell them whether he would accept the honour of being the next chief of the Brigantes.

Arthur turned to face the crowd and raised his hands to indicate he wished to speak. They looked upon a strong warrior, scarred and battle-worn, similar in build and height to the mighty Velocatus. Arthur framed his thoughts in the few moments it took for silence to return. "Dear people of the Brigantes. Venutius graced the rank that fell to him, and I would have it that he were here still, but he is not. Yet he and I fought together in battle and knew each other's mind. This great honour you offer, to be your chief, is unexpected. But today I say to you, yes. Yes, I accept it and undertake to lead you with courage and without favour!"

Roars of approval met his acceptance. To the hard-pressed Brigantes he was a real, tangible warrior who had shown bravery in battle beside their own men, and therefore more welcome than any other, including a distant boy-king whom they did not know.

Merlyn moved to Arthur's side and whispered some advice. "This is your first title, but shall not be the last. We shall make alliances for you across this land until a day will come when you are welcomed as a king."

"But will I have to stay here?" Arthur whispered in reply.

"For a few days. Lead some training of their warriors, dine with them, buy their wares and invite them to hunt with you. Then ride to join us at Vindolanda to discuss wider matters pertaining to the safety of the north."

"I would welcome your guidance here, Merlyn."

"Then I will stay," the healer replied with a smile of relief.

Chapter Five

"THESE PAST TWO years of peace, since the defeat of the Angles and the battle with Caradoc, have been most welcome," Bors reflected aloud to his companions. Wounds had healed and they were now travelling on the undulating road westwards from Vindolanda to the neighbouring fortress of Birdoswald, to a feast hosted by their neighbours, the Rheged. He chuckled and added, "News of your betrothal, Arthur, has spread the length of this land. Expect many well-wishers at your nuptial celebration today!"

Gawain spurred his horse forwards to ride abreast of Bors. "Since Arthur became Chief of the Brigantes, he has charmed his neighbours far and wide. The headman in every valley eats from his hand. 'Welcome Arthur, take my best goat.' And this union confirms him as Lord of the North," he announced.

"Charming is hard work, but I thank you for conferring titles on me, Gawain – although it is frustrating that the obstinate Deirans under Colgrin would not agree with them," Arthur replied, keeping pace with his comrades.

Percival led the procession, proudly bearing Arthur's bear and dragon banner. Smiling, he listened to the joyful banter behind him, a fitting complement to the bird chatter above the flower-strewn meadows basking in the warm spring sun.

Merlyn, who had been listening quietly, now shouted from behind, "And fewer raids from north of the wall, Arthur, since Lot and his Gododdin rabble have been your prisoners. This alliance with the Rheged will strengthen us further."

Arthur now divided his time between Vindolanda and the new Brigante capital. Since becoming their chief, he had moved their capital from a crude picket-fenced enclosure on a hilltop to the strengthened Roman fort of Cataractonium, called Cataract by the locals, halfway between Ebrauc and Vindolanda on the old Roman road.

"Your marriage to the Rheged chief's daughter will unite the wall-watchers in an alliance to command the lands both north and south of the Wall. Well, they say it is the quiet ones you have to watch!" Bors added, his huge body swaying in his saddle when he laughed.

Arthur, resplendent in his finely quilted wedding doublet, red cloak edged in purple, polished armour and winged-dragon helmet, was content with the arrangement.

He smiled at the memory of being waited on at table by a young woman who moved with high-born grace and smelled of a sweet spring meadow, her delicate hands unused to kitchen work, her skin unblemished, her face appealing and her light brown hair hanging in braids. He knew she was no serving wench, but kept his thoughts to himself, catching her soft green eyes and exchanging coy smiles. He was at the table of Chief Meirchion of the Rheged, who joked in private with his nobles until they had had enough and he announced that the girl waiting on Arthur was his first-born daughter, Gunamara. Now a year had passed, and their marriage was to be blessed by Bishop Samson.

The wedding procession descended from the last hill and entered the fort through a stone gatehouse, proudly led by Percival who bowed to left and right, acknowledging the cheering townsfolk who threw flower petals before their horses and chanted Arthur's name. The interior was a mixture of well-kept Roman buildings, livestock pens and some mud-brick thatched huts at the outer edges. They alighted in front of the chief's residence, once the commanding officer's quarters, and mounted the steps to the waiting reception party.

"Welcome Arthur, from this day, my son," Meirchion boomed over the heads of the gathering crowd.

Arthur bowed to the tall chief and then took the hand of his bride, Gunamara, kissing her lightly on the hand. She smiled warmly as her oval green eyes met those of her betrothed. Arthur noted her flowing gown of cream linen, edged with gold and belted with a golden sash. A silver cross hung from a chain around her snow-white neck and on her arms she wore delicately carved silver bands. Her hair hung to her waist in braids intertwined with gold and silver threads and around her head a silver tiara set with a purple beryl glinted in the afternoon sunshine. She was tall, like her father, and stood eye to eye with Arthur, who took his place beside her as the invited guests gathered behind them.

Bishop Samson came before them and whispered his good wishes, adding that he would now bless them before the crowd and guests, before they progressed to the banquet. He positioned himself between Arthur and Gunamara and held his hands up to the boisterous crowd for silence.

"God is smiling on us this day," he began, to warm applause. "We are gathered here to witness the joining in marriage of Arthur and Gunamara, in accordance with the will of God. From this day, they shall be man and wife and shall live under the guidance and holy teachings of Jesus Christ, who died for us so that our sins may be forgiven."

He then took their hands and placed them together. The crowd cheered and shouted out sentiments that ranged from wishes of good fortune to hopes for a fertile coupling that would bring many children. Arthur and Gunamara showed their appreciation with bows and waves to the crowd. Bishop Samson then retreated and the guests waited to greet the married couple before entering the hall for the wedding feast. Arthur and Gunamara laughed and held hands with their family and friends as they passed before them in a sea of smiling faces.

"Arthur, I am so pleased to see you again," a smiling young noblewoman said, her eyes shining with mischief. Arthur gawped as his mind processed a memory.

"My sister Anne!" he cried out, causing those close to him to gasp. No mention had been made of Arthur's distant family attending the celebration. "But how…?"

She curtailed his question by stepping forward and hugging him warmly. "Merlyn sent a rider to inform us of your betrothal and the likely wedding date. I decided to come and surprise you on your special day."

"It is indeed a surprise, and a welcome one," Arthur gushed, grinning from ear to ear. "But what of my mother? We must talk…"

"And so we shall. But first, welcome your guests and we shall talk anon. I am escorted here by Sir Tristan and the lady Iseult." Anne stepped to one side as Tristan bowed to Arthur and shook his hand, followed by his wife.

"Welcome, Sir Tristan and Lady Iseult – I am… meeting you for the first time," Arthur stuttered. His head was spinning at this unexpected turn of events. Tristan smiled, bowed and moved on, leaving Arthur to complete the greetings in a daze, barely registering who stood before him until it was the turn of Gawain and his comrades from Vindolanda, whom he hugged with warmth.

"Thank you for the surprise of my sister," he whispered in Merlyn's ear as they embraced. The elderly healer smiled, nodded and moved on.

The couple passed their standing guests and took their places at the head of the table, next to Chief Meirchion and opposite Gunamara's mother and sisters. Once seated, the company were plied with flagons of wine and ale and platters of cooked meats, fragrant breads and steamed vegetables. Minstrels struck up a merry tune as conversations rippled around the table. The reunion of the knights who had fought under previous kings – Gawain, Percival, Bors and Tristan – enlivened the occasion and there was much laughter and clashing of goblets.

"This is indeed the happiest moment of my life," Arthur whispered to his glowing bride.

"And of mine, my love," she replied, placing a delicate kiss on his cheek. Her younger sister clapped and grinned, but blushed and looked away when Arthur winked at her.

Meirchion leaned towards his new son-in-law and slapped him on the shoulder. "Arthur, this union is well made. I have seen how much your friends love you – they will make powerful allies in our battles against the enemies who trouble us. But we shall not talk of such things this eve." He pushed back his heavy oak throne and stood, raising his goblet. "Friends, nobles and knights, I ask you to raise your cups to the newlyweds and wish them contentment and many strong sons!"

Once the remnants of the meal were cleared away, and those who wished to toast the happy couple had done so, minstrels played and Arthur saw his opportunity to talk to Anne. He asked Gunamara if she might spare him to this errand and she cheerfully released him, turning to talk with her friends and sisters.

"Little sister," he said, taking a vacated seat next to Anne, "please give me news of our mother."

She smiled and touched his hand. "Dear Arthur, our mother is content, but somewhat infirm in her dotage. She sends you her love. And there is a parchment missive and token that I shall give to you after the celebration."

Anne talked of their lives at the court of King Geraint in Exisca and of the attempted poisoning of Morgaise by Morgana. Arthur had not heard this and expressed his shock. She continued, "Geraint allowed Morgana to leave with Mordred and their retinue. He told Morgaise he was unwilling to challenge the king and his powerful mother openly. But he was incensed by the plot." Anne lowered her voice and glanced behind her. "Indeed, Geraint has pledged to resist any call to arms from the boy-king."

Arthur arched his eyebrows in wonder. "Has this response to a call to arms been tested yet?"

"It has not. Saxon raiders have returned to the south coast and the Dumnonians fight their own battles whenever their lands are invaded. We know not how Morgana organises the defence of their part of the coast further to the east."

"And what news of Caradoc? We clashed with his army some two years ago outside Ebrauc, and heard only that he withdrew southwards."

"We believe Caradoc is with Morgana and Mordred at Venta, no doubt plotting how to hold their lands. Their combined army is not big enough to make war, so we feel there is a stalemate. The Saxons now hold the adjoining kingdom of Ceint, covering the southeast corner of our island. We do not know if Morgana would oppose them or make a pact with them, as Vortigern did in the years before Ambrosius."

"And how is your sister, Morgaise?"

"She is the happy mother of a son, named Huwel. I also have news." She lifted her chin proudly, but the confidence didn't quite reach her eyes. "I am betrothed to the young King of Powys, Owain, from the land of Cymru."

"But who made this match?"

"He is an ally of King Geraint, who looks to build alliances in the west."

"I know Powys. Hector, who raised me, took me to the town of Viriconium where a Roman legion was once based. It is but half a day's ride from Glouvia where we lived."

"Yes, Viriconium is the town where I shall live when I am wed. He will be coming for me soon, so I shall not tarry here. Perhaps tomorrow we can talk some more, Arthur, for the next day I must be gone."

They hugged and Arthur stood to return to his place, but not before Gawain drunkenly remarked, "It is clear to see the family resemblance between you two. Let no one doubt that you are both the children of Uther and Ygerne."

"Now I have Excalibur at my side, no one would dare!" Arthur joked, returning to his bride.

THE GREAT ROMAN wall stretched away in both directions to hazy mile towers, a grey score across the green rolling hills. Meirchion and Arthur leaned on stone turrets, buffeted by random gusts of wind, surveying the bleak landscape that stretched to the fringes of a dark forest to the north. A month had passed since the wedding, and Meirchion had wasted little time in enrolling Arthur's support for his most pressing venture.

Meirchion pointed to his left. "Our road will take us up the coastal path to the settlement of the Scotti. There, we will force them to submit to our rule and take their warriors northwards with us to confront King Ceredig of Alt Clut. He commands the largest number of warriors in the north, and must be brought to heel or we shall never have peace."

Arthur nodded and fondled the round pommel of Excalibur. "We have divided our army in two – Gawain, Bedwyr and I shall lead our best horsemen. The rest shall remain to patrol the wall under the command of Bors and Percival."

"I see you have also brought your sorcerer," Meirchion observed, pointing his riding stick downwards at Merlyn who was wrestling with the reins of a skittish white stallion.

"Merlyn is our healer and a useful tactician," Arthur replied. "Besides, he asked to come, and I welcome his company."

Meirchion grunted and looked over the cavalry assembled below them, trails of steam rising to the cold, grey sky from the nostrils of over five hundred horses. In addition, there were four supply wagons at the rear. "Then we are ready. Lead your men to our western fort where they will join with my one thousand warriors. Together, we will be the largest army to march north of the wall since the Roman legions of Severus in the time of my great-grandfather. He was a scout for them."

"You have many more horses than I imagined, Father," Arthur said as they descended the stone steps to their waiting horses.

"My forebears were wise enough to begin breeding horses to sell to the Roman cavalry units positioned along this wall. Now we sell them at livestock markets across the land. There are a great many horses in the northlands, Arthur, and our stables are coveted by other tribes, including the savages north of the wall. That is why we must show them our might."

They rode to the most western fort on the wall, still called its Roman name of Luguvallium, and joined the camp of the

Rheged warriors to pitch their tents for the night. At dawn they would begin the long march north. Arthur, Gawain and Bedwyr ate with Meirchion and his commanders, discussing their strategy and sharing what information they had on the northern-most tribes.

Chapter Six

BY MID-AFTERNOON on the second day, the army of Meirchion and Arthur had reached the settlement of the Scotti on the rocky, windswept coast called Galwydell. Meirchion sent Gawain and his cavalry to by-pass the coastal village and surround them. Arthur waited with his father-in-law on a sandy dune looking down on the feeble picket fence that enclosed a settlement of no more than fifty dwellings in a crude semi-circle, their ships lying on the beach behind. These were single-mast ships that could take eight oars on each side and carry about fifty men. The Scotti, a fierce tribe from the island of Hibernia in the western sea, knew of their presence and had their men lining the inside of the fence, armed and ready. Meirchion kept looking out to sea away to his left, until he saw what he searched for – the sails of a fleet of at least half a dozen ships.

"Ah, there they are. Those are our cousins, the seafaring Setanti. I ordered them to come and cover our sea flank. We have yet to establish the numbers of Scotti settlers on this coast, so their presence can help us count and corral them."

"What do you intend to do with them?" Arthur asked.

Meirchion laughed and jabbed his heels into his horse's flanks, pointing ahead of him with his short spear to where Gawain's banner could be seen fluttering on a dune on the far side of the settlement. Horn blasts signalled the advance, and his foot soldiers marched through the sand and tufts of wild grass to take up a position within a hundred yards of the fence. Gawain did the same from the far side – a shallow stream separating the two forces.

Meirchion gathered his commanders to him. "These warriors, Arthur, are from the Novantae clan on whose land we are standing," he said, pointing to a group of stocky warriors with weathered faces, their dark eyes under thick eyebrows burning with passion. "They are keen to evict the Scotti and take back their lands, and we are here to aid them."

He pointed to the guarded settlement where ragged black banners fluttered in the strong sea breeze, and continued. "But first we must talk to their leaders. I will invite them to leave, provided they swear allegiance to me and give me warriors for our campaign further north." He instructed three deputies, including one who spoke the Scotti tongue, to ride to the gates and request a meeting with their leaders. By now, the Setanti ships had blockaded the harbour, cutting off any chance of escape.

They had not long to wait before the rickety gates of the stockade opened and three men walked out. Meirchion nodded to Arthur and they took a central position, out of arrow range of the platform above the gate, and waited for them. The Scotti leaders had plenty of opportunity to see the thousand or more men lining the dunes around them as they walked out. Their leader spoke through a bushy grey beard in the language of the Gaels, his arm bands jangling as he gesticulated. Meirchion waited patiently for the translation.

"Tell him that I am Meirchion Gul of the Rheged and this is Arthur of the Brigantes. Together we speak for the entire north of this land, below and above the wall. They have seized this place from our friends, the Novantae, who now want it returned to them. They also want your heads on spikes to adorn their hall." Meirchion paused for the translator to catch up. The startled looks on the faces of their opponents showed that they understood the full nature of the threat.

A garbled reply was translated as, "We have lost our home lands to raiders and have been forced to travel here, across the narrow sea. We are at your mercy, mighty lord, and ask only for land to settle."

"Who is your leader?" Meirchion demanded.

"They are led by their king, Fergus Mor, who is in a settlement to the west," the translator replied.

"Another king. That's all we need. Don't translate that," Meirchion muttered.

The Rheged chief looked out to sea, framing his response. "I am a reasonable man and can be merciful, given your full cooperation." He paused and leaned forward in his saddle as he looked down on the uncomfortable group before him. "You must move all your people, including your king, to the far west of this land that juts into the western sea, where we shall allow you to settle in peace, provided you swear fealty to Arthur and myself, and give us your best warriors for our northward journey." Once this was translated, the three engaged in animated debate. Soon they turned back to their tormentor and gave their assent to the arrangement.

Arthur caught the disgruntled tone of voice of the leader of the Novantae as he muttered to his men, clearly unhappy at being denied his part in a slaughter that he had perhaps been promised.

Meirchion raised his voice to the fretful elders, instructing them to prepare their people to leave immediately by boat, adding that they would be escorted westwards by his allies, the Setanti. They started to move back to the gates but Meirchion had not finished. He shouted after them, "But before you go, you must line up your men so we can choose half of them for our army."

Gulls squawked angrily overhead, ignored by Meirchion, who calmly turned his horse and beckoned Arthur to follow. "Leave it to my men. We shall make our camp in the dunes, away from the smells of these people. I have found that slaughtering your enemies without good reason leads only to resentment and defiance. It will come back to visit you like a wraith in the night. If you can make an alliance, then it is the best outcome. These Scotti will continue to come from Hibernia, but we have now created a manageable colony for them."

"But will they stay there? Arthur asked, frowning.

"I will set a Novantae guard to confine them. They have pledged their allegiance to us, and we will weaken them by taking their best warriors to fight against our other more determined enemies."

"You are wise, my lord," Arthur replied.

Pushing his mare, Venus, up a steep dune, they searched for a grassy patch of land. By not slaughtering your enemy, they can return to fight you another day, he mused to himself. He could have mentioned that Merlyn had negotiated a similar peace between Brigantes and Deirans, but chose to keep this to himself. Besides, that alliance had crumbled at the first test of it. Conflict over land seems neverending, he thought. Just as a wolf pack drives out another to protect its hunting territory, so man behaves in the same base way. Meirchion has used intimidation and then reason – after showing his might, he has given them a way out. If this peace holds, then his actions are well-judged.

ARTHUR WALKED ALONG the dunes with Herrig and Gawain for company, watching the sun dip into the far sea in a burning ball of orange, tinting the evening sky. Below them a fleet of ships was rounding the headland, making its way westwards to the far end of this rocky land. The Novantae warriors had reclaimed their village and were celebrating around a bonfire with loud cheers and laughter.

"They will send for their women and children and re-populate this place," Gawain idly observed, kicking sand at a crab.

"It is the land of their fathers. Meirchion has merely righted a wrong and his men will love him for it," Arthur replied.

"Why does Merlyn avoid you?" Gawain asked, looking directly at Arthur.

"We had angry words before leaving Vindolanda, but he still wanted to come. Something about his secret mission to find an answer to the unhappy plight of the Britons. He is still convinced I shall play a part in the restoration of a united land."

"And so you shall. But what did you argue about?" Gawain persisted.

Arthur noticed his friend's fair hair was starting to grey and thin on top, and lines were etched into his weathered skin beneath his eyes. Even Gawain was not immune to the advance of time. "I am tired of rumours and wanted him to tell me the truth about how Uther begot me. To say what his old knights whisper about. He remained evasive, saying the union of my parents was blessed with the son they desired and there is no more to know. This answer does not satisfy me. What do you know of this matter?" Arthur searched Gawain's face, hoping for something more.

"Every man has a right to know his own birth story," he began, hesitantly. "I was not there, but can tell you what I heard from others."

"Go on," Arthur urged.

"Uther was blinded by lust for the lady Ygerne and so Merlyn put the idea into Uther's head that he could deceive her into believing it was not Uther but her husband Gorlois she welcomed one night to her bed at Tintagel."

Arthur gasped. He had heard this before but had refused to believe it. "How could this happen?"

"By some magic, I am told. She was deceived and the deed was done. Shortly after, Gorlois came to Uther's camp and challenged him to a duel. Uther slayed him with this very sword, Saxon Sting." Gawain patted the blade by his side.

"Then my father is a villain," Arthur groaned.

"He was many things, Arthur. A brave warrior who never shirked his duty, for one. But yes, the rank of high king can twist a man's mind into believing he can cause offense without feeling remorse or suffering the consequences. But by the slaying of Gorlois and then taking his wife, he offended many nobles and the unity of the kingdom hung by a thread. The air at court tasted bitter from that moment."

"And yet the nobles rallied under his banner to fight the Saxons."

"Indeed, they did. Perhaps the coming of a deadly foreign army was the only thing that would bring them together. They united and won a famous battle, in which I played my part, leading the cavalry charge across the plain at Caer Badon. By that time Ygerne was queen and had birthed a daughter, Anne. The past was soon forgotten amid the victory parades."

"And so was I. The baby who was spirited away by Merlyn in the night and given to a knight bereft of his own son."

"Who raised you to be the man you are now, Arthur. Whether it is God or the fates guiding our destiny, yours is a special one. We can all see that, and will fight for you to the end. You shall be high king of the Britons, Arthur. That is your destiny."

Arthur did something he had rarely done – he stepped forward and hugged the big knight. A tear rolled from his eye onto Gawain's shoulder. Gawain held him and felt his body shake. It was only then that he noticed Herrig standing in the half-light. Gawain nodded his head, indicating Herrig should walk away and allow his master some privacy.

"You are like an older brother to me, Gawain," he mumbled. "So, I will say this. I never wanted anything more than to work on Hector's farm. I did not ask to be Merlyn's cause."

"Do not blame Merlyn. He is caught in the same strange web of fate in which we are all tangled. Look to the future, Arthur, and learn all you can from wise leaders like Meirchion. Now, little brother, wipe your nose and let us return to the campfire."

TWO DAYS OF marching and riding up the rocky west coast brought them into the territory of the kingdom of Alt Clut.

"Clinoch is high king of a vast kingdom stretching north and east. He has powerful allies in tribes under his rule led by Caw and Ceredig," Meirchion explained to his commanders. "We shall seize the settlement beyond that hill and wait for them to come to us."

"Will you draw them into battle, Father?" Arthur asked.

"If they will not agree to a truce. Remember our mission, Arthur – to remove them as a threat to us. To stop them banging their defiance on their shields. But they must first kneel to me and accept me as their overlord."

Meirchion sent his riders, led by Gawain and Bedwyr, out in a flanking movement to left and right, and then led his foot soldiers along the road to the gates of a fortified village. They lined up facing the wooden stockade whose platform was lined with silent warriors, their conical helmets glinting in the sunlight. The riders lined the meadow to left and right, two hundred and fifty strong on each side.

Meirchion waited. After thirty minutes a delegation came out through the gates and walked towards them. Arthur, Meirchion and a guard of six moved forward on their horses to meet them.

"Who has come to our land?" The spokesman's face was a sea of swirling blue tattoos above his bushy red beard.

"I am Meirchion Gul of the Rheged, and this is Arthur of the Brigantes. Who are you?"

"I am Ceredig of the Damnoni. You have reached the kingdom of Alt Clut, ruled by Clinoch from the great rock. What is it you want with us, mighty Meirchion?"

Meirchion paused and looked over their heads at the wooden stockade surrounded by a ditch. "We have come because we are tired of your raids to the wall, tired of you killing our people and stealing our horses. We have come to demand an end to your hostile actions."

The Damnoni leaders exchanged a few words. Ceredig responded, "You have come upon us with a large army, and we can see your resolve is hard as a stone. What can we do to assure you of our desire for peace?"

Meirchion laughed a deep, rolling laugh that spoke of confidence. "We would have you empty your fort so that we might occupy it whilst we wait for your master to come. March your people out and we shall pick half of your men to join my army."

"And if we refuse? Would you risk war with our most powerful lord?"

"It is a risk I am prepared to take."

They said nothing then, but started to back away. They turned and ran to their gates, fearing being ridden down or shot by arrows. Meirchion's guards moved forward in a line, dipping their lances, waiting for his command.

"Let them go," Meirchion said, turning back to his lines. "Cut a tree for a battering ram! Prepare the men to advance!"

In barely an hour a wagon was converted into a battering ram, and Meirchion sounded the advance. He knew he must take the fort before nightfall, as reinforcements may arrive for Ceredig by the morning.

"Such simple wooden gates are easily shattered, Arthur," he said, advancing slowly behind his foot soldiers. "Note how I have put the Scotti warriors to the front. Ceredig will see that and know they are now our allies."

"You have not covered the rear gate, my lord," Arthur said, putting up with the lecture but thinking for himself.

"No. Perhaps their leaders will run away?" He laughed and signalled for the cavalry to move closer and fire arrows at the men on the platform. The response was merely stones flung from slings. The battering ram broke through the gate, splintering the single spar holding it, and the men roared as they flooded in. The sound of steel clashing and the cries of men filled the air. Arthur ordered the ram be pulled back to allow the horsemen to ride in. Gawain and Bedwyr led their riders in and the slaughter began.

Meirchion and Arthur rode in behind the last of their men.

"They are killing women and children, my lord!" Arthur cried.

"I know. It is sometimes necessary. We have to subdue an enemy who will never be loyal subjects. We must reduce their numbers, for as soon as we return to our lands, they will plan their next raid." He fixed Arthur with a determined look – his warrior face.

Some were streaming out of the rear gate and running to the forest.

"I shall not cut down women and children," Gawain said, pointing his lance down.

"I will not command you," Meirchion answered. "My guard shall chase them."

Meirchion shouted some orders to his men who then rode out of the gates making loud whoops. Arthur and Gawain remained by Meirchion's side and they slowly made their way to the chief's longhouse at the centre of the village. It was empty.

"Ceredig no doubt rides one of my horses to report this brief battle to his master," Meirchion muttered, looking into the dark corners of the longhouse. "Do not look so black, Arthur. This is how it must be. I know these people. They will come and fight us. Only after we win shall they listen to talk of a peaceful union."

They walked out into the sunshine, dead bodies littering the ground. Meirchion mounted his horse and shouted to his commanders. "Burn the buildings! We will not be staying."

THE BATTLE ON a meadow beside the River Bassas was a bloody affair. Arthur led a unit of cavalry and fought with dogged determination alongside his men. Gawain and Bedwyr rode down the flanks of the thousand-strong army of blue-painted, screaming warriors on foot whose bodies soon littered the field. Kings Clinoch and Caw rode into battle in war chariots, flanked by horsemen whose riding skills were no match for Gawain's seasoned cavalry. Meirchion let the young men have their glory on the battlefield. He rode in when the fighting had ceased to take the surrender of High King Clinoch, the only surviving noble in the opposing army. The body of King Caw was carried to them, and Clinoch asked if he could be buried with honour. Ceredig had fled the field with some of his men. Meirchion agreed, making his first and only concession.

Meirchion insisted on taking Clinoch back to his hall on a great rock by a mighty river, to discuss the terms of the surrender. He had been told it was a marvel to behold by Christian missionaries who had dared to travel north and attempt to convert the pagan kings.

"I have long wished to see this, Arthur," he said as they approached King Clinoch's eyrie.

"It is the rock on the river, the Alt Clut, for which this kingdom is named," Gawain added.

Arthur surveyed the sight of a huge, rounded rock with a flattened top on which a picket fence with four corner towers enclosed a hall and outbuildings. And he watched his father-in-law, who had ordered the killing of children that same day, gasp at the workmanship. He thought, but said nothing.

Meirchion instructed his army to camp at the base of the rock and then progressed up the winding road cut into its back to the top, accompanied by his commanders and a guard of fifty riders.

Arthur, Gawain and Bedwyr dismounted and climbed one of the towers to look out over a widening estuary, with distant forts on the headlands guarding the approach from a great ocean beyond. Dozens of sea-going boats sat on the shingle beach and hundreds of thatched huts lined the shores, separated by animal pens. Men and women continued to go about their business, unmolested by the well-drilled soldiers.

"It is indeed a great kingdom," Bedwyr commented.

"And always beyond the reach of Rome," Gawain added.

Arthur noted the absence of Roman influence as they walked to the main hall, marvelling at the bright colours painted on clay pots of differing shapes and sizes. It was the biggest timber hall Arthur had seen, with high roof beams under sturdy wood struts and thatch. They joined the other commanders at a heavy banqueting table of seasoned oak.

Meirchion was seated on Clinoch's throne, talking down to the elderly king. "Swear fealty to me and accept me as your overlord, and I shall leave you here to rule your lands," he said in an even tone to the fidgeting older man. There was little choice for the defeated king who wanted to avoid the destruction of his hall and the slaughter of his people.

"You have defeated my army, Meirchion" he said in a cracked voice. "I shall swear fealty to you and pledge to be your ally north of the wall."

"Good. And also swear your loyalty to Arthur of the Brigantes. You will give me my pick of two hundred of your warriors to join our wall guards and so strengthen our ties. I will not raid your gold and silver, although I will choose a token for my wife, but we shall take a wagon of grain as we depart to feed my soldiers. Now kneel before me, and instruct your nobles to do the same."

A handful of stony-faced ancients and striplings, bereft of their daggers and their dignity, knelt and kissed Meirchion's hand, then Arthur's, ending with their high king, Clinoch. Meirchion leaned towards him and said, "When Ceredig is found, ensure he also understands."

Clinoch slowly got to his feet and nodded.

"Then let us eat and be merry, my friend," Meirchion chuckled, signalling to a stiff attendant to serve him ale.

Chapter Seven

TWO NIGHTS WERE spent camping at the base of the rock, so the men were well fed and rested before the march home. Meirchion was dismissive of Arthur's suggestions that peace with the Damnoni and other tribes was flimsy and would not hold.

"We have done what we can, and lost few men in battle. Yes, they may raid, but I don't expect that for a few years. One reason to take two hundred of their best warriors is to weaken them and make them hesitate, especially now they have seen our skill and resolute will on the field of battle. They also know of our pact with the Scotti who spill onto their shores. Others may have burnt their villages and slaughtered their people, but that would only deepen their hatred. It is a good outcome, Arthur."

"But what of the first attack? Those who did not flee to the forest were butchered, and the houses razed."

"That was to show that we are prepared to be ruthless in our advance and draw them onto the field of battle. It was important to show them who they are dealing with. Compassion comes after a harsh lesson, Arthur."

They rode at a gentle pace, keeping just ahead of the marching soldiers. On the second day, their road forked, with the most direct line taking them through the Celidon Forest. Merlyn rode forward and proposed they camp at a deserted fort in a clearing near the centre of the vast forest.

"How do you know that place?" Arthur asked.

"I know many things, Arthur. I shall ride ahead with your scouts to ensure it is indeed abandoned, as I have heard." The white-bearded Merlyn dug his heels into his white stallion and galloped off, his black cloak flapping behind him. He still wore an old cavalry helmet when riding, but had carved into it mysterious symbols, and soldered on strange shapes in different coloured metals. These added to the intrigue of his appearance.

Meirchion called forward Gawain and Bedwyr and proposed that half of the cavalry follow the coast road and visit the Novantae village to check on progress in moving the Scotti to their allotted land. Bedwyr agreed to this, and Gawain stayed with the main army.

The ancient trees stood tall as the soldiers moved deeper into the forest, whispering to them as they bowed in the breeze. "They say it is the home of witches and sorcerers," Meirchion remarked to Arthur, adding, "I think your Merlyn will be quite at home here."

Arthur was less inclined to defend Merlyn from such jibes since Gawain had reported his use of magic in the deception and rape of Ygerne. This still rankled with Arthur, who avoided his old teacher wherever possible. The scouts returned after an hour, confirming the presence of a deserted fort in a clearing up ahead. There was no sign of Merlyn, Arthur noted.

They made a rough enclosure outside the crumbling walls of an old fort, so the horses could graze in the grassy clearing. This was no Roman fort but one made by ancient peoples, with un-mortared stone walls, now in disrepair, and collapsed mud brick huts within.

"I wonder who lived here, and who they were afraid of," Gawain said as they looked for a space to bed down. They erected a canvas tent fixed to lances. Soon campfires were lit and the men prepared their evening meals.

After eating, the commanders and their deputies stretched out on their blankets and invited Gawain to regale them with stories of battles and bravery. He seldom declined such invitations and soon took a seat by the fire with his leather pouch of wine.

Through the corner of his eye, Arthur noticed Merlyn leading his horse away from the fort, heading towards the forest. Gawain had started telling a tale, but Arthur decided he would track Merlyn. He discreetly left, carrying Excalibur, then found Herrig and told him to saddle their horses and catch up with him. Arthur hurried across the clearing as the last rays of evening light filtered through the trees, picking up Merlyn's trail.

Minutes later, ahead of them, they could see the outline of Merlyn mounting his horse and trotting deeper into the darkening forest. They scrambled forwards through the brush and came out onto a path, then followed his lead and mounted their horses, urging them forward. They bent forward when their heads brushed low-hanging branches, and swayed away from squeaking bats that flew across their path. A half-moon rose above the tree tops to offer some light while they slowly made their way deeper into the Celidon forest. Owls hooted and unseen creatures snuffled and grunted in the undergrowth as Herrig followed Merlyn at a distance.

After half an hour he stopped and pointed. Arthur could just make out the glow of a campfire through the trees. They dismounted and crept forward. As they got closer, they saw a clearing where a crackling fire lit up the outline of three huts, and four people gathered nearby.

"Remain here with the horses," Arthur whispered to Herrig and then crept forward again. Arthur could then see Merlyn in conversation with three hooded figures in front of three mud-brick huts with moss-covered roofs. He could not hear them but saw that Merlyn was haggling over the cost of certain items on the ground. Soon they reached agreement and he produced one of his thin bars of silver and proceeded to cut some off for the items.

Arthur watched Merlyn bow to the three and bundle up his items in a cloak. Who were they? Witches, maybe? Arthur slowly crawled back to Herrig as Merlyn mounted his horse and sat on the trail, lit by moonlight, adjusting his cumbersome load in front of him. The healer did not turn back towards their camp, but rode on into the forest. Before long, he entered a glade and stopped, looking up to the moon, as if searching for a sign or direction.

Arthur decided to confront him and brushed past Herrig, saying, "Wait here." He moved to the edge of the glade, startling his old mentor who looked behind and grabbed his reins, about to flee, not knowing who was following him.

Arthur shouted out, "Merlyn, it is I. It is Arthur." He then walked Venus into the moonlit glade.

Merlyn turned towards him and asked, "Were you following me, Arthur?"

"Yes, Merlyn. You have been secretive, and I wish to know your intent. If Meirchion were here he'd think you were consorting with the enemy."

"But not you, Arthur. I am about my business, collecting some of the ancient treasures of Albany. They were here before the coming of the Romans and are said to have magical powers. I wish to test them."

"And what would you do with magical powers, Merlyn? This meddling justifies those who accuse you of being a sorcerer. Are you a sorcerer? What is your purpose?"

Merlyn moved closer to Arthur and unwrapped the bundle before him. "My only wish is to understand how the past reaches into the present and unshutters a window on the future."

"What are those items you have bought?"

Merlyn lifted up a small three-legged cauldron in one hand. He dipped the other inside and produced a drinking horn and a whetstone for sharpening blades. "These are gifts for you, Arthur."

Arthur was intrigued in spite of his disapproval and asked, "What are their supposed magical properties?"

"This is the cauldron of Dyrnwich that will feed a dozen from a portion for two; any blade sharpened on this whetstone will always kill those it wounds; and whoever drinks water from the horn of Brân Galed will taste whatever they wish for. These are but three of thirteen lost treasures of the ancient Britons." He held the objects out to Arthur.

But Arthur was unwilling to receive them and remained still. "I do not want to benefit from sorcery, Merlyn. I am a Christian and cannot be part of any witchcraft. This is a folly! You have been tricked and wasted your silver."

The moonlight briefly lit up Merlyn's benign smile. "There is more in this world than is preached by Christian priests. I will add these to my collection of ancient artefacts and study them..."

"No!" Arthur shouted, causing Merlyn to start, and some creature to scurry in the long grass. "You must give them up. I cannot allow you to practise sorcery from your dispensary at Vindolanda. What dread magic did you use to deceive my mother that allowed Uther to have his way with her?"

They glared at each other in the dim light, Merlyn unwilling to answer, until a fox's scream at the edge of the clearing broke the stand-off.

"Then let me show you the cloak of Eurfon," Merlyn said, unfurling the grey cloak with his free hand and covering his head and body. In an instant he disappeared, together with his horse.

Arthur's heartbeat raced and then slowed down, settling to a dull thud in his ears. He cautiously moved forward, squinting in the pale moonlight, to the place where Merlyn had been. He had gone without a trace. Arthur alighted and examined the ground for hoof marks but shook his head after a short while. Merlyn was gone.

Arthur called Herrig and they searched together, but could find no clues as to which direction he had taken.

"Let's get back to camp. He will return there eventually," Arthur huffed as they mounted.

There was just enough light from the moon to see the outline of the forest, now dimming occasionally as clouds scudded across the night sky. They followed the path back to where they thought they had joined it. Herrig dismounted and seemed satisfied there were enough snapped twigs and trampled undergrowth. They led their horses through the brush, heading towards the clearing where the army was camped at the old fort. Herrig stopped suddenly and Arthur came beside him.

"What is it?" Arthur whispered.

"Listen. I hear the sound of men running and maybe fighting."

They stood listening in the night air, Arthur at first hearing nothing but the clicking of crickets, but soon he heard faint sounds of conflict in the distance.

"How far?" he wondered aloud.

"Impossible to say with these trees. Let us advance with caution."

They crept on, the sounds growing louder. Before long, it became apparent to them that the fighting was taking place in the clearing where their comrades were camped. Herrig's horse snorted, sensing danger.

"We should leave the horses here and creep forwards to see what's happening," Arthur said. Herrig nodded and tied his reins to a tree.

Men with burning brands were spooking the horses and whipping up a stampede. Beyond the outline of the fractured fortress wall, Arthur could see men fighting with swords, shields, axes and spears. A large force had come upon them, attacking from all sides by the look of it.

"We will not be able to join our comrades," Herrig said, answering Arthur's thought.

"Then let us get to the forest edge and be ready with our swords," Arthur replied.

For the next twenty minutes they could do little more than watch as wave after wave of tribesmen threw themselves roaring onto the defenders who held the fort. The horses had been run off, and hundreds of tattooed warriors, many naked from the waist up, were pressing onto the defenders from all four sides of the dilapidated fort.

"Half of our cavalry are at the coastal settlement," Arthur whispered, "reducing our numbers."

"That may be a blessing, my lord," Herrig replied. "At least they still have their horses."

They could see the outline of the defenders' raised shields and hear the clash of steel and the screams of the wounded. Local tribesmen prowled about the clearing in front of them, and they knew they would soon be surrounded and cut down if they showed themselves. Slowly, the grey fingers of dawn began to creep through the trees, lighting up the scene of carnage around the fort.

"I think their leader is Ceredig of the local tribe," Herrig said, pointing him out covertly.

"Some of these have a look of Clinoch's warriors. They have escaped the fort and joined with the attackers," Arthur replied.

"Then Ceredig will know exactly how many he is up against."

A stalemate seemed to have settled over the clearing as visibility gradually improved, but from inside the ruins a curtain of arrows suddenly rained down on the huddled tribesmen outside, some of whom raised their small, round, cow hide shields. Gawain's men were horseless but they still had their weapons.

The two volleys of arrows were the precursor to a charge from the defenders, who flooded through the gates of the fort and fanned out into a row of shield-bearers, perhaps sixty wide. The front row pushed forward, bashing their shield bosses into the faces and bodies of their ill-disciplined opponents, whilst the second rank stabbed at them with lances through the gaps between shields. Behind the second row, Gawain led his archers who randomly fired arrows over the heads of their comrades. The effect was to concentrate the tribesmen into an enraged group who continued to hurl themselves onto the shields of their enemy, losing many men in the process.

"Let us move around behind their leaders," Arthur hissed, moving off to his right in a crouched run through the undergrowth.

Herrig followed, and soon they were behind Ceredig and his commanders, barely twenty yards away. From their new vantage point they could see Meirchion's shield wall coming towards them, and Ceredig was inching backwards as he yelled commands. He tried to initiate a flanking movement to get behind their enemy. At first few seemed to hear him, but in the end, the band of men nearest to him responded, split into two, and moved off in opposite directions to try and get behind Meirchion's army. Ceredig was left with just three for company.

"Come on," Arthur muttered through clenched teeth; then broke cover and charged towards the backs of the enemy commanders, with the unprepared Herrig stumbling behind.

Ceredig turned and drew his sword just in time to parry Arthur's lunge. Soon they were locked in a sword fight, with Herrig battling by Arthur's side.

Arthur, Excalibur in one hand and a dagger in the other, fought two men, whilst Herrig swiftly killed one of the sub-commanders and then fought the other. Arthur's attack had been too impulsive. He now realised he should have cut down Ceredig's comrade before meeting the muscular and wily chief in combat.

Ceredig grinned as he pressed forward, sensing the younger man had overstretched himself and was in trouble. Behind them, the shield wall had broken and the meadow was a riot of fighting, with duelling soldiers now all around them. Arthur needed help, and it duly arrived in the shape of one of Meirchion's sub-commanders, who had recognised him. With the second man taken care of, Arthur now focussed on his duel with Ceredig.

He crossed his sword and dagger hilts to parry a downward blow, then pushed his opponent's arms away with all his might, making him stagger backwards and opening a route to

Ceredig's midriff. Lunging forwards with Excalibur, he drove the point into the big warrior's belly. Ceredig groaned and his eyes bulged as he sank to his knees. Arthur followed up with a stab from his dagger to the man's thick neck. Ceredig crumpled at his feet, just as Herrig joined him at his side.

"Well done, master," the big Jute puffed, fending off another angry tribesman.

The tide of battle had turned, and soon the better organised defenders overcame the ragged tribesmen, many of whom, having seen their leaders fall, ran to the forest. A cheer went up from Meirchion's men, echoed by the men of Vindolanda. Soon Arthur was surrounded with generous pats to his back. Gawain pushed through the crowd and held his young protégé by his shoulders.

"Arthur! We could not find you when these devils attacked us. Where were you?"

"We were out of camp on our own mission. I shall tell you all anon."

"Arthur slayed Ceredig!" Herrig shouted, holding Arthur's sword arm up. The jubilant soldiers pressed around him, chanting his name. Arthur was enjoying the plaudits until Meirchion forced his way to his side and the men fell silent.

"My congratulations, Arthur, on slipping out of camp and coming up behind our enemy. But I would still talk to your sorcerer concerning his knowledge of this place and advice to camp here."

"I too have searched for him, but cannot find him," Arthur meekly replied, adding, "I do not think he betrayed us – he is no doubt busy reading inscriptions on ancient stones."

Meirchion greeted this with a doubtful expression. He grunted, then grabbed Arthur's wrist and raised his arm, turning to his men for their adulation.

Chapter Eight

GUNAMARA CARESSED HER small bump and clung to Arthur's arm. "Our child shall be born when the leaves turn brown and the harvest is gathered," she said with a smile, pulling her cloak more tightly around her shoulder to keep the biting cold wind out.

"Then shall we be contented with our first child, my love," Arthur replied, kicking a lump of snow that had fallen from the roof of their villa at Vindolanda. Six months had passed since his return from the foray north of the wall. He was once again a hero in battle – at least that was what Ambrose had written from Gawain's effusive description of three victories. The threat from the north had been curtailed, at least for a while.

A servant met them at their door. "My lord, the commander has worsened and has asked for you," he blurted, in a trembling tone.

Arthur kissed his wife lightly on the cheek and opened the door for her to enter. "Stay warm by the fire, my love. I shall go to the commander's side." He followed the servant across the courtyard to the rear door of the dispensary and into a room containing six beds. It was warmed by the flickering flames of a winter fire in a hearth swept clean of ash. He tried not to react to the smell of a putrid injury and an underlying taint of urine and vomit. He dipped his finger in a pungent ointment in a pot by the door and ran it above his top lip.

Arthur glanced at the empty shelves and work benches vacated by Merlyn, who had briefly passed through ahead of the returning soldiers and cleared out his things, taking Pryderi and Ulla in a wagon loaded with his possessions. He had left without a word, giving no indication of where he was going, or if he would ever return. Arthur found Sir Bors in bed, attended by two healers and a priest. At least Merlyn had trained half a dozen apprentices to care for the sick, set broken bones, clean and dress wounds and treat common ailments.

"Bors, how are you this day?"

Bors groaned as he shifted his bulk on the straw mattress to face his visitor. "I am much worse and fear my ending will soon be upon me." His face was ash grey and he dribbled from the corner of his mouth. "I can no longer feel my legs, and fear the disease is creeping up through my body. Nothing these healers give me can stop it – only lessen the fever."

"I am saddened to see you in such a state, my friend."

"Send for Percival and Gawain, I wish to give some last orders," Bors said, his booming commander's voice now reduced to a faint whisper.

"Gawain is away on patrol, but I shall send for Percival."

Arthur sent the servant to find Percival and drew up a stool to sit and wait. Father Ninian mumbled some prayers in the background as the nurses fussed over their groaning patient.

Percival's entrance was accompanied by a flurry of snow flakes, his face set in misery and horror. "Bors, are you in great discomfort?"

"Indeed I am, Percival. Come closer, I wish to... tell you both my will."

Arthur and Percival sat close on stools and leaned in to hear his faltering voice.

"I have no kin, save for my bastard son, Adair. I now claim him and wish you to make him a deputy captain of the guard, so he may learn from his betters. And let him have my sword and pick of my things." Bors broke off to cough into a bowl. "Percival, you shall command Vindolanda. Rule with wisdom and strength of resolve. I know you can..." his voice trailed away and he fell back on the bed, moaning slightly as his eyelids fluttered, the exertion too much for him.

Arthur and Percival waited patiently as his nurses tried to revive him. He never spoke again. After five minutes a nurse pronounced him dead. Percival wailed and cried, as if his own father had died. Father Ninian moved in to say a final prayer, as Arthur hung his head and offered a silent farewell to a great and faithful knight. Arthur put his arm around Percival and guided the taller, grey-haired man to the commander's office. Percival and Gawain were the youngest of Ambrosius's knights, and both were now approaching their sixtieth year. Much had happened since that time of war which now seemed like a golden age of valour and doughty resistance to the plague of invaders.

"I cannot do this, Arthur!" Percival wailed, as he slumped into the commander's chair at Bor's big oak desk littered with tablets and parchments covered in neat rows of figures. He eyed the accounts. A banner depicting a charging black boar hung menacingly on the wall behind him.

"You can and you will, Percival. You have led men before and shall do so again. It is your destiny. You must embrace it. We commanders are few and new ones must be trained and prepared for the challenges of leadership, just as Bors, Varden and Gawain did prepare me. We can do this together."

Percival's dark eyes, like pin pricks in his narrow face, showed sadness and fear. He flinched slightly at his name being absent from Arthur's list of mentors. Arthur stood looking down on him, noting his unruly hair, worry lines and wrinkles, as Percival splayed his bony fingers on the desk top.

"Yes, I must try, Arthur. It was the final command of Sir Bors, a brave and unflinching commander who never shied away from his responsibilities. I must honour his memory."

"And so you shall. I will call the men and announce the passing of Bors and make arrangements for his burial. Then I shall announce you as commander. Put on your sword belt and wear a black headband and bear fur across your shoulders, Percival. You are now the commander – and must look like one before the men."

RETURNING A DAY later, Gawain had been distraught at being absent when his old friend and fellow knight had died. The frozen ground had proved a challenge for the men to break, but Bors was now laid to rest. Gawain and Percival returned to the commander's office from the burial ground, keen to turn their minds to more practical matters.

Gawain removed his gloves and hood, warming himself by the fire. "We are a rare breed, us few remaining Knights of the Bear and Dragon. Only you and I, Percival, and Tristan in Exisca, remain of the twelve. But let me wish you well in your appointment as Commander of Vindolanda and our stretch of the wall, dear friend."

Gawain had noticed that Percival's bearing was more upright and confident. "You have become friends with yourself again, I see. This return to responsibility has done you good."

Arthur bustled into the commander's office, followed by Bedwyr, his head down and forehead creased. Gawain offered them pewter mugs of mead he warmed with a hot poker. The priests had fermented it from the produce of their hives. It was one of many crafts with which they busied themselves in the grounds of their home beside the church that was once a legionaries' temple, in the burgeoning village outside the fort.

"You seem vexed, Arthur, what is the matter?" Gawain asked.

"I have received a report that King Icel and some of his men have escaped from our prison at Cataract. Also, that King Lot of the Gododdin died in the fight with their gaolers. It seems there was a breakout of many prisoners as they were fed. The Angles must surely have headed for the coast."

"Will you go there?" Percival asked.

"I must. I ride in the morning."

"And I will go with you, Arthur," Gawain offered.

"Yes, Gawain, for we must know more of this before we proceed much further. I fear the Gododdin will rebel when they hear their king is dead, in which case we may have to divide our forces. We may have two fires to put out, with escaped Angles roving the countryside. We must be ready for that."

Arthur turned to Percival and said, "We shall take most of the cavalry, leaving you with a hundred guards and Bedwyr, here, with fifty horsemen. If there is a Goddodin uprising, we must be ready for it." Arthur clasped Percival's forearm. "We shall take our leave and make preparations."

Arthur and Gawain rushed out, leaving the tall commander and Bedwyr to their thoughts. Winter in the north was never a good time to take an army on the road. Percival looked out of the window at the snow on the roofs of the barrack blocks, then moved to stoke the fire in his grate. "At least it has stopped snowing," he muttered, looking up at the younger man, his breath rising to the rafters.

IT WAS AN easy day's ride to the Brigante village of Cataract in good weather. In the slippery thin covering of snow, the horses took longer than usual, plodding steadily along the cobbled Dere Street, until finally arriving at the fortress gates as the last light of day faded to the west. Arthur and Gawain met with the local commanders at the chief's longhouse.

They listened in stern silence to the fuller account of what had happened, and the grovelling apologies of the guards over the slaying of Lot, who had looked no different from the other prisoners lagged with drab woollens. All sixty of the prisoners had been involved in a planned escape. Half had been killed or re-captured. But most of the surviving Angles and a handful of Gododdins had escaped and evaded their search parties.

Arthur glared his displeasure over his fawning men. "There will be punishments for this slackness, but they can wait. In the morning I want all available men ready to resume the search. Icel is a dangerous enemy who will surely return to trouble us should he make good his escape. What news of the Gododdins above the wall?"

His steward came forward and told them that he had heard the Gododdin and Votodani warriors had been called to a muster at their fortress on a high rock to the north.

"They cannot be many," Gawain said. "Shall I take half of the men northwards, Arthur, to stop their rebellion before it gathers pace?"

Arthur considered this for a moment and then nodded. "Yes, that would be best, but try to avoid a fight if their numbers are greater than yours," he cautioned.

"Agreed. Then let us taste some of the local ale and fill up on the victuals on offer." Arthur dispatched the offending gaoler and made peace with the remaining commanders. He needed them all to put right this mistake. He knew from his limited experience that peace in the north was a fragile thing that hung by a thread.

"At least the Deirans have stayed in their lands and not troubled us this year," he said by way of a toast, raising a mug of warmed ale to the gathering.

In the morning, Gawain took a hundred and fifty riders northwards to start the search for the missing fugitives and press on into the land of the Gododdins, leaving Arthur with a hundred cavalry, plus a hundred or so Brigantes on foot.

WHERE THE TREE line ended, miles of hardy marram grass sprouted from the sandy earth as far as the eye could see to left and right. After that came sand dunes, then the beach and sea. Arthur halted his riders in the tree line and dismounted, looking for any signs that men had passed this way. Wary country folk had told them that ragged men, barefoot and in sackcloth, had skirted their villages, stealing what they could and heading towards the coast.

"Look for footprints in the sand!" Arthur yelled to his men, who divided into two groups and moved along the fringes of the grass. In a short while, a shout went up, and Arthur rode to a soldier on one knee pointing at tracks, that were repeated a dozen times, heading towards the dunes and the sea. Arthur called to his men to move forward in a line, a hundred wide. At the top of the last dune, they saw the beach stretch away, long and flat, in both directions, but ahead of them, a group of men were boarding a fishing vessel.

Arthur led the charge through the soft sand and onto the harder shingle of the foreshore. Those in the boat had seen them and hurried to push the craft into the gentle surf, wading out to waist height before the last of them jumped in. Oars were shipped, three on each side, and the vessel pulled away, beyond the reach of the frustrated horsemen. Arthur saw the large frame of a man with an eye patch gloating from the stern. Icel had escaped.

"It is not a boat that can cross the sea, lord," one of his men remarked.

Arthur nodded. "You are right. They must surely move north or south along this coast and look to make port or meet with a longboat. Take a dozen men and shadow their movements, and report back to me at Cataract."

Arthur led his cavalry back the route they came, sending word to the Brigante foot soldiers searching the villages to desist and return with them to Cataract. No sooner had Arthur arrived than he was informed that Ebrauc was under siege from an Angle army.

"More Angles!" he exclaimed. "Maybe they believe their king is being held there," he wondered aloud. "Tell the men to eat and rest for we shall march to Ebrauc in the morning and see what misery has befallen our neighbours."

ARTHUR LED HIS army of a hundred skilled horsemen and two hundred ill-equipped militia on foot to the walls of Ebrauc. They had camped some five miles away and now arrived on a frosty morning beneath snow-filled clouds. From their vantage point on a hill, they could see trails of smoke rising from within the town, smashed gates and a discarded battering ram.

"The yellow-haired devils are within," a Brigante commander said, and then started at the angry glare from Herrig who removed his helmet to show his unruly blond mop.

Arthur laughed. "At least we have our very own yellow-haired devil, whose skill and ferocity in combat cautions us to not take them lightly. It seems we are late and the Angles are within, laying waste to the town, no doubt."

"They will spare no quarter," Herrig solemnly intoned.

"We need to know their number before acting," Arthur said. "Herrig, take two men and ride in the trees, unseen from the towers. Go to the river beyond the walls and count their boats. That will give us an idea of their strength. We shall wait here."

Campfires were forbidden as the men huddled in groups at the forest edge. Arthur sniffed at the grey sky – for now the snow was holding off.

After an hour, Herrig returned. "My lord, there are six longboats, each able to carry fifty or sixty. Ten men guard them."

"Then we can expect no less than three hundred of the devils within the town. I would prefer to meet them in the open where our horses can ride them down..." His thoughts trailed away at the sight of a line of Angles emerged from the gates, carrying looted items and shepherding some bound captives towards the port.

"Ah, there is our chance, lord," Herrig remarked.

"Yes. Tell the men to get ready. Herrig, you can lead twenty riders to the port to attack those by their boats, and I shall lead the rest through the gates. It would take five minutes for our foot soldiers to run the distance from cover to the gates, therefore I shall lead a charge to secure the gates. That should prevent them from blocking our entrance. We shall fight our way to the hall of Colgrin."

Arthur pointed to his Brigante sub-commander. "On entry, you shall lead a unit of fifty men to the gatehouse and walls, then on to secure the towers. The rest shall move out into the streets and kill the Angle invaders. Spread the word – we do not fight the Deirans today. But rally those who have fight in them to join us in purging the town of Angles. Let us make ready."

The men gathered their weapons and prepared for battle, whilst a priest who had accompanied them gave a loud blessing. Arthur, impatient for them to move to their start position in the trees closest to the gates, turned his mare to left and right, causing the priest before him to quickly move to 'Amen'.

Herrig picked men he knew from Vindolanda, and moved off along a forest trail. Arthur lined his riders in the shadow of the treeline, with the foot soldiers behind them, ready to run. The Roman walls enclosing the town were two hundred yards away across a snow-covered meadow and beyond a ditch. The grey skies above released a gentle fall of sleet as the horsemen charged across the ground, bearing down on the opening where the gates had stood.

Arthur's mare, Venus, was second to reach the gatehouse and he followed the horse in front into the dark space. The jabbing spears of Angle warriors were waiting for them in the market square they entered. The horsemen followed two abreast into the town, pushing back their enemies and hacking down on them with swords. Eighty horsemen had soon flooded into the town and they fought their way into the side streets. Barely two minutes behind them, the foot soldiers streamed in, their way having been cleared.

Arthur rode down those too slow to evade his mare, slashing to his left and right with Excalibur, bashing away any sharp points with his shield, and kicking out with his boots. He laboured along the main thoroughfare towards the forum and the king's hall. Townsfolk who had been hiding in upstairs chambers crept out onto their balconies to cheer on their rescuers. In the forum, the fighting was at it fiercest, as the Angle leaders ran down the steps of the hall to engage with Arthur's soldiers.

Dead Deiran guards littered the front of the hall, enraging Arthur and driving him on to greater slaughter. It seemed to him that his ferocity inspired his men to redouble their efforts. Arthur leapt from his saddle onto the stone steps to the hall and picked out the biggest Angle warrior. He knew this time he had no Varden, Gawain or Herrig by his side, and must be the great warrior his men expected. Eyes wide, his blood was up, and his sword arm wheeled over his head with frightening speed, striking down to devastating effect on shields, armour and limbs.

"Meet Excalibur!" he roared into the bearded face of his opponent, forcing him off balance with a blow from his shield and finishing him with a swipe to the neck. He looked about him, and saw the fight was going their way.

"On me!" Arthur shouted as he forced his way up the steps of the hall to the portico between high columns. The Angles, as expected, fought with great ferocity, swinging axes and swords at the Brigantes who flitted about them. But they were slow in their movements, and two smaller, lighter men could outmanoeuvre them and stab at the animal furs that were belted to their bodies.

Arthur held the top of the stairs until his men were around him, and then barged into the hall, squinting in the dim light. The vast space was littered with dead bodies, evidence of a spirited defence. At the far end, Arthur found a group of Deiran nobles surrounding their dying king. Colgrin was propped up on his throne, blood dripping from a deep shoulder wound. He had also been stabbed, and blood was pooling on the floor between his feet.

Arthur strode in front of him and the Deirans, recognising their former guest, parted.

"Arthur," Colgrin groaned, then coughed up blood. He was struggling to keep one eye open. "You have come... to save our town and... my people. For that, my thanks..."

He had summoned his final strength to speak, and now rolled off his throne onto the cold stone slabs. His attendants tried to raise him by his arms, but it was clear he was dead. His queen let out a cry of grief, and his body was carried to the back of the hall with her hand gripping onto his.

Arthur stood before the throne and addressed the dozen or so Deiran nobles. "The battle is not yet won. Are there any pockets of resistance from your men, or are you fully defeated?"

A white-haired elder replied, breathless in the face of this calamity. "My lord, all our men defended the walls and gates. And when they broke through there was bitter fighting in the streets. The king's guard bravely fought to defend us. To the last man." He shook his head.

"Then I will go and tell my men to search the town for any of the devils who may be remaining. Gather your people who have survived in this hall. I shall return to you."

With that, Arthur strode across the floor, his men falling in behind him. Outside, the Angle resistance had ended, and some prisoners were corralled in the centre of the square.

"Bind the prisoners and bring them. Follow me to the barracks," Arthur yelled to his soldiers.

He led them through the streets, to cheers and blessings from a few relieved survivors. The barracks was a scene of savage slaughter, with Deiran men, women and children pitifully butchered there. Arthur made a swift search of it and the outhouses, then gave orders to collect the dead onto carts and lock the prisoners in one building. And then he marched in grim silence back to the forum and took his place at the top of the steps.

The Brigante army thronged the square, chanting his name, and he smiled at the sight of Herrig leading his horsemen from a side street. Arthur beckoned Herrig and the Brigante sub-commander to join him on the steps.

"Fellow Britons, we have won a victory over godless and merciless invaders from across the sea!" He milked the applause, as more townsfolk crept from their cellars and joined the throng. "We are Brigantes who have come to the aide of our Deiran neighbours. Let this action end the feud between our peoples. Deirans, embrace your Brigante saviours!"

He then led his commanders into the hall and strode to the gathering of nobles by the blood-stained throne of their slain leader.

"Did Colgrin leave an heir?" Arthur asked, wasting no time with soft words.

"He has a son, my lord," the elder replied, pushing a trembling boy forward.

Arthur tousled the unhappy youth's hair. "What is your name?"

"Dermot, my lord."

"And I am Arthur, chief of the Brigantes. We did not meet when last I was here. I am sorry for the death of your father. He was a stout and much-loved leader to your people."

Dermot squirmed and shrank back from the tall and powerful Arthur. His mother came and stood behind him, wrapping her arms around him.

"You are not yet ready for leadership, Dermot, but I would teach you if you would let me." Arthur looked past him to the elders, who caught his meaning. "I would be your chief and unite the two tribes so that we are ready to repel these savage invaders."

"Your deeds in defeating the Angles and Gododdins have reached our ears, Arthur, and we would welcome you to tutor the son of Colgrin, but..."

Arthur cut him off. "...But nothing. You can only be led by a strong leader. You know what will happen otherwise. But I will not insist. I will not take it. You must give it freely." Arthur fixed the elder with a determined stare until the older man looked away.

The tribal elder sighed and nodded. "Yes, Arthur, you shall be our chief."

"And I shall take Dermot for my squire. He can learn from me, and perhaps, one day, be a leader himself. Now, let us go to the steps, where you can announce this pact."

Chapter Nine

ARTHUR SPENT ONE week at Ebrauc, supervising the repairs to the gates and other damage to the exterior of the former Roman legion town. Many Deirans had been killed in the Angle raid, and Arthur left a garrison of guards that was equal parts Deiran and Brigante. The Angles had rowed their longboats upriver to the quay that serviced the town, so Arthur had a stone tower that was being used as a henhouse restored to a defensive post overlooking the quay.

"They will come again, and you must be ready," he told his captain of the guards.

Arthur led his army north on Dere Street, staying a night in the longhouse at Cataract. There, the Brigante elements of his army returned to their homes.

Once back at Vindolanda, Arthur invited Percival and Bedwyr to meet him at the public baths, where they could exchange news. Through the rising steam clouds, Arthur described the battle at Ebrauc that lead to his appointment as chief of the Deirans on Colgrin's death.

"This is mightily good news," Bedwyr said, "and dissolves the tensions between those two tribes."

"And the Angles have suffered another defeat. I hope that will keep them away from our coast," Percival said, then added, "I also have good news." He dipped under the mineral-rich waters and reappeared, to heighten the drama of his forthcoming disclosure.

"What is it?" Arthur asked, humouring him.

"We received a messenger two days ago from Gawain. He was successful in putting down the Goddodin rebellion, and has followed your example and persuaded them to make him their new chief. He has remained at their citadel to the north."

Arthur reflected on this unexpected news whilst rubbing his arms with a porous stone. "That is good for Gawain, who perhaps is getting tired of life in the saddle. I shall send a messenger to him offering my congratulations. But I shall request that he return here at his earliest convenience. We four shall talk. In truth, I had hoped he would train up a new breed of knights – with your assistance, Percival."

"That would be most welcome," Bedwyr echoed. "Our young captains are greedy to learn the art of war as the Romans fought it, and this prized knowledge is ever rarer."

The bathers wallowed, lost in their own thoughts.

Arthur's mind was already on how he would rule his growing lands across the north. He needed a chancellor to recruit administrators who could collect taxes, in addition to young commanders. It was perhaps an indulgence of Ambrosius to have adopted the Germanic order of knights, although something similar, but with a distinctly Briton flavour, appealed to Arthur.

At times like these he missed the wisdom and influence of Merlyn. He was gone, perhaps for good. When he had challenged Merlyn's methods, laid out his worst suspicions, the healer had fled into the forest in a moonless moment. He now dismissed his own confusion at the time, brought on by talk of witches and magic most likely, or a poison mushroom in his broth.

Arthur broke the silence by questioning his companions. "Merlyn is no help, off pestering some old druid, I expect. Do you think I should be less suspicious of the old ways? Be more like Merlyn, endlessly curious, and passing no judgement?"

Percival furrowed his brows and replied, "Our absent friend Merlyn juggles many truths for the sport of it. Plain men are drawn to the one simple truth you wear on your shield, Arthur. It depicts a mother and child, the truth they already work and fight for." He carried on, reassuring the young chief. "You live by the Christian faith and tradition, and the work of priests drives pagan beliefs from our land."

Arthur searched the peeling scene of water nymphs on the ceiling, formulating his response. "In truth, the Angles, the Saxons and the wild folk from the far north are pagans who are our enemies, and of whom the people are afraid."

Bedwyr spoke up. "I agree with my commander. The age of the Romans, who countenanced many religions and gods, has passed. Your task of uniting this land is greatly aided by having the Christian priests and their flocks behind you, my lord."

"I thank you both for your wisdom and loyalty. My body is cleaner, my mind is clearer and my resolve is strong." He laughed and splashed water at his friends. "In the morning our messenger shall travel to Gawain, and I shall travel to Birdoswald with my wife to meet my father-in-law. I charge you both with making your plans for a commander's training school. We shall enlist the best from the Rheged, Brigante and Deirans."

MEIRCHION'S LAVISH VILLA was situated outside the walls of Birdoswald fort. It had a well-furnished guest wing on one side of a courtyard to accommodate Arthur, Gunamara and her entourage. Shortly after they had settled in, a servant came for Arthur, inviting him to meet with his father-in-law in his study. Arthur raised his eyebrows at Gunamara. His father-in-law was apt to be unpredictable.

"Ah, Arthur, come in," Meirchion smiled, offering him a goblet of sweet wine and drawing him to sit beside the fire. He stood in a bleached linen robe and jewel-studded leather belt by the fireplace, with poker in hand, jabbing at a burning log and sending up sparks. Arthur noted the grey hairs that peppered his dark beard.

"Congratulations, Arthur. In one swoop, you have routed the Angles at Ebrauc and succeeded Colgrin as chief of the Deirans. Although it is a pity Icel slipped from your grasp. The Angle king will rearm and return. But you are now Lord of the North, and as my son-in-law can command my army of a thousand men."

Arthur choked, dribbling red wine onto his tunic, stunned at the casual manner in which Meirchion described the situation as he saw it. "You are kind, sir."

Meirchion smiled. He was just warming up. "You have done so well already, winning your spurs at Lindum, making yourself indispensable to the Brigantes and the Deirans, and of course to us, your new Rheged family. We have together tamed our northern neighbours above the wall, and now you must show your intent to claim Uther's crown and claim this whole island. I have spoken to Bishop Samson and he is ready to crown you as high king in our church before our nobles."

Arthur sat in stunned silence.

Meirchion grinned and topped up his goblet. "The wine is good, yes? A wine merchant came by ship some weeks ago – the first for a while. There are signs that trade is returning as the movements of our enemies lessen. You see, Arthur, strong and firm leadership can lead to peace and prosperity – something we must endeavour to attain. There is no reason why we cannot continue to aspire to Roman methods and values."

Meirchion took his seat next to Arthur and placed a hand on his sleeve. "My vision is a lot to think on, I am sure. Let us sit and drink and I shall talk to you of other things."

He reached for a parchment and spread it out on his knees.

"What do you have there, Father?" Arthur asked him, thinking to divert Meirchion.

Meirchion held the curling edges of the map of Roman Britannia on his lap. "Samson has been teaching me about Roman history, about the records of the long dead scholar Tacitus. This map of Roman Britannia shows nothing above our great wall except empty space with the word, 'Caledonii'."

At that point in their conversation, Gunamara, heavy with child and shiny-faced, joined the men.

"Forgive me for interrupting, my dear ones, but I was lonely. What is that?" she asked, sitting on a settle and adjusting a cushion at her back with difficulty. And then she answered herself. "Oh, it is one of Samson's maps of Roman Britannia. Tacitus. He is Samson's pet theme. Did you know Tacitus described the tribes of Caledonia as cannibals, who enjoyed feasting on the flesh of their enemies?"

"I had heard that," Arthur replied, between sips, smiling his welcome. "A priest taught me to read the works of saintly Augustus and the historian Tacitus when I was a boy."

"Hmmm. Then you are a better scholar than me. Tacitus must have heard tales of the wild painted savages to the far north whom we call Picts," said his wife.

"We have been as far north as any civilised people have been, Arthur, to the hall of King Ceredig," said Meirchion, as he placed Gunamara's swollen feet on a footstool. "At least since the excursion of General Agricola who did not tarry long in the unwelcoming north."

Gunamara held one side of the curling map and said, "The map shows this island as a box, with two long sides and two short. But I do not believe the galleys of Agricola sailed around the north. In truth, no one knows how far northwards the land extends, nor how many flesh-eating Picts inhabit that wild place." She looked up with a smile, comfortable, as always, in the company of the two men she adored.

"This is your kingdom, Arthur – I give this to you." Meirchion rolled up the parchment and tied it with a red ribbon, handing it to the young man, humbled in that moment.

Gunamara looked at the gift with envy, but she didn't seem surprised by her father's words.

A family conspiracy, Arthur thought. "My thanks, Father, for your confidence in me," he mumbled. "I shall do all I can to live up to your expectations."

"I expect you to unite the squabbling tribes against these infernal barbarian invaders," he replied, standing. "Now, I have had some news from the south."

Arthur sat up and handed the roll to Gunamara.

Meirchion's expression was serious. "It seems that Morgana and Caradoc have met with their noisy neighbours, the Saxons, and made a peace treaty. This might spell trouble for your family at the court of Geraint, in Dumnonia."

Arthur's thoughts flickered to Anne and Morgaise, but of his mother, Ygerne, he had no image as they had not met.

"If this were not bad enough, your fair sister, Anne, has sent a messenger. She beseeches us to take an army south to her husband's lands in Powys, where a rival Cornovii chief raids his borders to test their resolve."

Arthur drained his goblet and placed it on the table, considering this news. "We shall soon have our first child, and I would wait for the first lambs of spring before taking an army south..."

Gunamara looked relieved; the lambing season this far north was a late one. Arthur put his hand on her shoulder.

Meirchion continued his thread. "...And by doing so repeat the migration of Cunedda from these parts. He populated the north of Cymru with our people, and some Gododdins, in the time of Vortigern, putting up a stout resistance to Hibernian raiders. You may find a welcome from his descendants who are the kings of Gwynedd and neighbours to Powys. I will send you with a letter to them, proposing an alliance, when the time comes."

"Let us hope they can read," Gunamara said, stretching her back.

Arthur stood and bowed to his powerful and wise father-in-law as their visit drew to a close.

Meirchion gripped his arm and winked an eye at Gunamara. "But before you march, Arthur, we must celebrate the birth of my grandchild and have a ceremony to proclaim you High King of the Britons."

ARTHUR PACED UP and down the path to the courtyard fountain, agitated at the cries of Gunamara. Eventually her cries gave way to joyful chatter and the wailing of a new born baby.

"You have a healthy son," a midwife announced as she placed a bundle of tightly wrapped bawling flesh into Arthur's hands.

"How is my Gunamara?" he asked, his eyes still anxious until the midwife reassured him of his wife's well-being.

"He has a powerful voice for one just minutes old," Arthur said, smiling and rocking the baby.

Meirchion appeared at his side. "He is your firstborn son, Arthur. In the language of Cymru where your destiny lies, 'Arthur's son' is 'Llacheu'.

"Then Llacheu shall be his name, and they shall come to know him there."

OVER THE ENSUING days, nobles arrived at Birdoswald for the coronation of Arthur. Gawain came from Vindolanda with Percival, Bedwyr and Ambrose, much to Arthur's joy.

Arthur embraced them all, and took Ambrose to one side. "My dear Ambrose. In addition to recording my achievements, I now wish you to be my chancellor and take charge of fiscal matters. You must spend time with my father-in-law who shall guide you."

Ambrose blushed and bowed, "My lord..."

Gawain barged his way before Arthur, elbowing the delicate scholar aside. "You know, Arthur, there is a precedent for two kings of Britannia at one time. This has happened before, and not so long ago," he said, slapping his protégé's shoulder.

"What has happened before?"

"Ambrosius was crowned after defeating Vortigern in battle, but Vortigern escaped and still paraded himself as high king for two more years. The youth Mordred may call himself king, but he shall taste the steel of Excalibur, and you shall unite the land."

"All that happened before I was born! And I have not yet set my mind on slaying my nephew," Arthur replied, gripping the rounded pommel of his sword. "One step at a time,

Gawain. Now, tell me about your new position as Chief of the Gododdins."

Gawain sighed and escorted Arthur to the church, where a cheering crowd had gathered. "They are a smelly bunch without manners. The inside of a sheep's stomach is a delicacy to them."

"Ha ha! But they did not put you in a pie!"

"I had thought to divide my time between Vindolanda and Monte Agned where their fortress sits, that is, with your approval, my king." Gawain made a mocking bow.

Arthur chuckled and slapped his mentor on the back, revelling in the cheers and shower of flower petals. "You may, with my blessing. Although I want you to help Percival establish a training school for a new breed of commanders."

"We have already started, Arthur."

"But I will take Bedwyr and Herrig for my journey south to rescue the kingdom of Powys," Arthur said, turning to enter the church. Those behind marvelled at his fine new cloak of red that fell from his broad shoulders, displaying his bear and dragon motif in thread of gold.

He walked alone, past hushed guests who stood grouped between high columns, to the altar where his queen held her head high and Bishop Samson rehearsed his blessing. Meirchion stood by Samson's side, holding a simple gold crown on a purple cushion.

"Now for another interminable sermon from our holy bishop," Gawain whispered to Percival from the back of the converted temple as a choir struck up a holy song in their own dialect.

"No Latin?" asked Percival, soon realising the departure from tradition.

They looked to the warbling boys and their animated conductor who turned and grinned at the congregation.

"Behold Gerwyn, the portly bard," Gawain muttered under his breath.

"Wherever nobles are gathered and coin pouches dangle…" Percival's reply tailed off as a blast of trumpets ended the fitful singing and signalled the commencement of the ceremony.

Bishop Samson delivered his welcoming remarks and then invited Arthur to kneel on the step to the altar where his father-in-law stood over him. Meirchion raised his arms up, holding the crown, then slowly lowered it onto Arthur's head.

"Arise, King Arthur of the Britons!" Meirchion's voice boomed, echoing off the painted ceiling where Jupiter, now called 'God' by the priests, looked down from his cloud.

Arthur turned to face his followers, a modest smile playing on his lips. A momentary silence was ruptured by a throaty cheer from Gawain that was taken up by the congregation, rising to a joyful crescendo.

"Now the hard work starts," Percival whispered to his raucous friend.

"This land will soon know his name, and look with hope to his banner," Gawain replied, before mischievously leading another cheer as Bishop Samson waved his hands in vain to quell the noise, eager to restore order and give his blessing. The stone gods of Rome looked down impassively, from their alcoves high up on the walls, bearing silent witness to the dawning of a new age.

Arthur, Dux Bellorum

Author's Note – In Search of the Real Arthur

Many readers will be familiar with the legend of King Arthur and the knights of the round table, his court at Camelot, the ill-fated love affair between his queen, Guinevere, and Sir Lancelot, and the search for the Holy Grail. These romantic and chivalric embellishments were added by various writers in the Middle Ages to a less glamorous King Arthur in a story first told by Geoffrey of Monmouth in his *History of the Kings of Britain* in 1136 AD. The effects of these additions to an already fantastical tale is to leave the impression that King Arthur is a made-up character, invented to fill the black hole in British history known as the Dark Ages (specifically, the late fifth and sixth centuries).

However, Geoffrey did not invent Arthur. There are earlier sources, mainly from Welsh literature, who mention a valiant military leader named Artur, Arthur (or Artorius in Latin) who may or may not have been a king. Undoubtedly, one of Geoffrey's main sources would have been Nennius, the first compiler of early British history, in his work, *Historia Brittonum* (*The History of the Britons* c. 820 AD).

Historian Miles Russell in *Arthur and the Kings of Britain* (2018), describes this work as, "a structurally irregular mix of chronicle, genealogical table, legend, biography, bardic praise poems, itinerary and folklore." It is Nennius who gives us our first tantalising glimpse of a 'real' Arthur in the listing of his twelve battles. Nennius tells us, "Arthur fought... together with the kings of the Britons and he was Dux Bellorum." He describes Arthur as a Dux Bellorum (a leader of battles), who leads the combined armies of the kings of Britain against their enemies, primarily the Angles and Saxons. Some interpret this to mean that Arthur was not a king, just a hired military commander. Others argue that Nennius assumes the reader knows that Arthur is one of the kings of Britain and that as Dux Bellorum, he was first amongst equals.

Miles Russell is of the opinion that Geoffrey originated the legend of King Arthur by taking the name of a real character in Welsh folklore and then deliberately constructing a Dark Ages superhero by piling on his shoulders the deeds of earlier heroic Briton leaders. This was perhaps done to satisfy his sponsors. It was a record of history they would welcome, the story of a Briton hero who fought against the unpopular Saxons whom they had recently defeated. His story of a busy and destructive Arthur fuelled the imaginations of later writers, who further embellished the legend and imbued him with the more romantic and chivalrous qualities of the day.

In my search for a 'real' Arthur I came across an article by historian David Nash Ford (www.britannia.com/history/arthur) who speculates on the locations of the twelve battles of Arthur as outlined by Nennius. Ford suggests that Arthur's first five battles could have taken place in the modern English county of Lincolnshire. He then places other battles further north in Yorkshire/Northumberland and has a further two, possibly three, battles in Scotland. These locations may or may not be correct, but they suited my storytelling, as I send Arthur and his comrades on a journey north, finally arriving at one of the many Roman forts on Hadrian's Wall. From his base on the Great Roman Wall, Arthur sallies northwards, fighting northern tribes at three locations in Southern Scotland.

I think it perfectly achievable that he could cover such distance (some historians have suggested the spread of locations is too wide) – travelling by horseback on Roman roads. It is a mere three hundred miles from Winchester, where the story begins, to Newcastle, at the eastern end of Hadrian's Wall. He had plenty of time, as my story covers roughly a ten-year period, taking Arthur from late teens to late twenties. There is scope for a second book that takes Arthur southwards to the English Midlands and Wales for more adventures and to complete Nennius's battle list.

There are other problems with Nennius's list. For one, he mentions Badon Hill, most likely a battle associated with an earlier king such as Aurelius Ambrosius (or, as in my previous book, Uther Pendragon). Also, he doesn't mention Arthur's final battle, Camlann, mentioned by earlier Welsh sources and included in Geoffrey of Monmouth's story.

My description of Arthur is partly based on the picture I chose for the book cover ('Arthur Dux Bellorum' by Gordon Napier). I was instantly drawn to this superb work of art when I recognised one element of Nennius's scant description of Arthur: "The eighth battle was in Guinnion fort, and in it Arthur carried the image of the holy Mary, the everlasting Virgin, on his shield and the heathen were put to flight on that day, and there was a great slaughter upon them, through the power of Our Lord Jesus Christ and the power of the holy Virgin Mary, his mother." The artist had clearly been inspired by this description in his portrayal of the young leader. Yes, Nennius was a Christian monk who was clearly keen to portray Arthur as a Christian leader fighting the pagan Saxons and Picts – a theme reflected in my storytelling.

What really happened in the late fifth and early sixth centuries? Perhaps one day a lost manuscript will be found, or archaeologists will uncover a definitive battle site or evidence of Arthur's fortress (almost certainly not called Camelot) or his burial site (almost certainly not Glastonbury Abbey). A recent theory by historian Graham Phillips in his book, *The Lost Tomb of King Arthur*, makes the intriguing case for the location of Arthur's kingdom, his final battle and burial place to be in Powys, central Wales.

His entertaining, if tenuous, case hangs on the possibility that 'The Bear' or 'ur Arth' was a title given to the kings of Powys, and one particular king was the Arthur of legend. There are still plenty of 'ifs', 'buts' and 'maybes' in his extensively researched and passionately-argued case, but perhaps the most lasting impression is his enthusiasm for the search and deep commitment to the task of uncovering the definitive lost history of Arthur.

If you enjoyed reading *Arthur Dux Bellorum*, please leave a review.

Also, if you have not already, then please have a look at the earlier books in this series, that starts in the year 410 when the last Roman Governor left Britannia for good, precipitating a slide into a dark age:-

Abandoned - http://mybook.to/Abandoned

Ambrosius: Last of the Romans – http://mybook.to/Ambrosius

Uther's Destiny – http://mybook.to/Uther

Printed in Great Britain
by Amazon